SUMMER LIGHTNING

SUMMER LIGHTNING

Pamela Oldfield

This first world edition published in Great Britain 2006 by
SEVERN HOUSE PUBLISHERS LTD of
9–15 High Street, Sutton, Surrey SM1 1DF.
This first world edition published in the USA 2006 by
SEVERN HOUSE PUBLISHERS INC of
595 Madison Avenue, New York, N.Y. 10022.

British Library Cataloguing in Publication Data

Oldfield, Pamela
    Summer lightning
    1.   English - Portugal - Fiction
    2.   Copper mines and mining - Portugal - Fiction
    I.   Title
    823.9'14 [F]

    ISBN-10: 0-7278-6324-X (cased)
                  0-7278- 9159-6 (paper)

To John and Madge Measures with love

Typeset by Palimpsest Book Producti
Polmont, Stirlingshire, Scotland.
Printed and bound in Great Britain by
MPG Books Ltd., Bodmin, Cornwall.

Prologue

The bird flew low over the familiar territory – a wide expanse of uninhabited land, flat grassland broken only by outcrops of rock, an occasional small and twisted oak tree and small patches of the prickly bush that bore the white cistus flowers. Already the fierce June sun had started to bleach the grass. In another month it would be parched to a dull brown and there would be no more green growth until the rains came in the late autumn and winter seasons. The bird, a blue rock thrush, alighted on the branch of a dead, twisted tree and ruffled its slate blue feathers before surveying its surroundings with wary eyes. For a long moment it watched a lone grey wolf which was stretched out on an outcrop of rock. In its turn, the wolf watched the nearby cluster of buildings on the edge of the much larger complex that was the isolated mine. The mine of San Domingos held no interest for the bird; it had been there a great many years and was part of the scenery but for the wolf it was a different matter.

The animal, a large male with a damaged ear, was intrigued by the sights and smells of the alien area. It was fascinated by the tiny figures moving among the rows and rows of whitewashed houses and the wolf's sharp eyes noted a horse and rider coming in his direction. Without understanding, the wolf smelled the fumes and smoke emitted from the belching chimneys of the industrial buildings. It heard the roar of the furnaces and the steady chunk,

chunk of machinery and sometimes felt the rumble of underground explosions as the ore was blasted from the rock. It was familiar with the sounds and sights of the open cast area and the large lake of water contaminated by the ore washing process. Loping cautiously within sight of the clanking engine with its tubs of crushed ore, the wolf had once before followed the trail of the narrow gauge railway as it snaked its way from the mine to the small town of Pomerau on the river. From there the ore from the mine was transferred to the larger vessels which would carry it downriver to Vila Real and from there to the Mediterranean Sea.

The bird watched as two more wolves joined the first one. Together, crouching low, they all crept closer to the town, heads down, their bodies taut. At that moment the faint jingle of bells from a herd of goats caught their attention and as one, they hesitated, tempted by the distraction. From its position in the tree, the bird saw the man and horse draw closer to the wolves and, moments later, the man on the horse fired a warning shot into the air. The three wolves turned sharply and fled. Instinctively the bird also took flight, soaring upwards and away.

The Alentejo plain was an unforgiving place.

One

Eduardo Lourdes paused for a moment to watch the four young English people playing tennis on the court near the bandstand. He was leading a young filly who tossed her head, impatient at the delay. Returning from a schooling session, the horse was eager to return to the stables and a feed of oats. Twenty-eight-year-old Eduardo was the assistant doctor at the hospital in San Domingos but his real passion was horses. He bought them young, usually unbroken, schooled them until they were suitable for riding, then sold them and bought another horse to train. He had a way with animals and his father teased him that this had given him a good bedside manner with fractious patients.

His parents were both Portuguese and this was reflected in his dark looks – brown eyes, smooth dark hair and fine features. Now he laid a soothing hand against the horse's neck and murmured to her.

On court he recognized the two Staffords, Jane and her husband Hugh. Playing opposite them was Andrew Shreiker, one of the mining engineers who had recently been a patient – suffering from sinus trouble – in the hospital, and Marion Barratt, the senior doctor's niece. Watching them chase about in the mid-morning heat, he shook his head, bemused. They said the English were mad and he didn't doubt it.

Jane missed the ball, shrieked with dismay and they all laughed.

A fifth person, a young woman, sat on the seat and watched the game from beneath her parasol. Fair curls, bright blue eyes and an impetuous nature – this was Lucy Barratt, Marion's younger sister; rumour had it she was soon to be married to Shreiker. For some reason which escaped him, Eduardo felt offended by this rumour. In his opinion Lucy Barratt was too young to know her own mind – caught halfway between child and woman. While in England he had heard the phrase 'Marry in haste, repent at leisure'. His mother, however, took the opposite view and had encouraged his sisters to find husbands and leave home early. To her it was important to 'settle down' but she was never in a hurry to get rid of her only son. His father Jorge saw marriage as something of a lottery and urged caution.

Beside Eduardo, the horse grew restive and skittered about and Lucy Barratt turned at the sound. Eduardo raised a polite hand in greeting. She smiled and, to his surprise, abandoned her seat and walked across to join him.

'Good morning, Miss Barratt.'

'*Bem dia, senor.*' She smiled suddenly. 'You see I have learned a little Portuguese but it is a difficult language for us. I can understand a little but can say much less.'

He raised his eyebrows. 'English is also difficult.'

'But you speak it so well. You put us all to shame. But then you went to school in England . . .'

'Mr Grosvenor has been very good to me. As you know, he paid for my education.'

At that moment the horse tossed her head and she glanced at it nervously and took a step backwards. 'What a beautiful animal. Does he have a name?'

He smiled. 'It's a female and no, she has no name. I'm schooling her and will sell her on. Her new owner will name her. Do you ride?' He could not imagine her doing anything quite so energetic. With her fair hair and slight figure she appeared almost frail and, beneath her parasol, her complexion was pale and unblemished.

'Ride? Oh no! Even if I wanted to I'm certain my parents would disapprove.'

He was amused. 'Do they consider it unladylike?'

'I don't think so. I think they would consider it rather dangerous. Afraid I would fall off and hurt myself.'

'That wouldn't happen if you were taught properly. I'm going to teach young Leo Grosvenor when he arrives for his school holidays from England. He's a very pleasant boy.'

'A little precocious, don't you think, but very sweet.' She twirled the parasol and the horse shied nervously and rolled her eyes. 'Oh sorry! I didn't think.'

'Don't apologize. She must get used to these things.' He gave the horse a couple of friendly slaps.

'Poor Leo must get rather lonely out here. There are very few other children around. He does speak Portuguese rather well, though. I dare say he used to play with Portuguese children when he was younger. Will he ride this horse?'

'Not this one, she's not ready for a rider. I have other horses and one which will suit Leo.'

There were more shrieks and laughter from the tennis court and for a moment the conversation languished while they both watched the game.

Eduardo asked, 'Why do you not play tennis?'

She shrugged slim shoulders. 'I woke with a headache but . . .'

'It's very humid today. The English find it tiring.'

She nodded. 'It was so close in the house, even with the overhead fans. I couldn't face the thought of rushing about after a ball but I wanted to come outside. I thought the fresh air would help.'

'And did it help?'

She considered. 'A little.'

'And your uncle – how is he?'

'Uncle John?' She looked at him in surprise. 'Why do you ask? There's nothing wrong with him . . . is there?'

Cursing his carelessness, Eduardo shook his head. 'Nothing serious. But I know doctors. They hate to take their medicine.' The doctor had recently become aware of a heart problem which apparently ran in his family. He had known he was vulnerable but, being one of those people who hated to delegate, he ignored the fact and was also inclined to overwork. When the problem was discovered he reluctantly agreed to take some pills and rest more but Eduardo had noticed no lessening in Barratt's workload. Obviously his nieces knew nothing and Eduardo wondered uneasily if he had even confided in his wife.

Lucy moved her hand tentatively in the direction of the filly's velvety muzzle. 'Will she bite? Is she very wild?'

'She might.' The hand was quickly withdrawn. 'She is not wild, exactly. Still very nervous but we're making progress. I've had her six months now.'

On court Andrew Shreiker groaned. 'You duffer, Marion! Now we are going to lose the last set.'

Marion laughed. 'I told you I was no good at this stupid game!'

'Hugh served to Andrew and he returned it, lobbing it high over their opponents' heads amid wails of protest, and moments later the match came to an end in a wild exchange and much laughter. The four exhausted players sat down, the two women on the seat and the men sprawled on the grass verge beside them. Lucy made no move to join them.

Instead she turned to Eduardo and asked, 'Will you come to the wedding?'

He smiled. 'Will I be invited?'

'Oh, of course you must!' Her eyes widened. 'I'll tell them to send you an invitation. I know Uncle John likes you. He thinks highly of your work. I know all about you,

Senor Lourdes. You worked for two years at St Thomas's hospital in London, your father is one of the miners, you were the only boy and you have six sisters!'

He laughed. 'You *do* know a lot about me! I'm impressed. I know nothing about you.'

'There's not much to know. You know I have one sister, Marion. We both went to boarding school in England because my father's health was poor and we were in the way at home.' She shrugged. 'Later Marion married, I was sent out here to live with my aunt and uncle and Paul, their son. Aunt Sarah always hoped for a girl but had to make do with two nieces.'

'Should I know your cousin Paul?'

Lucy understood the question. 'Probably not. He works in the assaying department. He's very clever but rather shy. His hobby is stamps. Always has been since he was a boy ... I met Andrew out here and that brings you up-to-date on my uneventful life.'

'And soon you will be on your way to Australia.'

'Don't remind me!' Her face clouded for a moment but then she thrust the thought from her and changed the subject. 'My uncle talks about the hospital here all the time but I've never actually been round it. He says the patients are entitled to their privacy and are not animals in a zoo!' She brightened. 'So you see, as we are inviting family, friends and colleagues to the wedding you must surely be included.'

'Then I shall hope to see you when the great day dawns.'

'My sister has brought my wedding dress from England. It's ... Oh no! I mustn't tell anyone about it because it's bad luck but I can say it's wonderful!'

Amused, he replied, 'I'm sure you will look very beautiful, Miss Barratt.'

'Thank you.'

Her sister called over, 'Lucy! We're talking about you. Andrew is saying terrible things!'

7

'I am not!' he protested.

Lucy said, 'I'd better go.'

Deciding he had made enough small talk for one day, Eduardo gave a polite nod, made his excuses and led the fretful horse back towards a shady stall and a manger full of hay.

Later that evening the main hospital ward – for men only – was quiet apart from a wasp trying desperately to find a way through the window glass. The overhead fans were busy and the curtains round each bed had been drawn back to allow the air to circulate. Sister Meadows sat at her desk in the middle of the room scribbling purposefully on a pink report pad while, under her stern gaze, a nurse scurried purposefully to and fro, ministering to her patients. Both women kept a wary eye on Doctor John Barratt who, in an immaculate white coat, was doing his evening rounds.

The ward was only two thirds full and for that John was thankful. Although he would never admit it, he felt extraordinarily weary lately, overwhelmed by his job and the personal problems which beset him. He had been uncharacteristically bad tempered. His niece's wedding was causing him particular trouble because it would be expensive. Nobody else knew that the Barratts had no private income and had long since used up his wife's family money so that they now relied solely on his doctor's pay. They managed to keep up appearances but Lucy's wedding would put a strain on their resources. Sarah insisted that they should ask Lucy's parents for help but they too had little money and John was reluctant to do so for fear of embarrassing them. John had assured his wife that Lucy's parents would almost certainly send a contributory cheque which might even now be in the post.

Rubbing his tired eyes, he took the clipboard from the end of the next bed and studied it. A broken wrist from a minor accident in the mine. They were never free of them which is why the men's ward always held more patients than the women's ward. The miners came in with strained shoulders, pulled back muscles, head traumas from the tunnel roofs, knee injuries from tripping. The conditions underground were cramped and difficult and he marvelled that there weren't more injuries. He had been down the mine once many years ago, rashly insisting that he needed to understand the men's environment, and could still remember the claustrophobic conditions, the damp heat, the noise of the explosions as the ore was blasted free, and the overpowering smell of the men's sweat. There was also the constant stench from the manure deposited by the rugged pit ponies that dragged the filled tubs back towards the shaft. Having finally escaped from the awful depths, he had privately sworn never to go down there again.

He exchanged a few words with the grizzled miner, nodded and gave a brief reassuring smile.

'We'll be sending you home tomorrow,' he told him in his almost fluent Portuguese.

'Why not today?'

It always astonished him that they didn't appreciate their good fortune to be in such a place receiving such excellent care. 'Because tomorrow is the day!' he said. They seemed determined to get back underground, filthy and sweating, as soon as they could. 'And because I say so!' he added.

The next bed contained a young man with a stomach ulcer. He was fast asleep so John could examine his notes without facing interrogation. At least he was responding to the treatment – unlike the unfortunate man next to him who was suffering from a severely diseased lung and was dying.

'And how are you this evening, Senor Modesto?' John asked the latter.

'Nothing wrong with me,' growled his patient, his face set in surly lines. 'I want to get out of here! I want to go home. I don't . . .' His complaints were interrupted by a burst of heavy coughing which left him breathless and red in the face.

'All in good time,' the doctor told him, frowning at his notes as he stood at the end of the man's bed. 'You are sick, Senor Modesto. Very sick. You should be grateful you're in here and not a hundred feet underground. We are taking good care of you.'

He should be thankful, John reflected, that Mason & Barry, with their Portuguese partner, had seen fit to build a decent hospital, complete with up-to-date equipment and first rate medical staff. Probably the best hospital in the area and certainly one of the first to have the benefits of electricity. The doctor was keen on telling people that the authorities had spared no expense.

Carlos Modesto glared at him. 'I'm not ill and I want to get back to my family!'

John sighed. The man was dying of tuberculosis of the lung but the Portuguese were sturdy, independent people. Left to his own devices the man would probably return to work and die with a shovel in his hands.

As he continued his rounds, moving on to the wards for women and children, he felt a moment's dizziness. His heart speeded up suddenly and then, just as suddenly, slowed and returned to its normal rhythm, causing his mouth to tighten with anxiety. Perhaps young Dr Lourdes was right and he should rest more. He was nearing sixty and no longer as fit as he once was.

But to reduce his hours would arouse his wife's suspicions and Sarah was nervous enough already. Knowing that there was a history of heart trouble in his family she watched him like the proverbial hawk and fussed over him. No, he mustn't alarm her about his health, especially now that she had the wedding preparations to deal with. Poor Sarah. She had been so eager for their nieces to visit yet the extra work and the responsibility weighed heavily on her.

Nurse Robbins hurried forward and he exchanged a few words with her. The young boy with a snake bite was ready to go home and his mother was coming to collect him, hopefully within the next hour. They exchanged a few words and John mopped his brow and thanked God that he was now free to go home. All he wanted was to sit down in the cool of the garden and smoke his favourite pipe.

Saturday 7th June. I talked to Uncle John's junior doctor, Eduardo, this morning. He was walking a horse which he is training. He seems very pleasant but rather serious compared with Andrew who is such fun. And such opposites. The doctor dark and Andrew so fair.

Doctor Lourdes asked me how Uncle John was, as though he thought there was something wrong. I do hope not but if there is Aunt Sarah will know about it. I have decided not to ask any questions as it is none of my business and Mama insists I am too inquisitive and it is not a trait men like in a young woman. I watched Andrew serving to Jane and I'm sure he was making it easy for her. I wonder if Marion noticed. The trouble with Jane is she doesn't take the game seriously and has no competitive streak in her nature.

I shall ask Aunt Sarah to add the young doctor's name to the guest list for the wedding. I keep wondering how I will like Andrew's parents when they arrive. I expect they are having the same thoughts about me . . .

The homes of the English administrative staff were grouped in a rough horseshoe around the *praca*. This area (pronounced prassa) contained attractive gardens, a tennis court and a bandstand with seats arranged around it. It was Sunday evening and the band was in full swing; the music supplied by enthusiastic Portuguese musicians with instruments paid for by the administration. They were playing a set of popular songs from the English theatres as Marion and Lucy sat together, listening and relaxing in the cooler evening air. Opposite them, out of earshot, Mrs Garsey sat with her small white poodle on her lap. It was a delicate animal, its short curls cropped for comfort in the heat, a red studded collar around its neck. Everyone knew Flossie but only Mrs Garsey loved her. The dog yapped a lot and had been known to snap at the hands or ankles of the unwary.

Lucy sat with her sister and wondered what it was like to be a young widow – Marion's husband had died three years ago. Lucy had insisted she travel out to Portugal so they could share a few months together before she married Andrew and disappeared into the wilds of Australia. The peaceful existence, she insisted, would be just what Marion needed and her sister had finally agreed to come out for the wedding. Lucy hoped that, with the passage of time, Marion would grow to enjoy the calm, well-ordered lives of the English community.

As if reading her mind, Marion said, 'I think I'm beginning to recognize a few faces at last.' She pointed out Elliot Grosvenor, the mine's Chief Administrator and his elderly sister Agatha Warren, also a widow. To their left Joanna – Elliot Grosvenor's daughter – sat alone, reading a book. 'And that's Mrs Garsey with her dog and her husband. What does he do?'

Lucy smiled. 'He's the mine's accountant by day but more importantly, he coaches the football team three evenings a week. He used to play when he was younger and has never fallen out of love with the game.'

She watched Jane and Hugh Stafford who were strolling in the garden. Aunt Sarah was missing, of course. She was on duty in the library where she thoroughly enjoyed the responsibility. It was open six evenings a week from seven to nine and was rarely too busy for one person to manage.

Lucy normally found the *praca* a haven of calm but tonight it failed to soothe her. She felt uneasy and suddenly sighed deeply.

Marion glanced at her, surprised. 'Is anything wrong?'

Lucy said, 'I don't know . . . Did you notice that Andrew served very easy balls to Jane?'

'No. Did he?' She turned her attention to Elliot Grosvenor. 'We don't often have the pleasure of the big man's company, do we? I've only seen him once before and I've been in San Domingos for five weeks.'

Lucy ignored the comment. 'He did. Andrew, I mean. I noticed particularly – and he also applauded every time she managed to win a point which wasn't very often. And last time we played as a foursome, and I partnered Hugh, Andrew didn't serve me easy balls.' Silently, she waited, daring her sister to mock her complaints.

Marion turned to look at her. 'Does it matter?' she asked. She sounded genuinely surprised by her sister's attitude. 'It's only a game, Lucy.'

'But don't you see? I'm the one Andrew's marrying. He should serve me easy balls, not Jane.' Now that her grumble had been put into words Lucy realized how foolish they sounded. And she probably was being foolish but she could not shake off the frisson of anxiety. She hoped Marion could help her put the incidents into perspective and make her feel better. She pressed on. 'Didn't you notice the way she looks at him? At Andrew? As though he's some kind of God! I'm surprised Hugh hasn't noticed . . . but maybe he has.'

Marion patted her hand. 'Do I detect a touch of jealousy? Honestly, Lucy, you don't have to worry. Andrew absolutely adores you. Everyone knows that. You and Andrew are meant for each other.'

'But when I first came out here he was in love with Joanna!'

'Really?' Marion glanced at the young woman in question. 'I didn't know that. But that was more than a year ago and now he's in love with *you*! I think you're imagining things. Stop worrying. You'll be man and wife in a few weeks' time and sailing away to Australia. You'll never see Jane again – and neither will he.'

Mrs Garsey caught Lucy's eye and waved. The dog, a small white poodle, barked and tried to get down from her lap but her fond owner gave her a token slap and hugged her closer.

Lucy returned the wave. 'I know what Mrs Garsey's going to give me for a wedding present,' she told Marion. 'A framed picture of some of her pressed flowers. It's a surprise but Aunt Sarah told me.' She rolled her eyes despairingly and they both laughed. It was well known that their Aunt Sarah was an inveterate gossip and could never be trusted with a secret.

Looking round at the other members of the band's audience, Marion said, 'I like Agatha Warren. From what I've seen of her she's a no-nonsense sort of woman.'

'She is, isn't she? She is lending me a marcasite barette for my hair. You know the saying. Things a bride should wear for her marriage. Something borrowed, Something blue . . .'

'You could have borrowed my wedding dress.'

Lucy hesitated. She hadn't accepted Marion's offer in case the dress was unlucky and she, too, might end up a widow but she couldn't tell Marion that. 'I wanted the fun of choosing my own design,' she said instead.

The music stopped to a burst of applause as it came to the end of a selection of songs from *The Mikado*; the bandsmen smiled their thanks, loosened the collars of tunics and dabbed their shining faces with handkerchiefs.

Marion said, 'I saw you talking to the young doctor earlier on. He's very personable, isn't he. Is he married?'

Lucy pursed her lips. 'I don't know much about him but

if he does have a wife I've never seen them together. He's crazy about horses, apparently, and is also a very good shot. He killed a wolf recently.'

'Good heavens! Was it attacking him? Are they dangerous to humans here?'

'Not that I know of but the wolves have been carrying off the goats and the goatherds asked for help. They are always particularly hungry at this time of year because they've been raising their families. It was an old she-wolf.'

'Poor thing.'

'Marion! You wouldn't think like that if you'd lost a lamb or your pet cat! This is the Alentejo and life's tough out here. We might seem very genteel but all around us it's tooth and claw.'

She rolled her eyes and Marion laughed. 'You do exaggerate, Lucy! But it obviously is a hard life for many of the Portuguese people. Months without rain, for instance, and some of the isolated villages must need to be almost self-sufficient to survive . . . I wonder what life will be like in Australia?'

Lucy's expression changed. 'Don't! I'm so nervous about it. I could happily stay here in San Domingos because in the last year I've settled here or I'd happily go back to England . . . But the thought of Australia make me very nervous but . . .' She raised her hands in a gesture of helplessness. 'I couldn't say that to Andrew. He is so keen to go there. He likes the adventurous side of it – pioneering, he calls it. Not that we will be pioneers. I don't think that but . . . I don't want to spoil his pleasure by being negative.' She sighed. 'And worst of all I won't have any friends. Not a soul.'

'You'll make new friends, Lucy. You're the sort of person that makes friends easily. Look how quickly you made friends with Jane and Hugh.'

This comment, instead of reassuring her, simply brought Lucy's thoughts back to her recent worry. 'You don't think Andrew is . . . a fickle sort of man, do you? Seriously?'

'Fickle? No! He flirts a bit but in a jokey way. Most men do that, don't they.'

'Do they? Did your husband flirt in a jokey way?'

'No, but . . .'

Lucy could not wait for her to consider the question and said, 'There's something else I haven't told you. Andrew was *sort of* engaged to someone before he came out to Portugal. A girl named Elenor.'

Marion stared at her in surprise. 'When did he tell you that?'

'Soon after we met. But by then it was all over. They were supposed to be having a big engagement party but then the date of his contract was changed and he came out in such a hurry they postponed it. The party, I mean. He'd given her the ring . . .'

'Oh dear! It was serious then?'

'No! It wasn't at all because as soon as Andrew met me he realized that he had made a terrible mistake with Elenor and wrote to her to cancel everything.' She glanced at her sister who was looking distinctly unhappy at the revelation. 'I don't think that matters, do you?'

'I suppose it mattered to Elenor but . . . these things happen.' She gave a slight shrug. 'Anyway, now he's marrying you. He's settled in his mind. Forget all about Elenor and be happy.'

Lucy nodded dubiously and Marion smiled. 'Don't worry so much. It was nothing.' A new thought struck her. 'And consider Andrew. *He* might be worrying about *you* being fickle!'

'Me? What have I done?'

'You stopped watching him on the tennis court and wandered off to talk to the doctor. You approached *him,*

16

remember. Andrew might have wondered. He might think *you're flirty.*'

Lucy blinked. 'Oh you don't really think so, do you?'

Marion laughed. 'Of course I don't but I'm just pointing out that men *and* women are entitled to last minute doubts. It's pre-wedding nerves, Lucy. I promise you.'

The band struck up again, three lively pieces from the old music hall. Lucy gave a sigh of relief, accepted her sister's promise gratefully and settled back against her seat to enjoy the music.

Monday evening found Sarah Barratt in the library which was open six days a week in the large administration building known as the Palacio. It was held in a cool, quiet room where Sarah Barratt felt safe. She was a timid soul at heart who shunned crowds and noise and life at San Domingos suited her perfectly. It was a small enclosed world which the outside rarely impacted upon. What happened in Europe or Asia was of no interest to her and she only learned about the rest of the British Empire by way of visitors.

The captain of *The Roda* steamboat – which regularly brought passengers upriver from Vila Real – was sometimes invited to dinner by the English at San Domingos, not only for his company but for the news he brought them. Sarah knew that one of the suffragettes had been killed under the hooves of a racehorse at Epsom during the Derby at the start of the month but since she disapproved of the movement and also horse racing, she felt very little sense of shock or loss. Young women stridently demanding the vote embarrassed her and as for tying themselves to railings and kicking the police . . . Well! It simply wasn't ladylike. Modern young women were a race apart as far as Sarah was concerned.

Even Lucy, of whom she was very fond, was often silly and feather-brained. Her parents had spoiled her – probably to compensate for their neglect of their daughters.

17

Thankfully her own son, Paul, was a serious soul – a son they could be proud of. When he was given a place in the assaying department he chose to accept the accommodation which went with it and had moved in to one of the houses to share with another member of the assaying staff. She missed him but she knew he needed some independence. Her only worry was his health. He had had a bad attack of malaria when he was younger and it returned from time to time but he had learned to recognize the signs – the headache followed by a rise in temperature plus a heavy night sweat. He put himself to bed and drank plenty of fluids and John checked on him. She smiled. Paul had been a wonderfully docile child, always tucked away in a corner poring over his stamps. She frequently thanked the Lord they had successfully raised him to manhood.

Sarah had also heard only a few days ago that poor Isadora Duncan, the famous dancer, had lost her two young children in a terrible car accident and that *had* upset her but now she tried not to think about it. Wars, pestilence, political upheavals and other traumatic events passed her by. She was fond of saying that 'What you don't know, can't hurt you'. To Sarah's way of thinking San Domingos was 'an island of calm' and, fortunately for her peace of mind, she had no idea that this tranquil state was about to be shattered in more ways than one.

Sarah flitted from shelf to shelf with a clean duster. She didn't simply run the duster along the edges of the bookshelves but took out three books at a time, dusted the shelf and returned the books. She had volunteered years ago to run the library and had once shared the work with Mrs Jackson but the Jackson family has gone back to England and she was now in sole command. She kept the blinds half drawn to keep out the sun and regularly applied beeswax polish to all the wooden surfaces she could reach. She made the polish herself and flavoured it with the wild lavender that grew around San Domingos – one of the few plants that somehow survived the fierce sun and lack of rain.

The cool tiled floor also received loving attention and was now mopped with soapy water once a week. Liliane, the Grosvenors' senior housemaid, had once tactfully advised that more frequent applications combined with the high temperatures would cause mildew to form on the walls and might spoil the books.

The bookkeeping was simplicity itself – the borrowed books were entered into a thick ledger against the name of the borrower. When the books were returned a line was drawn through the entry and the books replaced on the shelves.

Today she had worked backwards from Z and had reached M when Agatha Warren came in. She returned her books and then made a surprising offer.

'I thought perhaps on the day of Lucy's wedding, you might like to borrow our maid, Liliane,' she suggested. 'There's so much to do and hiring someone from Mertola would mean she would have to come the day before and in a way that would cause you extra work.'

Taken aback by the suggestion, Sarah was immediately alarmed. What would John say to the idea? was her first thought. Would it dent his pride to accept the offer of help? Worse still was the suspicion that Agatha may have guessed they would be hard pressed to provide a suitably elegant wedding feast but was too kind to say so. Even worse – her eyes widened – was the thought that Elliot Grosvenor might think the same way.

She sat down heavily, thinking frantically and wondering what to say. 'That's a very kind thought, Mrs Warren. I'll ... I'll discuss it with my husband.' It would be nice to have an extra pair of hands but she certainly hadn't even thought of hiring someone. And Liliane, of course, was very experienced and spoke reasonable English. She spoke much better English than Sarah spoke Portuguese.

Agatha also sat down. 'I expect you are busy preparing a menu for the great day. I remember my wedding as if it were yesterday. We were married here, of course.'

Sarah knew that her dead husband, Charles, was buried in the small cemetery reserved for the English community.

'I am, yes. I'm wading through Mrs Beeton at the moment,' she confessed. 'Trying to find suitable recipes. The climate here is so different. I have a light hand with pastry but in this heat nothing turns out the way you expect it to!' She gave a nervous laugh while her thin hands twisted and untwisted the duster.

Agatha smiled. 'I have to admit we didn't even attempt an English menu. Clementine, my mother, suggested a traditional Portuguese menu and it was very successful. You might like to consider it for Lucy. I could give you the recipes which are reasonably simple and can't go wrong.' She laughed. 'We had *arjamolho* – that's a tomato and onion soup. Very light but tasty. In Spain they call it *gazpacho*. Then roast boar – the wild boar here is so good, isn't it – and last but not least an iced gateau called *bolo de principe*. We put a ruched white ribbon round it and it looked quite spectacular decorated with candied . . .'

'*Principe?*' Sarah queried.

'It means "prince". It's often served at festivals.'

Sarah was intrigued. A Portuguese menu would be different and the local ingredients would be much cheaper than importing everything from Harrods.

'You've given me food for thought,' she told Agatha, 'if you'll forgive the unintentional pun! I'll see if I can persuade my husband.'

Ten minutes later, when she was once more alone, Sarah resumed her dusting and she hummed as she worked, her mood lightened considerably by Agatha's timely visit.

Two

Eduardo sat at the kitchen table with his father while his mother and sister, Mariana, prepared the food. Mariana was the only sister still unmarried and she was sixteen and courting. She would marry and leave home before she was seventeen and Jorge and his wife would once more have the small whitewashed cottage to themselves. Eduardo had his own quarters among the English as part of his salary but he felt isolated there and often had breakfast with his family.

'So,' he asked. 'What news?'

The table was laid for two as the women had already breakfasted. Mariana had already been to fetch water and her mother had been to the communal wash place to soak her washing.

Jorge bit into a thick slice of flat bread which he ate without butter. He chewed it slowly and swallowed before replying. 'The men are still grumbling. Much good it will do. They'll never strike. Not again.'

'But they'd like to?'

'Course they would. Wouldn't you on our wages? Time they went up. It's been nearly six years.'

Mariana said, 'They're too lazy to strike!'

Her mother frowned. 'Cut more bread, girl, and keep your opinions to yourself.'

Mariana caught Eduardo's eyes resentfully but said nothing. She cut two more slices of bread while her mother cut chunks of ham from a bacon hock for them.

Eduardo nodded his thanks and Mariana fetched a jar of honey. A hen wandered in with five fluffy chicks and they pattered round the men's feet in search of crumbs.

The room was small and dark, the only light that entered it coming in through the open door. Their home was like hundreds of others laid out in neat rows and built to house the workforce and their families.

Eduardo said, 'Will you strike if the others do?'

There was a thoughtful silence. Jorge said, 'We owe them a lot. *You* owe them a lot. Grosvenor educated you. Where does that put me if I strike?'

Mariana said, 'Where does it put you if you don't?'

The mother gasped with anger and slapped the girl's face. 'I told you. This is not your business!' Turning to Eduardo she said, 'Always she has envied you your chance. She has never forgiven them for ignoring her.'

Mariana burst into tears and ran into the bedroom. Jorge shook his head.

Eduardo said, 'She is a bright girl, Mother. She's frustrated.'

'But she's a woman! Grosvenor can't educate every bright child. She knows that in her heart. And she's courting already. What good would an education do her? All she thinks about is this boy. She worships him! Her friend has a child and Mariana wants one too. Foolish girl!' She shrugged irritably and shooed out the hen and her brood.

Eduardo raised his eyebrows. 'Cecilia has a child already? But how old is she?'

'Old enough to know better, I'd say!' She snatched up a bag of pegs and set off for the washhouse.

Reluctant to continue that particular discussion Jorge enquired after Carlos, his friend, who was in the hospital. Eduardo had been dreading the question. The two men had been lifelong friends and had married two sisters.

'He'll never recover, Father. You do know that, don't you? He has advanced tuberculosis in his lungs.'

His father cursed and struck the table with his fist. 'Another one on the way out!'

Eduardo eyed his father wearily. 'I wish you would get out while you can.' His father's second cousin was a boot-maker in Mertola and was eager for Jorge to join the business. Jorge, knowing nothing else but the mine, was stubbornly refusing on the grounds that he would never abandon his mates. With his left leg damaged in an earlier accident, Jorge was no longer fit enough to shovel ore but was instead responsible for the care of the pit ponies. The animals lived down the mine for months at a time, in stables blasted from the rock. At the end of their stint they would be brought to the surface to recuperate and fresh ponies would be collected from the fields and taken down into the darkness.

Jorge forked cold bacon into his mouth. Eduardo ate little. There would be food at the hospital. He stood up. 'I must go or I'll be late.'

His father nodded wordlessly. There was no more to be said.

That same afternoon, when Andrew Shreiker returned from his shift underground, he opened his front door and sighed. A letter had been pushed under the door. Another missive from Lucy, he guessed and was correct. He picked it up feeling guilty. When she had started sending the letters he had found it amusing; funny that she wrote to him since they met almost every day his work allowed and lived only a few hundred yards apart on opposite sides of the *praca*. Lucy had explained that every man should have a bundle of love letters and she didn't want him to miss out because of their circumstances. Occasionally he sent her a letter in return but he hated writing letters. He opened it without enthusiasm.

'My darling Andrew,
  Our wedding is so near I feel I must ask you to
understand this letter. Put it down to pre-wedding
nerves if you will but I do need your reassurance that
you still love me and that I am the only woman . . .'

'Damn! She's twigged!' He stared at the letter as his heart
started to thump. How had she guessed? What had he done
to alert her? Or had someone else warned her?

'. . . in your life. I do not think you have changed towards
me but I have been aware that your attitude to Jane Stafford
is friendlier than it used to be – or am I imagining this?
You must be honest with me, darling. Much as I love you,
I could not bear to marry you if your feelings have changed.
We must talk, obviously, but I thought I should prepare the
ground and give you a chance to reply in writing as that is
so much easier than face to face. Marion assures me . . .'

So she had confided in her sister! Who else? Her aunt?
He felt cold with fear. Had Jane said something to her? No,
surely not. She wouldn't be stupid enough to tell Lucy. His
hand holding the letter shook slightly. A fresh thought struck
him – did Hugh know anything of this? God! It was a
disaster. He read on.

'. . . that I am making a mountain out of a molehill. If that
is indeed the case I shall be the happiest person alive.
  Your loving fiancée, Lucy.'

He sat down heavily and read the letter again. Please
God, Hugh had no idea what had been going on between
him and Jane. Not that it meant anything. It was just a bit
of harmless fun but Lucy wouldn't see it like that and
neither would Hugh. He must get hold of Jane somehow

and warn her – and tell her that it was over. Now. He wondered how he had ever allowed himself to get drawn into the web of deceit. He raked his fingers through his hair and groaned. He must decide what was best to do – and do it fast!

While Andrew was panicking, Lucy and Sarah were sitting together at a small table in the garden, beneath the welcome shade of a slim eucalyptus tree. They were discussing the wedding invitations and drawing up a list. Lucy tried to concentrate as her aunt told her of Agatha Warren's generous offer of her maid, Liliane.

'She's very experienced, Lucy, and will be a great help. Your uncle has agreed to the idea. I thought he might argue but he didn't. He is so preoccupied at the moment. But Liliane! Another pair of hands. Isn't that wonderful?'

'It is, yes.' Lucy sipped her ginger beer and wondered if Andrew had found her letter and if so what he was thinking. The moment she had pushed it under his door, she had regretted it. If only she hadn't been so rash. Fools rush in where angels fear to tread! Marion had told her many years ago that the saying must have been made with Lucy in mind!

Her aunt smoothed the sheet of paper and dipped the pen into the ink. 'The tenth of June already and we haven't done the list of invitations. Oh dear! I'm all at sixes and sevens but now we can make a start on it. We can start with family,' she suggested. 'Me, your uncle, Paul and Marion. That's four.' She wrote the names down carefully then looked up suddenly. 'But what am I thinking of? We don't have to invite ourselves, do we!' She laughed and crossed out the names.

Lucy nodded distractedly. She was trying to hide her growing agitation. She now wished that she had ignored Andrew's behaviour on the tennis court. Suppose he *had* served a few easy balls to Jane – did it signify anything? Probably not. And maybe Hugh had served *her* easy balls. Would she have noticed that? She should have let sleeping dogs lie.

'. . . do you think? We can't possibly leave them out.'

Lucy frowned. 'I'm sorry. Who are we talking about?'

'The Grosvenors, dear. Aren't you listening?' Her aunt stared at her reproachfully. 'Mr Grosvenor can be rather intimidating but we must ask him. He might not come, of course. So that's Mr Grosvenor, his daughter Joanna and his sister Agatha. That's another three. That makes seven.' She resumed her writing.

Lucy took a mouthful of ginger beer which went down the wrong way and made her splutter inelegantly. She snatched for her handkerchief as her aunt pretended not to notice. A terrible thought had struck her. Suppose Andrew took the letter the wrong way and was annoyed with her. Suppose, because of the letter, he saw a different side to her – a less flattering side, thinking her small-minded and ridiculously hysterical. Suppose they ended up having a row about her letter! Why had she been so stupid? She felt positively ill at the prospect of a falling out.

Her aunt said, 'And then there's your particular friends, Jane Stafford and her husband Hugh.'

Lucy hesitated. 'Jane and I aren't quite as close as we once were but we must invite them because Hugh is Andrew's best man.'

Her aunt looked up, surprised. 'Not so close? I thought you four were inseparable!'

'We are in a way but . . . I find Jane rather silly sometimes. Don't you? Rather childish.'

'We-ell, I don't know . . .' She blinked. 'Young people today *are* rather skittish compared to when I was a young woman. My generation had more common sense. As a child I was brought up to respect my elders and speak when I was spoken to. That was one of the things your uncle admired about me – so he says. That I was modest. I will agree that Jane is somewhat loud. That laugh of hers.'

Lucy felt vaguely mollified by her aunt's criticism of Jane. 'She does have a rather loud voice,' she agreed. The question was, did Andrew find her exciting? Didn't he notice her faults?

Her aunt shrugged. 'Still, nobody's perfect and I like Hugh. He's a gentleman. So . . . they seem quite a pleasant couple. I'll add them to the list, shall I?'

'Of course. And Mrs Garsey and her husband. We'll have to hope she leaves Flossie at home. And the doctor, Doctor Lourdes.'

Sarah glanced up from her writing. 'Doctor Lourdes? He's hardly a close friend, Lucy.'

'But I said we would. I promised. He has a father who . . .'

'Lucy, dear, you're getting carried away!'

'What about Captain what's-his-name from the steamboat? He comes to dinner sometimes.'

'For heaven's sake! Be reasonable. You'll be including the postman next and the police chief! We agreed it would not be a lavish affair. A few discreet guests – people who mean something to you. Portuguese people won't want to come. They won't speak much English and . . .'

'Doctor Lourdes speaks very good English but I take your point about his father. We don't actually know *him*.'

'We do have to strike a balance, dear. We can't invite everyone you've ever spoken to – it would be impossible and the expense would be enormous.' She scribbled on the paper again. 'There. I've added Doctor Lourdes. Does that satisfy you? And you've made me lose count!'

While she was counting the guests again there was a knock at the door. Her aunt looked up. 'Do go and see who that is, Lucy. I'm not expecting anyone. I did want a quiet

27

afternoon with you to sort things out. There's the food to discuss. If it's anyone for me say I'm busy and ask them to leave a message.'

Reluctantly Lucy rose to her feet for she had a feeling it would be Andrew. She made her way along the passage with mounting trepidation. She opened the door and saw Andrew on the step. 'Andrew, I'm sorry . . .'

'My poor darling girl!' He put his arms round her and hugged her. 'I read your letter and I'm so, so sorry you've been worried.' He lowered his voice. 'You are quite wrong. There is nothing happening between me and Jane. Nothing at all.'

'Oh, thank heavens!' She clung to him, weak with relief. 'Dearest Andrew. I should never have doubted you and I shouldn't have written that way. It was foolish of me. I had a moment's panic.' Lucy closed her eyes thankfully. It was all over. He still loved her. She should never have doubted him. 'Aunt Sarah is on the patio. We were making a list for the invitations.' She drew back a little and gazed up at him, her eyes shining. 'So you do still want me to be your wife. To be with you for ever. It's a long time, for ever.'

'Not with you beside me. It can never be long enough!' He kissed her. 'I won't come in, Lucy. I'm in the middle of a long letter to my parents. They are coming, of course, but I want to tell them all about the preparations. They'll want to boast about it to all their friends. You will send them an invitation, won't you? They can show it to people. And don't forget my friends when you make the list. I'd like to invite my boss, Stephen Benbridge.'

'Isn't he engaged to Joanna Grosvenor?'

'The same, so invite them both . . . and Will Hawks. I work with him quite often.' He smiled. 'We blow things up together! I also have to write to my grandmother so I shall be busy. You don't mind, do you, dearest? Once we're married we shall have so much more time together, not to

mention the sea journey to Australia.' He kissed her again.
'And no more panics, eh? Promise me!'
'No more panics. I love you, Andrew.'
'So trust me!'
'I will.'
With a cheerful heart she watched him stride away in the
direction of his home, returned his final wave then closed
the door gently. Everything was going to be all right. Now
who were those friends of his who must be added to the
list . . .?

Later that day Dr John Barratt was in his consulting room
catching up on some paperwork when Nurse Robbins
rushed in without knocking. He looked up, annoyed by
the interruption but was at once silenced by the expression of distress on the nurse's face. She was red-faced and
breathless.

'Please, Doctor Barratt, it's Senor Modesto.' Her voice
had risen with alarm. 'He's out of bed and . . . and Sister
says you're to please come at once. He's getting dressed
and we can't stop him. He hit out at Sister – at least he
tried to but she ducked and he swore at us . . .' She stopped
for breath, one hand to her heart.

He had risen to his feet. 'Do calm down, Nurse Robbins.
I'll come immediately. I should have expected something
like this!' Together they hurried back along the corridor.
'And you're sure Sister wasn't hurt in any way?'

'She was unhurt when I left but he's in a very violent
mood.' Beads of sweat were forming on her forehead as
once more she was forced to exert herself. Never a slim
person, Nurse Robbins found the long corridors tiring even
on a good day when she was under no duress.

By the time they reached the ward even the doctor was
out of breath. 'The man's as stubborn as an ox!' he muttered.
'It will be a mercy to be rid of him if he's so insistent.'

'He wouldn't take his medicine this morning, Doctor, and threw his breakfast on to the floor. He's in a very difficult mood, Doctor, and . . . Ah! Here he comes!' she said, her voice rising to a squeak.

Carlos Modesto was staggering out of the ward door, half dressed and with bare feet. Wearing only pyjama trousers and a grey wool shirt, he made unsteady progress, clinging to the walls for support and swearing loudly with every step. Sister was doing her best to try and hold him back but he gave her a push which, catching her off-balance, sent her sprawling. Nurse Robbins screamed and ran forward to help her.

'Senor Modesto!' John bellowed in Portuguese. 'What do you think you're doing?' He grabbed the man's arm and held on to him while Nurse Robbins helped the Sister to her feet. 'Are you all right, Sister? Are you injured?' He glared at his disruptive patient, gave him a shake and said sternly, 'Behave yourself, senor! This behaviour is quite intolerable!'

The Sister stood up nervously, checking that no bones were broken then straightened her uniform and cap. She drew in a long, unsteady breath. 'This wretched man refuses to . . .'

Carlos Modesto roared suddenly, snatched himself free from the doctor's clutching hand and began to resume his escape along the corridor.

John shouted, 'Stop right there, Senor Modesto!' and ran after him. Nurse Robbins ran with him and together they caught and held their unwilling patient.

Furious, John said, 'Now listen, senor. If you want to go home this badly you shall go – but not like this. I shall notify your family and they can come and collect you. Be it on your own head. If you choose to shorten your life by going home, who am I to argue?'

The man regarded him sullenly and said nothing. Now

that his escape had been officially agreed all the fight appeared to have gone out of him.

John said, 'I'll prepare discharge papers for you and you will sign them before you leave the hospital. It is a serious matter, senor. I will no longer be responsible for your health. Do you understand? I can't have this kind of behaviour in my hospital. And you will apologize for pushing Sister.' They urged the man back towards the ward where the Sister regarded him with barely concealed distaste.

He muttered something and John shook him again. 'That won't do. Say you are sorry properly. And in English. Say "I am sorry"'

'I sorry!' The apology was obviously an effort and was accompanied by a scowl but the Sister accepted it with a sniff of disapproval and between them they manhandled him back to bed. A porter was found and dispatched with a message to the man's home and John withdrew to his office and sat down to the necessary paperwork. He felt very shaken and also annoyed with himself for almost losing his temper with the man. He felt he had been unprofessional and that bothered him. Never before had he lost control of himself, even for a minute, and the lapse frightened him. He filled in the form with a shaking hand and then sat with his head in his hands, trying to recover.

He had just decided he needed a cup of tea when the first pain hit him. His chest seemed to tighten, there was a sudden ache in his right arm which quickly intensified. He tried to call for help but realized no one would hear him. The agony enveloped him and with a groan, he lost consciousness and fell forward on to his desk.

He was still there thirty-five minutes later when Senor Modesto's wife arrived with her son to collect her husband and her screams brought Nurse Robbins running to the scene. The patient and his family were quickly dispatched to wait in the office and a porter was sent to fetch Doctor

Lourdes. In his absence John slowly regained consciousness, to their huge relief, but remained in a very weak state, barely able to remember what had happened. The pain had gone but they were afraid to move him but he was able to sit back in his chair and sip some cold water.

'I think I fainted,' he muttered, his voice little more than a croak. His face was ashen and his lips were grey and both women had enough experience to recognize the truth about his condition before Doctor Lourdes arrived and confirmed their diagnosis. Doctor Barratt had had a heart attack. He was carried on a stretcher into the ward he had so recently left, gently undressed and propped up on some pillows in a bed next to the nurse's desk. The curtains were pulled around him and strict orders were given by the young doctor for round-the-clock monitoring.

'Someone must notify his family,' Doctor Lourdes decided when the patient was as comfortable as possible in the circumstances. He scribbled a note and sent it to the Barratts' home.

Sister regarded him gravely. 'He's not going to walk away from that too easily, is he?' she asked. 'Poor Doctor Barratt. I suspect he won't be the most co-operative patient. I'm not surprised this has happened, though. He's been overworking for months now.'

Doctor Lourdes nodded. He was deeply worried about his new patient. 'We'll run some tests tomorrow,' he told her. 'Try and discover how much damage has been done. He's going to be forced to rest now, I'm afraid.'

'He won't like that at all!' She sighed. 'And we can blame it on Senor Modesto! If he hadn't been so difficult . . .'

He put a hand on her arm and shook his head. 'It was nobody's fault,' he said. 'It was waiting to happen. If it hadn't been today it would have been tomorrow or the day after. Or the next month. At least he was in the right place and we could help him quickly. Let's hope he has a strong constitution. Let's hope he's ... What do you call it in England?'

Sister managed a faint smile. 'A tough old bird?'

'And you, Sister. I understand Senor Modesto pushed you over. Are you sure you're not hurt?'

'No bones broken, doctor, but I think I'll have some nasty bruises tomorrow! And if I'm honest, it did shake me up. I'm not as young as I used to be!'

'None of us are, Sister. Do you need to take a day off?'

'No thank you. Without Doctor Barratt you're going to need me!'

'Then leave a little early tonight and rest. As for Doctor Barratt, we must hope for the best and ask the padre to say a special prayer for him on Sunday.'

That same afternoon, at the Palacio, Elliot Grosvenor played with a paper knife as he stared across his desk at Andrew Shreiker who stood opposite, trying to look at ease. Andrew always found his boss rather intimidating. He held the most senior position in the mine and was also a tall, burly man, who had once been handsome in a rugged way. He had a brusque manner, always spoke his mind and had no time for weakness of any kind. Rumour had it that his unhappy marriage to Catherine and her accidental death had left a bitter legacy but Andrew was unable to imagine him as a younger, happier person. He had never remarried but his daughter Joanna, son Leo and sister Agatha were obviously fond of him so presumably he had some good points which were hidden from most people. Andrew gave him a tentative smile which was acknowledged with a curt nod.

'Sit down, man!' Grosvenor barked. 'What I want is your view of the men's mood. You see them on a daily basis. I feel uneasy.'

Andrew crossed his legs and then immediately uncrossed them in case he looked too casual. 'I think there is some unrest, sir,' he said guardedly. 'I wouldn't like to say how significant it is. There's a lot of grumbling, a lot of men taking time off, a lot of minor accidents. Always a bad sign. There was a fight recently in the lowest level and one man is in jail for inciting trouble.'

Grosvenor nodded. Andrew wondered just how much or little to tell him. There had been signs of a growing rebellion and some hostility towards the English staff. At least, there was towards him but was it personal or were the other engineers noticing anything? He had no way of telling short of asking them and that meant revealing his own difficulties.

Grosvenor sighed. 'We had a strike here in 1907. Before your time but no doubt you've heard about it.'

'Yes, sir, I have.'

'Nasty, bitter business. I'd hate to go through that again. I thought we could beat them but I was wrong. In the end we had to give in to certain demands. We had to reduce their hours after we heard on the grapevine they might have been planning to disrupt the pumping system. Of course they didn't. They would have put themselves at risk and they're not stupid. Far from it! How much was bluff we couldn't tell but we wanted to avert a major disaster so we had to give in.' He drummed his fingers on the desk. 'So what is it this time? Don't we do enough for the blighters? School, hospital, band, football stadium. For God's sake, man!'

'From what I glean, sir, it's the wages.'

'Wages!' He shook his head in disbelief then frowned. 'What sort of hostility are we getting now? Anything ominous?'

Andrew hesitated. Better not to say too much or it would reflect badly on him, and Benbridge and Hawks who were the other men held responsible for managing the workforce.

'Just the small things, sir, hard to pin down. Time wasting, disrespect to authority, ignoring the safety rules. Things like that. Last week one of the ponies broke free and held up everyone else because we couldn't move the truck. They said it was a faulty strap. Maybe it was. The week before some dynamite went missing and . . .'

'What? You've lost some explosives? Good God . . .'

'It's all right, sir,' Andrew said hastily. 'We found it but . . .'

'I should damn well hope so!' He glared at Andrew who cursed himself for mentioning it.

'We tried to investigate, sir, but nobody knew a thing. At least, nobody admitted to knowing anything.'

'Come down on all of them hard, Shreiker! Don't be afraid to make an example of anyone you suspect of inciting trouble.'

Andrew hesitated. 'They do have some reasonable complaints, sir. There's rarely enough drinking water. At those temperatures the men get thirsty. The doctor says they can easily get dehydrated. One day we had three men pass out. If you could allot more drinking water . . .'

Grosvenor held up a peremptory hand. 'Right! See to it. I want no excuses for malingering, you hear? When I see the hospital ward filling up then I'll wonder what's going wrong.'

'Yes sir. I understand. I'm sure we all do our best to . . .'

'I know.' He stood up and crossed to the window. 'And keep me informed. I want a weekly report either from you or Benbridge. On morale. That's it. You can go!'

As Andrew rose eagerly to his feet there was a tap on the door. Hugh Stafford, the secretary, put his head round the door. 'Sorry to interrupt, Mr Grosvenor, but Doctor Barratt's had a heart attack. He's in the hospital and very poorly.' He withdrew.

Grosvenor struck his forehead with the flat of his palm. 'That's all I need!' he muttered. 'Never rains but it bloody well pours!'

*   *   *

35

Half an hour later Lucy was sitting beside her uncle's bed when Elliot Grosvenor pushed his way in through the swing doors and marched up the ward followed by an anxious nurse who was explaining the rule about only one visitor at a time.

Within the curtains, Uncle John was sitting propped up against pillows, wearing a standard blue hospital gown while Lucy helped him drink from a feeding mug. A single white sheet covered him and a black canister of oxygen stood beside the bed. His face was grey and drawn and his lips were almost colourless.

Lucy saw the nurse's agitation and guessed the reason. 'Should I go?' she asked.

The nurse glanced over her shoulder to see if the Sister was in sight. 'It might be all right for just two or three minutes,' she said, 'but don't say I said so. Pretend I don't know.'

Lucy nodded and the nurse disappeared leaving Lucy to deal with the General Adminstrator of the San Domingos mine. Elliot stood at the end of the bed, towering over her, and stared at the patient. 'I suppose you've been overdoing it, Barratt. I warned you weeks ago to take it easy.'

Impossible man, thought Lucy. Not even a 'How are you?' or a 'So sorry to hear about this'. Was he totally devoid of social graces?

Her uncle whispered, 'There's always . . . such a lot to . . .' He stopped to recover his breath.

As firmly as she could, Lucy said, 'My uncle's not to be upset in any way!'

Grosvenor said, 'I'm not upsetting him, Miss Barratt, I'm talking to him.'

'He's been on oxygen.' She indicated an oxygen mask on the bedside locker. 'He's just taken it off to have a drink.' Trying not to be overwhelmed by Grosvenor's importance,

Lucy forced herself to return his gaze. From where she sat he seemed a giant of a man and she knew from Andrew that he had temper.

Grosvenor turned back to her uncle. 'You were dealing with a recalcitrant patient, I hear. The Portuguese can be very stubborn. Gone home, has he?'

Her uncle nodded. Lucy offered him more water but he shook his head weakly and closed his eyes. Lucy said, 'Dr Lourdes says my uncle has to have lots of bed rest and no worries. Nothing to trouble him until he's stronger.'

'So where's your aunt? Shouldn't she be sitting in your place?'

'Aunt Sarah fainted when she heard the news.' He rolled his eyes at this but Lucy pressed on. 'She hit her head when she fell and isn't in a fit state to go anywhere at the moment. Marion is sitting with her. Naturally my aunt will come along later if she feels up to it.'

'And where's Lourdes?'

'Elsewhere in the hospital, I suppose.' She didn't care for his manner and was starting to feel resentful. Did the man think her uncle had had his heart attack deliberately to annoy Elliot Grosvenor? Was he always like this? She felt sorry for Agatha. She must be devoted to her brother if she put up with this bullying behaviour day after day. She stood up, removed the feeding mug and reached for the oxygen mask which she placed gently over her uncle's face and mouth. With his mouth covered, she thought, he could not be expected to hold a conversation with anyone. 'Try to sleep, Uncle John,' she told him pointedly. 'Rest is the best cure. You must listen to Doctor Lourdes.' She smiled. 'I know what they say – doctors make the worst patients! But Aunt Sarah may be along later and I'd like you to look a bit better by then.' She picked up his hand and kissed it. 'I won't be far away and I'll be back later to sit with you.'

Her uncle raised a weak hand in acknowledgement and closed his eyes. Lucy looked at Elliot Grosvenor. 'I think we should leave him to rest, don't you? He's not up to conversation.'

His lips curled into a brief smile. 'You're an expert now, are you, Miss Barratt?'

'I *have* spoken with the doctor. I don't pretend to be an expert but I am well informed.' She smiled to soften the reproach.

Wondering how she dared to speak that way to Elliot Grosvenor, Lucy led the way out of the cubicle, carefully closing the curtains behind them and walked firmly towards the swing doors. To her relief Grosvenor followed without further argument. Outside in the corridor they paused, looking for signs of life. They found it eventually in Doctor Barratt's consulting room where Eduardo, a woman and Carlos Modesto – the latter now dressed in shoes, shirt and trousers – were talking together.

Grosvenor said, 'Ah! Here's the man that caused all the trouble! Going home is he? Good riddance!' He spoke in English and fortunately only the doctor understood.

Lucy and Grosvenor waited while the patient scribbled his name on a blue form and then a green form. The doctor spoke to them in Portuguese and they answered and stood up.

To Grosvenor, Eduardo said, 'I'll see them to the door. They have his friend's mule cart waiting to take him home.'

As the three of them moved carefully towards the door, Eduardo caught Lucy's eye and winked. Elliot Grosvenor sat down and stared round impatiently, his large hands resting on his knees. Lucy, unwilling to make further conversation, crossed to the window and looked down on to the forecourt where a small cart and a large mule waited in the care of a young man who was presumably the patient's friend.

Grosvenor said, 'So you're the reason for the wedding preparations. It's all I hear. Wedding this! Wedding that!'

His voice was gruff and Lucy bridled at his tone.

'Your own daughter Joanna will be getting married next year, I believe. To Mr Benbridge. You'll have to go through it all then!'

He seemed not to hear. 'Marrying young Shreiker. That should settle him down. Let's hope so. And then off to the wilds of Australia. Land of opportunity if you don't mind hard work. I've toyed with the idea of going there myself but not for a few years yet. Looking forward to it?'

Lucy turned. 'Very much,' she said, giving him a bright smile. No need to share any of her anxieties with Elliot Grosvenor. 'We have a pretty bungalow reserved for us and we've been offered a year's free subscription to the tennis club.'

'The *tennis* club! Hah!' He made no attempt to hide his amusement. 'Well, you can't go far wrong then, can you. The tennis club! It's a long way, Australia. Good sailor, are you, Miss Barratt?'

'Reasonable. I'll survive.'

To her relief they heard the young doctor returning. 'Sorry about that,' Eduardo said with a grin. 'I wanted to be sure he had left the premises.' He said to Lucy, 'I'll be a while with Mr Grosvenor. If you want to go back to your uncle I'll come along and see you shortly.'

'Thank you. I hope I shall find him sleeping.'

With as much dignity as she could muster, Lucy left the room and walked back to the ward. Resuming her seat beside her uncle she was pleased to see that he was indeed sleeping and settled herself to think about Andrew. Grosvenor had suggested that marriage would 'settle him down'. Adding that he hoped so. Grosvenor's careless comments had disturbed her more than she realized

*   *   *

39

The following morning, which was Wednesday, Marion joined Lucy at the hospital and spent a few minutes with her uncle, bringing a message from his wife that she would call in to see him later in the day. They eventually left their uncle in the capable hands of Nurse Robbins and walked home together.

'He has to have rest and more rest and light foods,' Lucy said. 'I'm going to ask Aunt Sarah if I can make one of my almond custards and take it in with me when I visit – they're so easy to digest.'

'Good idea. Aunt Sarah is going to take some lemon barley water with her tomorrow. Poor thing. She had such a fright. When she came round she was in a dreadful state. Almost hysterical. She kept saying, 'He's dead, I know he is! You're afraid to tell me!' It was some time before we could convince her that he was still alive. Poor Aunt Sarah. She'll have a huge bruise on her forehead from where she hit it on the corner of the table. It's a good thing we're here actually.'

As they reached the *praca* Lucy frowned. 'You don't think Uncle John will die, do you? I mean . . . sometimes people have more than one heart attack. I don't even know if the one he's had is mild, moderate or serious. They vary, don't they? He looks terrible. I don't think he could survive another one.' Deeply troubled, she looked at Marion. 'I wonder how old he is.'

'I don't know. They never talk about their ages, do they.' She sighed. 'We'll have to say extra prayers for them. I wrote home this morning to let Mama and Papa know what has happened.'

They paused for a few minutes to watch Joanna and Agatha playing tennis together on the court – a leisurely game with little or no evidence of competitive spirit.

Lucy said wistfully, 'I shall miss Joanna's wedding. I'd like to have seen it.'

'I'll be back in England by then so we'll both miss it,' Marion said.

'Will you marry again . . . ever?'

'I doubt it.'

'Suppose I don't like Australia. I'll be trapped there for years and years. For ever, possibly. They have a great many poisonous things – like spiders that can kill you with one bite! Not to mention crocodiles . . . or are they alligators? And there are those strange people – the originals – that live out in the bush.'

'I think you mean aborigines. They live in the bush. They're not so much strange as different. Clever in their own way. Nothing to be scared of.' She gave her sister a sharp look. 'You'll like it, Lucy. I'm sure you will.'

'Do you wish you were going to Australia?'

Marion hesitated. 'I haven't given it much thought but I'm sure you'll get used to it. There'll be good and bad things about it and you'll enjoy the good things and learn to put up with the bad things.' Marion gave her a closer look, her head on one side. 'You're not usually so . . . so unenthusiastic, Lucy. You wrote to me most excitedly about Australia before I came out and now suddenly you seem full of doubts.'

'Do I?'

Marion slipped an arm through hers and they walked on. 'Is it really Australia or is it Andrew? If you've changed your mind about him it's not too late to . . .' She let the sentence die.

Probably afraid to put it into words, thought Lucy. Marion meant well but how could she admit to her that it was Andrew who might have changed his mind? On the other hand, who else was there she could talk to in confidence about what was worrying her?

She said, 'Yesterday evening, quite late, I decided to take a walk in the cool air and I went past his house. It was in

41

darkness. Not a sound. He wasn't in. I looked in all the windows. So where was he?'

'Was he out secretly meeting Jane? Is that what you mean?'

The bluntness of her question took Lucy aback. Why did her sister have to be so direct? 'I suppose I do.'

'Then you'd better ask him – or ask Jane . . . or Hugh. You could find an excuse to pop into the Palacio and see Hugh and ask him if Jane was at home all of last evening. If he says "Yes" then you can stop worrying.'

'And if he says "No"?'

'Then you can tackle Andrew. Or I will. I'll ask him outright on your behalf.'

'Oh no!' Lucy grabbed her arm. 'Promise me you won't. That would be awful! Promise me you won't talk to anybody about it. I told you in strictest confidence!'

By this time they had arrived at the Barratts' home and with Marion's promise, the subject was dropped.

Wednesday, 11th June. My mind is in a complete whirl and I hardly know which way to turn! Why don't I trust my dearest Andrew? I feel so ashamed of my suspicions especially when he has assured me there is nothing at all to worry about. In desperation I talked to Marion and she suggested I speak to Hugh privately about it. Probably that will set my mind at ease. Andrew and I ought to trust each other if we are going to spend the rest of our lives together. But if we don't – what then? I am at my wits' end!

As if I haven't enough worries, poor Uncle John has had a heart attack and might well have died! Suppose he does die? It doesn't bear thinking about. I feel very frightened for him but I know people do recover from such attacks so I should have faith in Doctor Lourdes. I have lit a candle on my dressing table and will say my prayers for Uncle John kneeling beside it as though I were in church.

Summer Lightning

I'm feeling rather sorry for myself at the moment. It should have been a wonderful summer and I ought to be happy but suddenly everything seems to be going wrong. What on earth have I done to deserve this unhappiness?

Three

O n Thursday Lucy made her almond custard and took it along to the hospital for her uncle who, to her gratification, was able to enjoy a small portion and thanked her profusely for her kindness. She stayed with him for half an hour until Marion arrived bringing Sarah who had made a good recovery from her fall.

Lucy then made some excuse, left the hospital and hurried in the direction of the Palacio where she made her way up to Hugh's office. She felt ashamed that she needed to see him but determined to allay her fears about Andrew once and for all. Hugh would realize that she mistrusted the man she was about to marry but she had decided it was worth it for peace of mind. She drew in her breath, paused, then knocked on his door.

'Come in!'

Hugh looked up in surprise as she entered. Pen in hand, he was seated behind a large mahogany desk with a small pile of papers in front of him. 'Lucy! What brings you here?'

It was strange to see him in formal attire in his place of work. 'I need to ask you something, Hugh,' she began. 'I don't want you to think . . .'

He stood up, indicated a chair for her and they both sat down. Immediately Lucy decided she had made a mistake by coming but it was too late. Once she had asked her question his peace of mind might also be shattered – depending on his

44

answer. But she could think of no other reason for being there and stared at him helplessly as the seconds ticked by.

'What is it?' he repeated, twirling his pen absent-mindedly. 'There's nothing . . . Oh God!' His expression changed. 'It's not Jane, is it? She's all right?'

'Yes . . . At least . . . maybe not. I don't know. This isn't easy for me, Hugh.' She drew another shaky breath. 'Can I ask you something in strictest confidence, Hugh? I have to know something and . . . depending on the answer . . .' To her horror she heard her voice break and knew that if she didn't hurry, she would end up in tears. 'In confidence,' she said again.

'Yes, of course!' He looked concerned.

She swallowed hard and blinked back the tears. 'Was Jane with you all yesterday evening, right up until bed time?' She crossed her fingers for luck.

He frowned, puzzled by the question. 'I think so . . . No! Tell a lie. She did pop out for half an hour or so just after nine. Maybe just before. She wanted to talk to Mrs Barratt at the library about some books she'd ordered from Foyles. Why do you ask?'

Lucy's body temperature seemed to drop and she shivered involuntarily. 'Did she see Aunt Sarah?' It was almost a whisper.

'Yes. She never closes promptly at nine. The books hadn't arrived but . . .'

'Aunt Sarah wasn't at the library yesterday evening because she'd fainted much earlier when she heard about Uncle John's heart attack. She was resting in bed after her fall.' For a moment Lucy thought she was going to be sick but she fought the feeling. She watched Hugh's good-natured face and saw the moment when he experienced the first jolt of doubt.

'But Jane said . . . She repeated some of the conversation they had had. Are you sure about this?'

45

Too late now to hold back, thought Lucy desperately. 'Quite sure. I went round to see Andrew and he was also out. I think they were together.'

The pen fell from Hugh's hand, splattering ink on to the topmost paper but he seemed unaware of it. Lucy reached over, turned the sheet upside down and pressed it into the blotter then replaced it on the pile. Throughout the small manoeuvre Hugh hadn't moved. He sat back in his chair and stared past her into the distance and Lucy guessed he was replaying the scene in his mind.

She said, 'I'm sorry, Hugh. But I'm rather worried. I had to talk to you.'

'You mean Jane lied to me?' he asked, his tone expressionless.

'I think so. I've been suspicious for some days now. Haven't you had the slightest inkling?'

'No . . . That is . . . Truly, Lucy, such a thing never entered my head.' He leaned forward abruptly. 'We mustn't jump to conclusions. There may be nothing to worry about . . . Jane wouldn't . . . They wouldn't surely! Dammit!' He pushed back his chair and walked to the window. 'Suppose they have been seeing each other – they aren't likely to admit it. Andrew and you are getting married in a few weeks' time.' Turning, he stared at her, his face pale. 'I shall ask her, naturally. Oh God! I hope you're wrong but . . . last night! It all sounded so natural. I can't believe there is anything happening, Lucy.'

'I'm so sorry.' She sighed heavily. 'Do you forgive me for asking you? I didn't know what to do. How can I marry him if this is what I think it is?' Her mouth trembled and she bit her lip hard. 'I did ask him about it – in a letter. He denied it.'

He seized the hope. 'There you are then.'

'Then last night happened. What will you do, Hugh? Will you ask her? Or keep a watch on her?'

He sat down again and ran his fingers through his hair. 'I can't spy on my own wife. I'll ask her outright and risk a scene if I'm wrong. I'll have to tell her why I'm asking and that will bring you into it. If she's completely innocent she won't be very happy with you!'

Lucy shrugged. 'And you'll believe her if she denies it?'

'I don't know until the moment comes. And of course I forgive you. But if she has been lying to me . . . Oh God! What will I do?' His eyes opened wider. 'You don't think they're planning to elope? Could it be that bad? No! What am I talking about!' He rubbed his face tiredly then looked up. 'I suppose we could do nothing. Just wait and see. Would that be cowardly?'

'Hope it all goes away, you mean? Can we risk it, Hugh? Suppose it doesn't go away but gets worse. Your marriage will be ruined and mine will never happen!'

He raised his shoulders helplessly. 'You're right. Look, leave it with me for the moment, Lucy. I'll ask her. Then I'll come back to you whatever the outcome. Is that all right?'

Lucy nodded.

He went on. 'I don't want you to do or say anything hasty. We must try to keep a lid on this. I don't want Mr Grosvenor to get wind of it.'

'Mr Grosvenor? What's it got to do with him?'

'He's very strict about such matters. Quite Victorian, really.'

'But didn't he have an illegitimate daughter by the Portuguese woman? Joanna is the child of that relationship. He's hardly in a position to blame others for . . .'

'It's because of that. It caused so much trouble and heartache.' He stood up. 'But let's leave him out of this. I'm sorry I mentioned it. We'll do the best we can and keep each other informed. Let's hope it has all been a misunderstanding.'

He saw her to the door and gave her arm a friendly squeeze which was meant to reassure her but as Lucy left the building she had the suspicion that she had made matters worse. But she would do as Hugh recommended and say nothing until he had spoken to Jane and reported back. She would somehow stay calm and give them the benefit of the doubt. Her own instincts, however, told her that there *was* something going on.

'I'd like to wring your neck, Jane Stafford!' she muttered. 'And yours, Andrew. Or maybe bang your stupid heads together!' She spoke aggressively in an attempt to hide her growing fear and to give herself courage. Nothing in her life had prepared her for such a catastrophe and she had no idea how to deal with it. Hardly looking where she was going, she stumbled as she crossed the *praca*, aware that a dreadful weight had settled on her young shoulders.

Around five that afternoon Elliot Grosvenor looked up from his work as Doctor Lourdes tapped on the door and entered. He scowled at his visitor. 'I sent for you two hours ago.'

'I was needed,' Eduardo replied, unperturbed by his welcome. 'One of the trucks turned over and a man was caught under it. His leg is broken and I had to set it.' He made no apology. Grosvenor could be very abrupt but Eduardo had known him a long time and had learned to ignore it. He was a good administrator and a fair man and Eduardo respected him. 'May I sit down?'

'Of course. I'm sorry. This wretched business with Doctor Barratt. How long is he going to be away from his job?'

'I can't say for sure yet. It's too early but he has taken some nourishment and . . .'

'Yes, yes! How long? Weeks, months?'

'Certainly weeks. If he doesn't make a complete recovery or if he has another attack it may be never. Ask me again in a week or two and I can give you a better prognosis.'

'God Almighty!' He shook his head in disbelief. 'How will you manage single-handed?'

'I won't be able to manage. I was planning to ask for extra help. I might be able to cope if I had some extra nursing help. Unless there is an emergency of any kind. I suggest . . .'

'Extra nurses? From where? They don't grow on trees!' He rolled his eyes.

Eduardo kept his face impassive. 'I suggest some of the young English ladies might care to volunteer their services – on a part-time basis.'

'Young English ladies?' He looked astonished at the very idea. 'But they aren't trained. How could you expect them to help you? I shouldn't care to be bandaged by a young English lady!'

'They could undertake the more menial tasks and relieve the qualified nurses who would then have more time to work under my supervision. Nurse Robbins is very experienced and could help me with the more complicated procedures. It would only do as a temporary measure and if Doctor Barratt doesn't return we would have to recruit another doctor.'

Shocked, Grosvenor regarded him stonily. 'You think the young English ladies would volunteer for *menial* tasks?'

'Don't you think they will? This is an emergency.'

His look was challenging and the administrator drummed his fingers on the desk and stared past him while he wrestled with his thoughts.

'You mean . . . bedpans and suchlike?'

'Yes. And they could learn to take temperatures, help with the washing, take round the meals . . . Our qualified nurses have to do a lot of work that does not require any medical training. It is a constant complaint in the profession.'

He could see that Grosvenor was struggling to admit that this was probably the only way out of their immediate problem.

'Leave it with me, Doctor Lourdes,' he said finally. 'I'll come by the hospital later and let you know. Now you'd better get back to your patients. Thank you for your time.'

'Not at all. I'm sure we can deal with the problem.'

He was halfway to the door when Grosvenor asked, 'That overturned truck? Was it deliberate? Sabotage?'

'I have no way of knowing that, sir. I think you should talk to Mr Shreiker or Mr Benbridge.'

As he retraced his steps to the hospital, Eduardo allowed himself a faint smile. How would the genteel English ladies react to the idea, he wondered. The smile faded. What did Grosvenor mean by sabotage? If he knew there was serious unrest he should be taking steps to diffuse it.

It was Saturday before Hugh Stafford felt able to talk to his wife about Lucy's suspicions. Even then he waited until they were in bed before summoning enough courage to take the final step. Her answers, he knew, might bring about a major upheaval in their marriage. If she said it was true but the affair was over where would that leave them? Could they survive . . . and was survival enough? He knew he would never be able to forgive her. Even if he could he would never forget the agony of her betrayal. He would certainly never trust her again. It would be the beginning of the end. And yet if he tried to ignore the matter and say nothing he would never be at peace. It would be there at the back of his mind and not knowing would eat away at his confidence in the relationship. Lucy had raised the doubt in his mind and now he had to react.

He had been trying to decide how best to broach the subject. Perhaps he should mention that Sarah had been missing from the library on that fateful Tuesday. It would be interesting to see how Jane reacted to the news that he may have caught her out in a lie. Suppose she didn't react. What would that mean? That she was innocent? It couldn't mean that. If she hadn't been in the library with Sarah Barratt then she must have been with Andrew because otherwise there would have been no need to lie.

Closing his eyes, he said, 'I hope you're still awake, Jane. I have to talk to you about something.'

There was a long silence. He relaxed marginally. If she was asleep he could delay it until tomorrow.

At last she said, 'I have something to tell you, Hugh. It won't be easy.'

Equally shocked, they lay together in the darkness without speaking. Then Jane sat up and switched on the bedside lamp. She looked warm and tousled and utterly desirable but Hugh could not bear the thought of touching her. Reluctantly he sat up. He had hoped to talk under the cover of darkness but Jane had decided otherwise.

Looking past her, he said, 'I hope it's not what I think it is.' He heard a sharp intake of breath.

'What do you think it is?' He turned towards her and saw how disturbed she was by the small exchange. So there was something. He felt a prickle of fear.

'Lucy came to talk to me the other day – about you and Andrew.' His voice was hoarse but he had said it. It was out in the open. He tried to read Jane's expression but failed.

She said slowly, 'I'm in love with him, Hugh. I'm so sorry it's happened but I am. I don't know what to do and I don't suppose you can help me. And why should you?'

Horrified, they stared at each other.

He said, 'Were you ever going to tell me?'

'I thought I was. I thought Andrew wanted to marry me and I was going to ask you for a divorce. Now . . . he tells me he can't go through with it. He's going to marry Lucy.'

51

Her face crumpled and she covered it with her hands but when she looked up again her eyes were still dry but there was pain there.

Hugh struggled with a mean thought. She had betrayed him, her husband, but now she had been betrayed by someone she loved. He was fiercely pleased that Andrew had failed her yet part of him was angry that he had treated her so badly. But now at least Jane understood what *he,* Hugh, was feeling. But it solved nothing. He felt sorry for her humiliation and furious with Andrew for treating Jane so callously. Andrew was an utter swine to play with her affections and it would give him great pleasure to tell him so. So much for friendship!

'So he thinks Lucy will still want to marry him after this?' he asked.

Alarm fluttered in Jane's eyes. 'How will she know about it? You don't have to tell her.'

'She has already guessed. She's no fool, Jane. She came to me with her suspicions but I couldn't believe she was right. My best friend with my wife! And I had no idea. God! What a fool I was to trust you!' He sagged back against the pillows.

Jane's face paled. 'She knows? Oh no! I must warn Andrew.'

'Andrew knows. She wrote to him. One of her famous letters! He denied it but she found out anyway. She knew he was out Tuesday night . . . and you said you were in the library. Remember?' She was silent. Guilty as charged, he thought sadly. 'You weren't because the library was closed. Sarah Barratt had fainted earlier when she heard about the doctor's heart attack. It wasn't difficult to put two and two together for her or for me.'

He watched a variety of expressions flit across her face – guilt, shame and fear. 'So were the two of you going to run off to Australia? Was that the plan?'

She nodded. 'I have to tell you, Hugh, that I still love him.'

He swallowed but his throat was still dry. 'And you don't love me?'

'No. I'm still fond of you as a friend . . .'

'Some friend! My God, Jane! Listen to yourself!'

He felt so tired. A dreadful weariness had taken hold of him but he would never be able to sleep. He wondered what she was thinking. She couldn't run to her lover because . . .

He sat up abruptly. 'How far did this go, Jane?'

'I've told you. It's over.'

'No. I mean how . . . how familiar were you? Were you lovers?' He was amazed that this question had only just occurred to him and the image of them in bed together shook him physically so that he felt a wave of nausea.

'We weren't . . .' She avoided his eyes. 'Nothing like that. I can promise you that.'

'And I'm supposed to believe you?'

'You asked.' She drew in a long shuddering breath.

'And if Andrew says differently?'

'He'll be lying. We both wanted it but I couldn't go that far.' Her face changed and tears ran down her cheeks. 'I wish to God we had! There! Now you know!'

He felt as though she had slapped his face and he recoiled slightly. Then he got out of bed and pulled on a wrap. 'I can't stay here. I can't sit there and look at you and know what . . . and know how you and Andrew . . . I suppose you've been laughing at me and Lucy! Planning how to keep your horrid little secret!' He shook his head as his eyes filled with tears. 'I never took you for this kind of woman – never! You've shattered my whole life!'

He fumbled under the bed for his slippers and made his way unsteadily downstairs and headed for the whisky.

*   *   *

53

On Sunday, the next morning, Lucy was awakened very early by a commotion in the road outside and hurried to the window. She saw Hugh standing outside the gate, a bottle in his hand. He saw her and waved, swayed and almost fell. Glancing at her bedside clock she saw that it was twenty past five.

'Oh God!' she exclaimed. She knew at once what had happened. Hugh had confirmed her suspicions. She grabbed her dressing gown, pulled it on and crept along the passage. She must silence him before he woke the entire neighbourhood and alerted their neighbours to the scandal which loomed larger than ever.

Opening the gate she caught Hugh by the arm and tried to steady him. He was very drunk. But what to do with him? Where to go? Neither of them was properly dressed and if anyone saw them they would jump to the wrong conclusion.

'Come inside, Hugh, but keep very, very quiet!'

He slumped against her and she had to put an arm round him and steer him towards the front door. Once inside she closed the door quietly and led him into the kitchen. She sat him down, removed the almost empty whisky bottle from his hand and made him drink some water while she brewed a pot of tea.

'Eat this!' she told him and handed him a thick slice of bread covered with marmalade. 'Eat! Don't talk!'

He took one bite, struggled to swallow it and then began to cry large silent tears.

She watched him helplessly for a moment then put a comforting arm round his shoulders.

'We'll think of something,' she told him. 'There's always an answer. We'll find it, Hugh!'

This was her fault, she thought. I'm to blame for the state he's in. I should never have told him.

He whispered, 'You were right . . . and she still loves

him. What am I going to do? She still loves him! I want
to see him. I want to *kill* him!' He looked up through his
tears, making no effort to stop them. 'I thought we were
happy. We *were* happy . . . Now it's finished.'

Bit by bit the story of Jane's confession came out and
Lucy listened wordlessly as he spelled out the end of her
own marriage as well as his. She made tea and insisted he
drank a few mouthfuls. He was trembling violently and
she put that down to a combination of shock, grief and
alcohol. Why did men turn to the bottle for help, she
wondered. How could they have a rational discussion about
what to do while he was in this state? All he was fit for
was sleep, she decided, and came to a decision. She would
dress, take him home and deliver him to Jane. Let her see
what a mess he was. Let her feel some of the guilt. Then
she would come back, wash and change and go to see
Andrew.

Ten minutes later she was outside the Staffords' house,
knocking on the door. Leaning heavily on her for support,
Hugh was almost stupefied and muttering incoherently. She
heard footsteps, the door opened and she came face to face
with Jane. She was wearing a white nightdress which accen-
tuated the pallor of her face, her eyes were dark and
anguished and her hair was dishevelled. Lucy felt a
moment's compassion but promptly hardened her heart. Jane
looked utterly bewildered.

'I'm returning your husband,' Lucy said bluntly.

'I didn't know . . . I thought he was asleep . . .'

'Well, he's not. He's tired, he's drunk and he's broken-
hearted! You'd better put him to bed before he collapses.'

Hugh took a couple of faltering steps and fell against his
wife who staggered back under his weight.

'Help me, Lucy, for God's sake!'

Lucy stepped forward and then checked herself. 'You're

responsible for the state he's in. You look after him. I don't envy you your conscience.'

Jane's face paled but she made an effort to rally herself. 'I didn't ask him to get drunk!' she said as she struggled to keep him upright. 'I suggest you mind your own business, Lucy.'

'He made it my business! He came to our house and woke me up. Would you rather I had left him there to rouse all the neighbours?' Lucy was aware of wildly growing anger. She must get away before she said or did anything she would regret.

Jane's mouth tightened as she tried to shake her husband into some kind of wakefulness. She obviously felt no pity for him. Lucy felt a tight knot of anxiety forming within her stomach. Had Jane *really* fallen out of love with him? If so, there would be no going back for them. If they separated and then divorced, Jane would be free to marry Andrew.

With an unexpected surge of energy Hugh broke free from his wife and stumbled a few steps towards the bedroom.

Jane watched him. 'Look at him – he's pathetic! I don't want him here.'

'He's entitled to be here,' Lucy snapped. 'This is his home. I could hardly say the same about you!' Her voice had risen and she recognized the warning sign of her temper rising.

'It's my home too.'

'It's the home of Hugh and his wife but you don't want to be his wife!'

Still Jane made no effort to help her husband. 'I love Andrew,' she repeated stubbornly. 'He loves me. Why don't you release him from his promise?'

Lucy said, 'Because he swore to me that he doesn't want to be released. It was just a silly affair! A last minute fling. He says you mean nothing to him and that he still loves me.'

Perhaps she had exaggerated a little, she thought, but as she saw from the look on Jane's face, the message had struck home. Before Jane could recover Lucy said, 'I think you should go and see to him. He might be ill.'

For a moment their eyes locked. Jane hissed, 'I do wonder how I ever came to like you, Lucy Barratt!'

'The feeling's mutual!' Lucy listened for signs of life from Hugh's bedroom but he did not respond. She had no real knowledge of men and alcohol. Was he ill or simply drunk? She said, 'You might need to call in Doctor Lourdes. He looks ill to me. There is such a thing as alcohol poisoning but I don't know how much he's drunk. He had an empty bottle of whisky in his hand when I . . .'

'Thank you.' Jane turned on her furiously. 'I think I can look after my own husband without your advice!'

The words 'Do you?' hovered on Lucy's lips but she bit them back. She had already come close to losing her self-control. She took three deep breaths then turned and walked away. Time to go back to her own bed.

As she reached the gate Jane shouted, 'I suppose you're going to run off first thing tomorrow and tell Andrew what's happened.'

Lucy turned, her heart full of bitterness. 'Yes, Jane. I certainly am.'

Sunday was Lucy's first day as a volunteer nursing aide at the hospital. Short of sleep, she walked reluctantly through the hospital entrance with her mind in a daze. Last night she had had a nightmare confrontation with Andrew and she had not slept following it. Now she must carry out her nursing duties as best she could. Thank heavens, she thought, that she was not a doctor. Even in her present state she imagined she could carry out menial tasks without killing anybody. And this fraught day might well be the best she would have for some time to come.

Inevitably the facts of their tangled relationships would become common knowledge. Being the subject of unpleasant gossip instead of the happy bride-to-be would prove humiliating. She was full of dread and sick at heart and wondered how she would get through the day without bursting into tears.

The Sister glanced up irritably as they met in the corridor. She looked harassed, and glanced at the watch pinned to her uniform. 'Are you one of the volunteers?'

'That's right. I'm . . .'

'I was told you'd be here at eight. It's now nearly quarter past. Surely you can tell the time!'

'I'm sorry. I'm . . .'

'You young ladies will have to set your alarm clocks if you can't be more punctual. We can't have you turning up when you think you will. Hospitals don't run themselves. So who are you?'

'I'm Lucy Barratt and . . .'

'The doctor's niece? Then you of all people ought to know how things are done.'

Lucy felt her face colour. She had never been spoken to like this and didn't know how to respond. She said quickly, 'How is he this morning?'

'As well as can be expected.' She regarded Lucy with an expression Lucy couldn't read. 'So is it just you today?'

'No, I'm on this morning's shift and this afternoon it's Joanna Grosvenor's turn. We've worked out a rota and tomorrow it will be my sister, Marion, and . . .'

Sister interrupted her. 'Never mind tomorrow. It's today I'm worried about. We need to get started. Follow me.' With a purposeful stride she led the way back along the corridor to the men's ward and Lucy hurried along behind her. Not all the beds were in use, she noted thankfully but counted thirteen patients.

Sister said, 'They've all been washed but breakfast is late

and they're all complaining. You know what men are. Great babies, most of them.'

She pointed to a large cupboard. 'Find an apron that fits – you don't need the entire uniform. You're not a nurse. That's the breakfast trolley.' She indicated a wooden table on wheels which waited just inside the door. It was laden with cutlery, bowls, cups, two large jugs of milk, a metal canister, sugar bowl and a small tea urn. 'Then ladle out the porridge into the bowls. Ask if they want sugar and milk and do they want a cup of tea. If you don't ask they'll call you back later and you'll be running to and fro like a headless chicken.'

'What do I do if they don't like porridge?'

'They go hungry. It's porridge or nothing and don't give them too much or it won't last. Oh, I see there are a few slices of toast. Don't stand for any nonsense from them. If they argue walk away and serve the next patient. I have a couple of dressings to see to and Nurse Robbins will be back here shortly. Do what she tells you and don't answer back. Now please get a move on.'

The nurse hurried to a cupboard to collect the dressings and disappeared behind the curtains of bed three. Overcome with nerves, Lucy froze momentarily as the man behind the curtains began to groan and then to curse in fluent Portuguese.

One of the other men called out to her. 'Eh! Senora! I hungry!'

She sprang into action immediately, full of apologies, and rushed to find an apron. She was soon halfway along the ward while the large canister containing the porridge grew emptier. Before she reached the last three men there was none left and they had to make do with rather stale toast which didn't endear her to them. Feeling rather pleased with herself nonetheless, Lucy was looking forward to a brief rest, but she was quickly disillusioned.

After the breakfast it was time to remake the beds, helped by another young nurse, and then it was time to take and record temperatures and then came the dreaded time to empty bedpans. By eleven o'clock, Lucy was exhausted by the unfamiliar work. Her back ached, her head was spinning and she was beginning to feel sorry for nurses in general. It was not an easy life, she realized, stumbling round the ward like the proverbial zombie.

Visiting time arrived and the ward filled with mothers, children, sisters and brothers, all only allowed in one at a time so that the corridors were packed with people waiting their turn to see the patients. Nurse Robbins rang a large bell at the end of the hour and Lucy was thankful to see the room clear as if by magic.

Doctor Lourdes arrived as she was beginning to serve the midday meal of rabbit stew with dumplings which, to her surprise, the men appeared to relish. He did his rounds, gave her a quick smile and disappeared again. A pity, she thought with a pang of regret. She would have enjoyed a little civilized conversation.

Her uncle had been put in a private room and she talked to him briefly. He was on a special diet provided straight from the kitchen by Nurse Robbins. For most of the day he was kept lightly sedated, still conscious but in a restful state of mind. This, the doctor assured her, would reduce the strain on his heart.

Ten minutes before she was due to leave, the doctor sought her out again.

'You look very strained,' he told her with a look of concern. 'Not just because you have worked so hard but . . . You looked unhappy when you first came in. Are you sure you want to continue this work?'

His kind words were nearly her undoing. They brought back all her worries and she had to fight back tears of weakness. 'It's not the work, Doctor Lourdes, and I do want to

60

continue. It's . . . It's something in my private life. Nothing I can talk about but . . .'

He touched her hand gently. 'You must come to me for help if you need it. You will soon be married and this should be a very happy time for you. I know you have your family around you but sometimes it is easier to talk to a stranger.'

'Oh, but you're not a stranger. You're a friend! You did get your invitation, I hope.' As soon as she had said it, she realized how unlikely it was that there would be a wedding for him to attend. It dawned on her with some force that all the preparations that had already been set in motion might come to nothing. A new worry to add to everything else.

'I'll be fine,' she lied, forcing a smile. 'I didn't sleep well last night. That's all.'

As he walked away, she had the distinct impression that he had not been deceived by her lie but at that moment she saw Joanna approaching and forgot all about him.

There was only one thing in favour of the hectic routine into which she had been plunged. It left no time for her own worries and for that she was grateful. Andrew had been appalled by the account of her early morning encounter with Hugh Stafford and even more upset by her exchange with Jane. What had worried him most was Jane's insistence that she was still in love with him and was still determined to divorce Hugh and go to Australia with him. That, Lucy noted, had frightened him. So, she reasoned, he didn't want that to happen. Which surely must mean he wanted to go with *her*. That thought gave her a small crumb of comfort and a little hope. Was it possible, after all, it *had* been nothing more than a silly flirtation? If so, *did* he really still love her, Lucy – as much as before? She desperately wanted to believe that this was so but lacked the confidence. And if they *did* go ahead and marry, how would she feel about this later on? Would his betrayal lurk at the back of her mind to spoil the relationship? Deep down she feared that all was lost.

As she stumbled away from the hospital, after showing Joanna where to find an apron, she knew there was only one person she could confide in and that was Marion.

The evening meal was always at nine o'clock, as soon as Sarah returned from the library, so Marion and Lucy had time for an hour on the lake. This was a popular spot with everyone at San Domingos. Early in the day, when free from their lessons, the Portuguese children splashed in the shallows, the older boys dived and swam underwater and the older people of both nationalities rowed themselves over it. Not all of it was safe for swimming. One area was covered with water-lilies – a favourite subject with the artists among them. Further round still, the Portuguese men stood on the bank and fished.

On this particular night Marion and Lucy seemed to be the only people on the lake and Lucy was thankful for the sense of privacy this gave her. While they took turns with the oars, Lucy filled her sister in on the latest details and Marion was justifiably horrified. She stopped rowing, pulled up the oars and let the dinghy drift while she concentrated on Lucy's account.

'Lucy, this is terrible! You must talk with Aunt Sarah. Someone ought to know what is happening. If you and Andrew are not going to marry . . .' She threw up her hands in dismay.

'But how can I stop all the preparations and then it goes ahead? Stop. Go. Stop. Go. People will think I'm mad!'

Marion was silent, thinking, one hand over her mouth. 'You could say it was being delayed because of Uncle John's health. No-one would think that odd. It would give you time to sort out your feelings.'

'I did drop a hint to Aunt Sarah along those lines and

she said she wouldn't dream of it. With Uncle John in the hospital, the only thing she has pleasant to think about is the wedding and she and Agatha are planning a menu together.' She sighed, adding, 'I keep wondering what's happening between Jane and poor Hugh.'

'I wonder if he went in to work this morning. It doesn't sound as if he'd have been up to it and if his breath smelt of whisky someone would have been sure to notice it.'

Lucy shrugged. 'I don't suppose he wants to be at home with Jane. Probably find it easier to work, as I did this morning. That way you don't have time to think. You'll find out tomorrow for yourself and Sister is very strict, she has to be because some of the men like to make her life difficult. She told me that swearing and loose talk are forbidden!'

Marion slid the oars back into place and resumed her rowing. She said, 'Doctor Lourdes asked me how you were? He said you looked "under the weather". I take it he doesn't know what's going on.'

'Not from me. I suppose it's the doctor in him. He sees us all as potential patients.' She smiled faintly. 'Which ward will you be on? Do you know?'

'The women's ward which I'm told is almost empty except for two new babies and their mothers. Apparently we're not allowed to go into the small ward where the infectious cases are in case we catch something. Something to do with the insurance for medical staff. Three men have malaria and . . .' She broke off, startled by a muffled thud. 'What was that?'

'A rumbling noise! Very loud. Maybe it was thunder.'

'I don't know.'

'Blasting perhaps?'

'It's not usually so noticeable.'

They both looked up at the cloudless sky but at the same moment the dinghy began to rock violently. As they clung

63

to the sides to steady themselves, wavelets raced across the surface of the water and they looked at each other in alarm. The rumble had come not from the sky but from deep underground.

Four

F rightened, the two women looked at each other. Lucy had paled. 'It's an earthquake!' Her first thought was that neither she nor Marion could swim. If the waves grew higher and swamped the boat they would be tipped into the water and would almost certainly drown.

Terrified, they regarded each other wide-eyed and fearful, but to their great relief the sound which Marion had heard was not repeated. As they sat there, petrified, they noticed that the wavelets had lessened and the boat was level. Nervously they searched the land around them for signs of upheaval or cracks in the soil but saw nothing.

Lucy said, 'It definitely wasn't thunder but could it have been an earthquake? Nothing seems to have happened.' With a start, it occurred to her that they might be very vulnerable, afloat in the middle of the lake. Suppose the waters opened and they were sucked down! Before she could pass on this thought a siren began its mournful note and the truth dawned.

Lucy cried, 'It's the mine!'

'An explosion!' Recovering first, Marion grabbed the oars, turned the boat and began to row back the way they had come.

'It *must* have been an explosion,' Lucy said fretfully. She closed her eyes and uttered a quick prayer. Andrew would have been down there.

Marion asked, 'Is Andrew on duty?'

'Yes.' Her throat was dry as dust and there was a tension pain building behind her eyes. With growing horror she watched the approaching shore as the sound of the siren swept eerily across the water towards them, heavy with the threat of death and destruction. For a moment Lucy was frozen with fear then she snapped back into action.

'Change places with me,' Lucy told her sister. 'It's my turn and I'm fresh. I can go faster than you.'

'No! I can do it!' But she was already tiring and after a few more minutes agreed to change places so that Lucy could take the oars. She rowed steadily, wishing they had stayed closer to the shore. She was trying to imagine what might have gone wrong deep underground and what it meant to the men below. In all the time she had been at San Domingos there had never been an accident of this type and she had become complacent. The thought that Andrew might be involved in such an event had never entered her head. She had taken his safety for granted. Now she could only guess at the terror of the men trapped in the darkness, hundreds of feet below. Please God, let Andrew be alive, she prayed.

Marion said, 'They'll have a rescue team, won't they? And doctors and . . . Oh! There's only Doctor Lourdes! We'll have to go and help – all of us . . .' She nodded towards the mine shaft. 'People are running towards it. God help the poor devils, injured and dying down there!'

'Don't talk like that! It may not be that bad. We must look on the bright side until we know for sure.' Lucy pulled harder on the oars. 'We don't know that anyone's been hurt. It might not have been an explosion. It might have been a fall of rock. That would send shock waves through the earth.'

'A rockfall? That would be almost as bad . . . possibly worse!'

Lucy cursed her sister's lack of taste but knew that Marion

was right. She had always been proud of being engaged to an engineer and felt vaguely superior but now she envied Jane Stafford. Hugh, as Grosvenor's secretary, was never likely to be in any danger.

She searched for a comforting thought. 'Not if the rock fall was in an area where none of the men were working.' She sent up a desperate plea to heaven. If you let him live, God, I'll forgive him anything.

They fell silent, both busy with their own fearful thoughts.

By the time they had made their way over to join the crowd at the head of the main shaft there was a little information forthcoming. It *had* been an explosion and not a rockfall which meant that the warning klaxon had sounded and men had left the danger area as normal. The problem seemed to be that the explosion had been greater than normal and some of the men nearest to it had been hurt. A few of them had already been brought to the surface and stood around, their faces blackened, their clothes and hair thick with dust, their expressions grim. They muttered angrily among themselves. Doctor Lourdes was attending to a small group of men seated on the grass. One had a head wound and blood seeped through the bandage. Another was unconscious. A third held his own arm, his face twisted with pain.

Agatha told them what she knew. 'It could have been much worse but it's bad enough. They had all retired to the normal safe distance but the explosion was bigger than normal so some of the men were caught by the blast and a few stray rocks.' She lowered her voice. 'They're all saying that too much explosive was used but that can't be right; Andrew Shreiker was in charge and he's considered totally reliable. Elliot thinks very highly of him.'

Lucy asked, 'Is there any news of him?'

'Yes. He's all right. He was virtually unscathed, by some miracle! He came to the surface to organize the rescue team then went back down with them.' She hesitated. One of the miners says he was in a strange mood. Hardly spoke. Not his usual cheerful self at all.' Seeing Lucy's expression change she added, 'Honestly, Lucy, it could have been a lot worse. There'll be an enquiry, naturally, but no one was killed. We can thank God for that!'

Sarah appeared beside her. She was out of breath and holding her side. 'Isn't it dreadful!' she whispered. 'And poor John. I've just left him at the hospital. He desperately wants to be down here helping but Doctor Lourdes absolutely refuses to allow him anywhere near the scene. In fact he's not allowed to set foot outside the bed and Nurse Robbins has been warned to keep a close eye on him.'

Agatha asked, 'How is he, generally speaking?'

'Very poorly, I'm afraid. This doesn't help. How can he lie there resting knowing what has happened? He feels that he's their doctor and he's failing them. Of course he wants to be here when needed.'

Almost as she spoke the door to the lift cage opened again and more stunned men stumbled thankfully into the light of day – among them a young man who held his hands over his ears. He muttered frantically in Portuguese and Sarah translated. 'He says he can't hear,' she explained. 'I expect the blast has affected his eardrums. It's probably only temporary.'

Three men were carried off on stretchers and loaded into a wagon which was then driven off in the direction of the hospital.

'What the hell happened?' shouted a voice behind them.

The question came out more like an angry roar and they all turned to see Elliot Grosvenor striding towards them. From the corner of her eye, Lucy saw Andrew emerge from the cage. He, too, was covered in dust, blood ran from his nose and he was limping. Lucy looked for Jane but there was no sign of her.

Marion saw him too. 'Andrew looks utterly defeated, poor chap. Oh Lord. They're sending him over to talk with Mr Grosvenor!'

Lucy couldn't bear to watch. 'I can't stay here. I'm going over to the hospital,' she told her sister. 'They'll need some extra help. Are you coming?'

Marion nodded. Turning their backs on the scene behind them the two sisters made their way towards the hospital, saying little. Anxious women from the miners' cottages passed them. One or two asked questions but Lucy said, '*No tengo Portuguese*' and Marion shook her head.

They had nearly reached the hospital building when Marion said, 'So he was spared, Lucy. Are you still angry with him? You might have lost him altogether. If he'd been killed in the explosion you wouldn't have had to make a decision.'

'I know. It does rather put things back in perspective, doesn't it.' She frowned. 'I keep wondering ... You don't think he tried to kill himself, do you? I can't believe he would do anything like that but ... Well, men can be just as emotional as women, I suppose.'

'Andrew?' Marion frowned. 'Hardly the suicidal type. Hugh, yes. If it had been him instead of Andrew. He *was* in a sorry state this morning from what you've told me. We shall probably never know. If he was trying to ... to end it all I'm sure he'd have succeeded.'

'He may have been careless. Not concentrating properly. Thinking about Jane. Oh dear! What will happen to him if they blame him?'

Marion put an arm round her. 'Follow your own advice, Lucy. Look on the bright side. No-one seems to have been badly hurt, not even Andrew.'

Halfway up the steps Lucy stopped. 'Suppose Jane is also here *in* the hospital. I can't work with her, Marion. What on earth can I say without feeling a complete idiot?'

The problem was answered moments later by Jane herself. She was halfway down the corridor, talking to Nurse Robbins, when she caught sight of Lucy. She then spoke rapidly to the nurse who turned and looked at Lucy. Seconds later Jane had disappeared in the direction of the children's ward. Marion winked at Lucy and whispered, 'Guilty conscience!'

Ten minutes later Marion was busy in the men's ward and Lucy, wearing the full nurse's uniform, was trying to hide her anxiety. Sister and Nurse Robbins were dealing with all the smaller injuries and Lucy had been told to assist the doctor. She was washing her hands in a small room next to the operating room where he was expected any minute to deal with a head wound. When she was called in the young man with the head wound appeared to be semi-conscious. When the temporary bandages were removed, a large gash was revealed which had to be explored for anything more serious before the stitches could be inserted to restore the torn flesh.

Eduardo smiled at Lucy. 'Don't look so frightened. This is a comparatively simple procedure and you won't be asked to do anything but hand me things and take things like this . . .' He gently removed the temporary bandage which had been put on while he was still underground. '. . . and drop it in that bin.'

She hid her revulsion as she accepted the bloodstained bandage and did as he had instructed.

'Now pass me those tweezers. There's a bit of grit here . . .'

Somehow she kept her eyes averted and managed to do what was required of her.

It was close to half an hour later before the work in the operating room was over and Lucy was given the task of cleaning up and wiping down while Nurse Robbins put in an appearance to deal with the sterilizing equipment. When it was over Doctor Lourdes escorted her home.

At the gate of the Barratts' cottage they paused. The doctor thanked her for her help. 'Are you all right?' he asked her. 'It can be an unnerving experience, being in an operating room for the first time but you handled it well.'

'At least I didn't faint at the sight of the blood,' she said.

'I did wonder.' She steeled herself to ask the question that was worrying her. 'Are any of the casualties going to die?'

He hesitated. 'I hope not. The head wound case troubles me a little but I'm very hopeful. And an older man has a fractured leg which may be difficult to heal – but it shouldn't threaten his life.'

'You know they are blaming my fiancé because it was his responsibility . . .' She swallowed.

'I believe Mr Grosvenor is a fair man. And you will soon be married and gone to the other side of the world. These things pass. Try not to worry.'

'But Mr Grosvenor must give my . . . my husband-to-be a reference. He has already given him one, in fact. If he were to officially blame Andrew, Mr Grosvenor might be forced to inform the Australian administrator. He might have no option.'

'I see now why you ask such a question. I cannot be more reassuring but I am hopeful there will be no fatalities.'

Disappointed, she nodded. 'It's been quite a calamitous day, one way or the other. I will pray for a better day tomorrow. Good night, Doctor Lourdes.'

'Good night. Sleep well.'

Later, Lucy almost fell into bed, she was so tired. She thought about Andrew and wondered what Mr Grosvenor had said to him. She thought about Jane and wished her at the bottom of the sea! Then she thought about Hugh and hoped their marriage would survive.

'I still have Andrew,' she whispered into the gloom of her bedroom. 'For better or for worse. That's what we shall promise each other.' Perhaps, she thought, this had been a test of her loyalty and love. Did she love him enough to put the past behind her? If *she* had erred, would Andrew have forgiven *her*? She hoped the answer to both questions was a rousing 'Yes!'

Saturday, 21st June. At last life seems to be returning to normal and I can breathe again although I still feel tired and a little depressed. I am trying hard to rise above it. The explosion at the mine is no longer the main talking point, thank goodness. It has been very hard for Andrew. His pride has taken a terrible denting but so far he has not been accused of anything except a mistake – that is bad enough. It could have been so much worse but Stephen Benbridge told me these things happen from time to time and the fact that no one died means it will eventually be forgotten by all but the men concerned. It was kind of him to say so. I suspect Joanna asked him to say something reassuring. I feel as if my life is being turned upside down and I am helpless to do anything about it.

Doctor Lourdes assures me that the majority of the injuries are minor ones and so far the incident has not found its way into the newspapers as Andrew feared.

Uncle John has made good progress – everyone is surprised that he is improving so fast. He is able to come out of hospital tomorrow, as long as he promises faithfully to continue to rest and take life very calmly. He reads a lot, of course. Aunt Sarah has also recovered from the shock and is once again busy with the preparations for the wedding. July 12th is rapidly approaching! I still can't imagine myself as a married woman but I expect all brides feel like that.

Andrew and I have decided we can put all the problems behind us and go ahead with our marriage with confidence.

He has promised never to see Jane again alone. Now it is only poor Hugh who needs support. He keeps away from us which is sad when I think how happy we were, the four of us, before all this happened. Jane also keeps herself away from me. I don't know how she is feeling towards us but she makes me nervous.

I now know how hard it is for people who have to work for a living. The hospital is very tiring work and I fall into bed at night exhausted. I suppose it is good for my soul!

Lucy awoke the following morning with a headache which threatened to spoil her day and she decided to miss the padre's Sunday service. All the confidence expressed in her diary the night before had vanished and she felt vaguely out of sorts. Marion and her aunt went to the service without her and she wandered round the house like a lost soul until Andrew made an unexpected visit. He was in a more positive mood than of late and that cheered her. She made an effort to shake off her gloom and inevitably her spirits began to rise.

'I've been thinking about Jane,' she told him, as they sat in the kitchen breakfasting on toast and tea. 'I'm going to behave in a very mature way.'

'I'm glad to hear it. No pistols at dawn, then!' Andrew said.

They both laughed.

'If we meet on the *praca* I shall be polite but distant,' she told him earnestly. 'I can hardly withdraw *her* wedding invitation because it was for both of them and I want Hugh to be there. I don't want to punish him. It's a little difficult.'

'I doubt if Jane will have the cheek to attend. Maybe she will pretend to be unwell and stay away.'

Lucy hoped so. 'You don't think, Andrew . . .' she began and felt again the cold dread within her. Another worry was troubling her. Since the explosion she had felt unable to express it, considering that Andrew had enough to worry about but now, in his present mood, she thought she could share it with him. 'You don't think Jane would deliberately disrupt the ceremony, do you? To punish you for letting her down – and to get even with me for the things I said to her that morning when Hugh was drunk?'

Andrew frowned. 'How could she disrupt it?'

Lucy took a deep breath. 'Suppose when the vicar asks for anyone "with just cause to speak or forever hold your peace . . ." ' She swallowed hard and ploughed on. 'The bit where they ask if anyone knows any reason why we shouldn't be joined in Holy Matrimony . . .' He looked blank as though the idea had never occurred to him. 'Would she do that, Andrew? She wouldn't, would she?' Lucy lifted the cup to her lips and tried to drink so that he would not notice her trembling.

'She wouldn't!' He spoke the words forcefully but he suddenly looked as fearful as she was and to Lucy he sounded horribly unconvincing.

For a few moments they were speechless, chilled by the image this created. He said, 'I'll speak to her . . .' Seeing Lucy's expression change he corrected himself hastily. 'No I won't! Of course I won't. I'll ask Hugh to speak to her.'

Lucy longed to be reassured but the fear remained. 'But suppose she hasn't thought of it and we put the idea into her head! Oh Andrew . . .' Tears pressed against her eyelids. 'I was so looking forward to the happiest day of my life and now . . .' To her horror the tears came. 'I'm dreading it, Andrew. This is impossible.'

Fortunately Andrew immediately recognized her need and took her in his arms and held her close. 'Cry as much as you want to,' he told her. 'Cry away all the grief and bad memories. It's been a difficult time for you, I know, and it's all my fault. It can't be good for you to bottle it up inside you.' He kissed her and stroked her hair. 'My poor little Lucy. What have I done to you? I'm such a stupid, thoughtless beast. I don't deserve you but at least I know it.'

Lucy let the tears flow. She no longer had the strength of will to hold them back and no longer cared to try. Gradually the storm of tears passed and he still held her in his arms and talked gently to her. This, she told herself, was the Andrew she had fallen in love with. Slowly she disentangled herself, kissed him, sat down again and poured them both a second cup of tea.

That afternoon Lucy was sitting on the patio with her uncle who had returned from the hospital with strict instructions to rest at home for at least three more weeks.

'And no excitement!' Doctor Lourdes had told him. 'Your heart won't stand it.'

So Lucy was reading *Gulliver's Travels* to him which he assured her was his favourite book and one he had loved since reading it as a boy. Unfortunately Lucy found it boring but such a heresy would never pass her lips and she read it with as much expression as she could muster. Her uncle was lying on a chaise longue that had been carried out for him and placed in the shade of a large carob tree. She kept an eye on him because he was supposed to be resting in bed but had insisted that the chaise longue would be equally restful and he wanted to enjoy the fresh air after being cooped up in the hospital. He was pale and had lost a lot of weight but he was cheerful enough and Lucy thanked God that he was on the mend.

He said suddenly, 'He's a good man. I'm sure of that.'

'Gulliver? Yes I think he is.'

'Not Gulliver, dear. Your young man. He'll look after

you, you'll see. Australia, by all accounts, is a strange country. We had a man here once who'd been there for five years. Can't remember the fellow's name but I can see him clear as day. Big moustache. Very brown from the Australian climate. He loved the place, Lucy. Wanted to stay there but his wife needed special medical care so he'd gone back to England and, blow me down, she died within six months!' He stopped, already out of breath and dabbed his neck with a large handkerchief.

Lucy said, 'Are you all right, Uncle John? Not too tired? This is your first day home, remember.'

'I'm fine, Lucy. Don't fuss. Where was I?' He frowned.

'Telling me about the man from Australia.'

'Oh yes! Poor chap. All alone in England – and he'd lost his job by then, of course.'

'And his wife!' Lucy said pointedly.

'What's that? Oh yes. And his wife. So he got a job with Mason & Barry and came out here.'

Lucy surreptitiously slid a bookmark into place and closed *Gulliver's Travels*.

'So is he still here?' she asked.

'No, no. He did the job Stafford does now but somehow – they never did find out how – he stole a lot of money and took himself off. Never heard of him since.' He laughed. 'Funny cove, old Simpson. Ah!' He looked at her triumphantly. 'That was his name, Simpson.'

'Did you know him?'

'Just to say "Good morning" to. Not a close friend, thank goodness.' He peered past her and Lucy turned her head.

Her uncle said, 'Is that who I think it is?'

Lucy saw the Chief of Police coming towards them on his large black stallion. They watched him dismount and walk towards them and something in his expression sent a shiver of alarm through her.

He came to a halt in front of them and saluted. 'I look

for Andrew Shreiker,' he announced, reading carefully from a small piece of white card. 'Mr Andrew Shreiker.' He looked at Lucy. 'I am told ask you where he is. I am come to arrest him.'

Uncle John sat up and stared at him. 'To *arrest* him. I think you have made a mistake, senor.'

Lucy's heart began to beat uncomfortably fast. She said, 'You must be mistaken, Mr Shreiker has done nothing wrong. You should speak with Mr Grosvenor. He will tell you. Mr Shreiker is innocent.'

He shrugged. 'He has been accused. I must make the arrest. It is my job.'

Her uncle said, 'What is the charge?'

The Chief of Police studied his card. 'He is charged with causing bodily harm through negligence. Where will I find him?'

Lucy said slowly, 'He's probably at work, down the mine. Mr Grosvenor will explain. Please go to the Palacio and see Mr Grosvenor. He is the mine's General Administrator.'

He scowled. 'I know who is Mr Grosvenor. I do not wish to see him. I must find Mr Shreiker. You are, please?' He looked from one to the other.

Her uncle said, 'I'm Doctor Barratt. And . . .'

'I'm Lucy Barratt. I'm Mr Shreiker's fiancée. We are to be married.'

He frowned. 'Married? When is this to be?'

'July twelfth.' She said it with as much conviction as she could manage.

He gave her a pitying look as he shook his head. 'The twelth of July? So soon. No. This is not possible!' He saluted, turned on his heel and retraced his steps. When he had gone they looked at each other in dismay.

Lucy said, 'Bodily harm through negligence?'

It had an ominous ring to it.

* * *

Hugh Stafford reported the arrest to Elliot Grosvenor who
was immediately furious. Hugh watched with secret satisfaction as his employer's face reddened and his eyes bulged
in their sockets as he brought a large fist down on to the
desk which he was sitting behind. The force of the blow
jerked the inkwell which spilled a stream of ink. He stared
at it savagely then snapped, 'Don't just stand there – mop
it up!'

Quietly Hugh blotted the ink and set the inkwell upright
while Grosvenor continued his tirade.

'Arrested one of my staff? Good God! I'm the man who
set up the police force in the first place! It's our police
force, dammit! We recruited him. We gave him the damn
job!'

He glared at Hugh who said, 'Yes, sir!' in a carefully
neutral tone.

He pushed back his chair and stood up. 'Arrested one
of my senior engineers? How does he think I'm going to
run the bloody mine if he waltzes in here and drags off
one of my key men? God! The nerve of the fellow. What's
his name?' Striding up and down the room, he snapped
his fingers impatiently in an attempt to improve his
memory. 'Juan Ribeiro!' he cried at last. 'That's it! I'll
nail him to the nearest tree if I get hold of him! I swear
I will!'

Wisely Hugh said nothing. He knew his employer very
well and knew the storm would blow itself out. Five minutes
later, as Hugh had silently predicted, Grosvenor stopped
striding up and down the office, seized a book and hurled
it at the wall. A single page fluttered free as the book fell.
Silently Hugh picked it up, restored the page to its rightful
place and waited while Grosvenor sat down.

'Sit down, Stafford,' he said heavily, 'and tell me what
this is all about.'

'It seems, sir, that the man who received the bad head

wound when the explosion took place is still in hospital. His wife has decided he is dying and that she will be left a widow with their four children who are all under six years old.'

Grosvenor rolled his eyes but said nothing.

'She has a male cousin in Lisbon who's a lawyer – his name's Manuel Cesario – and he has told her she can sue for compensation when her husband dies.'

'Is he going to die? Is he that bad? Why hasn't Dr Lourdes been in touch?'

'Because the man isn't going to die. Doctor Lourdes is desperately busy without Doctor Barratt. There were nine men needing hospital attention and he has to rely a lot on the young ladies. They mean well but can only do menial jobs and they're not used to hard work.'

'What's wrong with the victims?' Grosvenor had picked up a pen and twirled it unhappily.

Hugh took a folded paper from his pocket and began to read aloud from it. 'Three had inhaled a lot of dust and their breathing is temporarily impaired. A few had caught the blast. One man is still deaf but his hearing is gradually improving . . . One has a sprained wrist and . . .'

Grosvenor groaned. 'I suppose *his* wife's going to sue also!'

'He's not married, sir. Then there's the head-wound man – Augusto Cardoso. But he's not dying. There were no fatalities. Cardoso's wife alleges that Shreiker was negligent in using the wrong amount of explosive and must be held responsible.'

'His *wife*? What the hell does his wife know about explosives?'

'The other men are telling her that. If we want Shreiker released they will have to set bail at a special hearing.'

'Special hearing be damned! I want him released *now*! I'll deal with the matter.'

'Some of the other men are muttering, sir.' Hugh kept

his voice level. 'I think you should know. They say Shreiker's been in a funny mood lately. Not concentrating. Short-tempered. That sort of thing. The men don't like his attitude and they no longer trust him.'

'They don't?'

'Not really, sir. The explosion brought down some of the roof.'

'Very little, in fact. I've been down there.'

'But it could have been a real disaster. Men could have been buried alive.'

'Well, they weren't, thank God.' He leaned back staring up at the ceiling. 'It's being exaggerated out of all proportion. Having said that it was bad enough but . . . So they're saying it was his fault. Shreiker's fault.' He sat forward again. 'You know him well, don't you? What do you say?'

Hugh shrugged. 'I have to admit he's been moody lately. We're . . . not as close as we once were, sir. I'd rather not say any more.'

Grosvenor gave him a searching look. 'Fallen out, you mean? Over this business?'

'No, sir, but yes, we have had a falling out but it was personal, sir.'

'Hmm?'

'The lawyer's going to say Shreiker was distracted. There's a rumour that . . . Well, I hardly like to repeat it.'

'Do it!'

'Well sir, some people are saying that he was trying to . . .' he hesitated. 'That maybe he was feeling desperate and . . . because of his personal problems.'

Grosvenor made the connection. 'Trying to kill himself? God Almighty! He'd better not be doing anything of the sort! Not in the mine's time, anyway. Has he gone completely mad?' He thought for a while. Hugh waited for him to start drumming his fingers on the desk top and didn't have long to wait. 'D'you know anything, Stafford, about this "personal problem?"'

'I'm not free to say anything. I'm sorry, sir.'

'So he does have a problem?'

'It would seem so, yes,' Hugh answered. His expression was one of regret but inwardly he was rejoicing. He had never expected to get a chance to repay his erstwhile friend for the wrong he had done him but this was the perfect opportunity. He was relishing the fact that Andrew Shreiker had been arrested. Serve the arrogant sod right!

'And you can't say any more?' Grosvenor watched him closely.

Again Hugh hesitated.

Grosvenor said quickly, 'So if I guessed it was money . . .?'

Hugh shook his head.

'Not *women*?'

Hugh avoided his eyes.

'Good God! I never had him down as a womanizer! The man's about to get married – or was until he ended up in prison!' He shook his head, bewildered by this latest revelation. 'Does the Barratt girl know? No! Forget I asked. I won't pry further. I'll keep my mind on my own problems . . . which is to get him out of prison and back at work. Damn fool! If he's charged and found guilty it will reflect badly on the mine and I won't have it. We have a reputation to protect.' He sighed. 'I'll go and sort out Senor Ribeiro. Give him a flea in his ear! You take a message from me to the doctor, Stafford. Tell him to spare no time and expense to get this Cardoso fellow out of hospital and back on his feet. I'm not asking him, I'm telling him! Sue for compensation indeed! The chap is a miner, isn't he? It's a tough job but it's regular and it pays the bills! If he doesn't like it he can go off and tend sheep!'

Hugh let himself out with a feeling of triumph. Slow to

81

anger, Hugh Stafford was not normally an aggressive man and certainly not physical when angered. He could never have fought Andrew – and if he had, he would probably have lost – but he now felt tremendously cheered by the knowledge that he had found the perfect way to punish Andrew. As he walked back to his own office he was smiling for the first time since Lucy had broken the bad news.

Monday morning dawned and with it came the post which was brought down from Mertola once a week. A cheerful postman, with a round face and humorous eyes, escorted a train of mules to carry the various parcels, packages and letters, both commercial and domestic. Food and clothes were sent out from various London stores and small pieces of equipment could also be carried. Monday's postal delivery was always eagerly awaited by the English as news from home was important and frequently shared. The inhabitants of San Domingos were alerted to its arrival by the sound of the bells with which each mule was decorated and by the time the postman was dismounting a small crowd had formed. The postman told them in his broken English that a motor car had been seen in Mertola and that people had watched its progress through the village with amazement and some alarm.

'Chickens and cats – they run! Dogs bark!' He rolled his eyes. The postman held up circled fingers and thumbs to illustrate the goggles the owner of the car, a rich man, had been wearing.

Someone asked what colour the car was.

'What colour? It was . . . grass.'

'Green.'

'Yes, yes. Very much green. And wheels, they yellow! It was noisy and it belched smoke.'

He handed out some letters and postcards. The rest of

the mail would go first to the Palacio to be signed for by Hugh Stafford. Later it would be collected individually.

Lucy's envelope contained tickets from the steam company for their journey from Lisbon to Australia and the sight of them threw her into an immediate panic.

A quarter of an hour later she sought out her sister who was in the sitting room examining a pair of leather shoes which had been ordered from Harrods before she left England.

'My walking shoes have come at last!' she cried proudly. 'Do you like them? I rather like the colour. They are lighter than I thought but I suppose light tan . . .'

'Very nice.' Lucy gave them a cursory glance and then showed Marion the tickets. 'What am I going to do?' she demanded. 'Are we going or aren't we? Because if not Andrew will have to return the tickets and . . .' She trailed into silence.

Marion began to take off her sandals. 'I assumed you were going ahead with everything. If not you should have told people. Really Lucy! I thought because you dropped the subject that you had forgiven him. You have, haven't you?'

Lucy sat down. 'I had, in a way, although we didn't actually talk about it. I was afraid to. I didn't want to have to turn up at the hospital with red eyes and I knew I'd cry. And now he's under arrest. Everything's hopeless! I know I ought to tell Aunt Sarah but you know what she's like. She'll be panic stricken.'

'What do you think?' Marion held out her feet, now encased in the sensible lace-up shoes.

'They're fine.' Lucy looked reproachfully at her sister. 'If you're not going to listen to me . . .'

'I am listening. If you are asking me for advice I'd say talk in confidence to Agatha Warren. You can trust her – she never gossips – and she'll be able to advise you. You can explain that you don't want to upset Aunt Sarah or cause your uncle any worry because of his heart. That's what I would do in your shoes. And talking of shoes . . .' She stood up and walked carefully around the room, trying her new shoes for comfort. 'What do you think?'

Lucy glared. 'They're wonderful shoes! Fabulous! I've never seen such enchanting footwear! Is that enough praise for your shoes? Can we get back to what's important? It's just the rest of my life we're discussing!'

Marion rolled her eyes. 'You asked my advice and I've given it. How can you expect me to take you seriously, Lucy, when you've been like this all your life.'

'Like what?' Lucy glared.

'Dithering. Changing your mind! Remember your tenth birthday. You wanted a picnic and then you wanted a party and then you wanted to go to the ballet with friends and then it was the picnic again! Mama was losing patience!'

'I was only a child then!'

'And your pet rabbit that you desperately wanted – until you reached the pet shop and then you wanted a parrot and . . .'

'Mama wouldn't let me have it because . . .'

'She said it would learn unsuitable words!'

They both smiled at the memory.

Marion said, 'Now it's "Shall I marry Andrew or shan't I?" Nobody but you can decide.'

'But you've been married. You should know more about it than I do! Please help me make up my mind.'

Marion sighed. 'Right. I'll do my best.' She considered. 'Men aren't like us, they're like children at times. As far as I can see, Andrew is basically a good man and I think you love him and I'm sure he loves you. If I were you – and I'm not – I'd forget about his silly adventure with Jane.' She shrugged. 'Did it mean anything? I doubt it except that maybe his judgement is far from perfect. I'm sure he regrets it. If you're still not sure, think about how you would feel if you break off the engagement and Jane leaves Hugh and the two of them elope to Australia. Would you then realize that you'd made a mistake? Would you immediately want him back? Would you envy her the children they would have?'

Lucy looked stricken at this scenario. 'And would I ever fall in love again? Could I ever love anyone else?'

'Precisely. And I don't think he'll be in prison long. Mr Grosvenor will get him out. Mason & Barry has lawyers.'

She took off the new shoes and replaced them in their cardboard box, re-wrapping each one in its sheet of tissue paper.

Her sister's words made sense and Lucy felt marginally reassured. 'I could make him swear on the Bible not to be unfaithful again,' she suggested.

'*Ask* him, Lucy. Don't *tell* him.'

'Yes. You're right.'

Marion said, 'Aunt Sarah says that a cheque has come from Papa towards the wedding expenses. I'm so pleased. I admit I was getting a little worried.'

'That's good . . . I wonder if I should tell Hugh that we're going ahead with the wedding. It would put his mind at ease.'

'It would, I expect . . .' She hesitated. 'But if he tells Jane you've been in touch it might provoke her and we don't know what sort of mood she's in. It might make her vindictive.'

'Andrew will have to find another best man.'

'I should let him worry about that,' Marion said turning her full gaze on Lucy. 'I think you should go full steam ahead. First try on your wedding dress. I suspect you've lost a little weight with all the worry you've had. If it needs altering I can help you but we don't want a last minute rush.'

Lucy, greatly cheered, thanked her and agreed to do so. Really, she thought as she left the room, Marion could be very trying at times but her heart was in the right place.

Five

Agatha's letter was from Leo – Elliot's son by his marriage to Catherine – the marriage which had ended in her death. Agatha was immensely fond of his son but she read the letter which Elliot had passed to her with dismay.

'Dear Papa and Aunt Agatha and Joanna and the horses,
I am coming home ten days early for the summer hols and Mr Garner has changed the tickets for me because Simms and Carter and Betts have all got chicken pox and Old Beaky says we all have to go home or there will be an outbreak and we shall all be in quarantine. I shall be at Pomerao on Friday 27th. Please remember that I am not going to wear anything stupid at the wedding or else I shan't go and I hope Doctor Lourdes remembers that he is going to teach me to ride one of his horses.
Love to you all,
Your son, nephew and half brother Leo'

Agatha looked at her brother and smiled. 'I love his letters,' she confided. 'I keep them all. But I do see the problem. He couldn't be coming at a worse time with all that's going on though he must never know his early return is inconvenient.'

Elliot sighed. 'We'll never be able to keep matters from him. He will insist on gossiping with the servants. And I dread his questions. He is so perceptive.'

87

'He's older now, Elliot. Growing up rapidly. I'll have a word with him if you like – and hopefully Mr Shreiker will be out of prison by then so he needn't know about all that.'

'Joanna will tell him. They are as thick as thieves. But as you say, he mustn't know the change of dates is unwelcome,' he said frowning. 'Who will meet him from the boat? Isn't Friday the day you do your duty at the hospital?'

'Mine and Joanna's. We're on duty together but I can try and change days with someone – unless Lucy Barratt would like to meet him. She loves going down in the carriage behind the wagons. According to her it's exhilarating!' She laughed.

'No accounting for taste!' he replied. 'Did you know Leo was going to learn to ride with Doctor Lourdes?'

'He probably did ask permission but if so I'd forgotten but you know how independent he is. The way you were, Elliot, when you were his age. I'm happy with the notion. He'll be in good hands. Eduardo Lourdes would be a good role model and Leo must get tired of female company. Not many boys his age in San Domingos – except the Portuguese lads, of course. I know they play football together,' she said. 'Sport has a universal language, it seems, but Leo is fairly fluent in Portuguese.'

Elliot nodded. 'I wish I could say as much for our otherwise charming ladies! Very lazy, aren't they? The servants quickly learn adequate English but most of the women . . .' He stopped abruptly, warned by her expression. 'Sorry, Agatha. I'm on my high horse again! I will say you are the exception but then you embrace all things Portuguese. I'm glad you're here.'

'Thank you, Elliot.' She hid her surprise. Her brother was not given to compliments and could rarely be relied upon to say the right things when socializing. In recent years he had learned to hide behind his work – a habit he had developed during his marriage to Catherine, a marriage which had proved to be an unfortunate mistake. Except, of course, for the son she had given him. He was inordinately proud of Leo.

Many people found Elliot dour, she knew, but he had once been a happier person and she clung to the hope that he might one day come out of the shell he had built around himself. He ought to remarry. She tried to interest him in the idea but he gave her no help in what might have become a project for her.

'I'll seek out Lucy,' she told him, 'and ask her to meet Leo.' With a brief sigh, she left him to his work.

Lucy seized on the idea with great enthusiasm. 'Meet Leo from the boat? Oh yes! I'd love to. Pomerao fascinates me. So tiny and yet so important. I think of it as a cog in the San Domingos wheel . . . And shall we bring back some fish? There are often men fishing along the river. Do you remember last year one of them sold Joanna a lamprey? I didn't care for it but everyone says it's a delicacy.'

'Fish? Why not? If there are enough we'll share them. If not, you keep it. Your aunt will be delighted with fresh fish for the larder.'

Lucy made her way home with a spring in her step. Marion was right. Now that she had spoken to Andrew and they were reconciled she felt better altogether. Humming cheerfully, she hurried upstairs to try on her wedding dress. It was hanging from a hook on the wall, covered by a white sheet which hid it entirely.

Reverently she removed the sheet and gazed in awe at the ivory silk with its cream lace overlay on the bodice. Thank heavens she was going to be able to wear it. Slipping out of her clothes she lowered the dress gently over her head and fastened the row of covered buttons down the front of the bodice. Looking at herself from all angles she saw that she *had* grown a little thinner so that the bodice no longer fitted her round the waist but hung down, spoiling the shape. She pinched in the sides and it was at once restored to its original glory.

'Thank heavens!' she muttered. It could easily be taken in. For fun, she slipped on the shoes and lowered the tiara of white wax flowers on to her hair. This is what Andrew would see, she thought and some of the earlier magic returned to warm her anxious heart.

It will be a perfect day. It *will* be a perfect day! It *will* be a perfect day! she thought. If wishing could make it so she would surely be rewarded by a day to remember.

A photographer had been hired from a studio in Mertola and would travel to San Domingos the day before the wedding and sleep in one of the rooms reserved for visitors. Mrs Garsey was going to create an arrangement of artificial flowers for the church. There was a large marquee stored at the Palacio for such occasions along with chairs and trestle tables. Several friends were lending white table linen, glasses, cutlery and tableware.

Lucy sighed as she considered the list she had made. Had she forgotten anything? Jane should have been the matron of honour but nothing more had been said on the subject. Nothing needed to be said. Lucy hoped desperately that Jane would choose not to attend the ceremony. She would certainly assume the role of bad fairy if she did, Lucy thought bitterly.

Uncle John was standing in for her father and would give her away – *if* he was well enough. Doctor Lourdes had given very cautious approval as long as he retired to bed, or the chaise longue, when he returned from the ceremony.

There was a tap on the bedroom door.

'Come in!' She expected Marion but it was her aunt.

Sarah gasped in delight at the sight of her niece in her wedding finery and her small dark eyes lit up. 'Oh Lucy! You look wonderful, my dear. Turn around slowly . . . Oh, it's beautiful. I'm so looking forward to the wedding. It's the only good thing that's happening at the moment with poor John ill in bed, your Andrew being arrested and the trouble at the mine.' She sat down. 'I keep saying to myself, "Never mind, Sarah, we have the wedding to look forward to." It cheers me up, you see.' She took a quick breath. 'It's usually so dull here in the summer. Too hot to do much at all. When I was younger I used to like drifting about on the lake among the lilies but now I find the reflection of the sun on the water too much for my complexion and it dazzles my eyes.' She sat down on the top of the clothes chest and clasped her hands. 'Mind you, this summer I think I would settle for dull, given the choice. It's one thing after the other! A bolt from the blue! The heavens have opened above us and unkind Fates are leaning down to punish us!'

'Punish for what exactly? We haven't sinned, have we?'

'*We* haven't but we don't know about everyone else!' She laughed. 'All we need now is a plague of locusts.'

Lucy laughed. 'Locusts? They wouldn't find much to eat round here. What grass there is, is eaten by the sheep and goats. The pigs have the acorns from the cork trees, the bees have whatever flowers survive . . .'

'Yes dear, I know.' Her aunt was already tired of the subject. 'If only your poor dear parents could see you in that dress, Lucy.'

'They'll see all the photographs, Aunt. That will be a thrill for them.'

Lucy gave another twirl, enjoying the excitement on her aunt's face. With the return to something approaching normality, Lucy's battered confidence was slowly building again. All would be well, she thought. She would allow herself the luxury of hope.

She said, 'It will be a perfect day. I know it will.'

Aunt Sarah clasped her neat hands. 'I shall pray for you both,' she said.

* * *

Thursday, 26th June, dawned with yet another row of clouds on the horizon; clouds that would never bring the much longed for rain. What it did bring was the meeting between Elliot Grosvenor and Manuel Cesario. The meeting was for ten o'clock but that hour passed with no sign of a lawyer from Lisbon.

Elliot Grosvenor sat in his office and glared at Michael Jay, one of the firm's lawyers. 'Where is he, dammit?' he asked.

Michael Jay was a large, shapeless man with a florid complexion and bulbous eyes. Elliot thought he resembled a snail but kept this strictly to himself. Appearances, he knew, were often deceptive and Jay had a sharp mind and was an experienced lawyer who had been with the firm for many years. Jay smiled slowly, seemingly perfectly at ease in his tight fitting collar, tie, shirt and heavy worsted suit he wore in all weathers. Rumour had it that he only had one suit. Others argued that he had several identical suits. No-one asked.

'They'll be here soon,' he offered. He leant back a little so that the overhead fan cooled his face.

As if on cue there were footsteps on the stairs and Hugh Stafford came in followed by a tall, good-looking man with smooth dark hair who, to Elliot's eyes, seemed to be no more than eighteen.

Elliot scowled. 'About time!' He stood briskly, offered his hand and sat down again.

Hugh Stafford made the introductions and left. Elliot called him back. 'We'll have a tray of tea, please, Mr Stafford, in fifteen minutes.'

'Right you are, sir.'

They all sat down. It seemed that the young lawyer, Manuel Cesario, spoke very good English.

He seized the initiative by opening up his briefcase and producing a sheaf of closely typed paper. 'I think we are

here to discuss Mr Andrew Shreiker,' he said, 'and to . . .'
Jay glanced at Elliot then interrupted the speaker. 'We
are here to reject the ridiculous accusation made against
one of our employees. A man of the highest integrity in
whom we have the utmost faith.'

Cesario crossed one leg over the other, ostensibly to make
himself more comfortable but also to show how much at
ease he was with the situation.

Elliot decided he was an upstart and should be put firmly
in his place. 'Mr Shreiker is a fully qualified engineer
brought out by me from the mining establishment in Redruth
in Cornwall, England. He has been with the company for
more than a year and has proved eminently satisfactory. He
works with explosives every day of the week and has a first
class safety record. There is no way he would make a
mistake. Your client is mistaken and Mr Shreiker must be
released immediately.'

'My client's husband alleges that the amount of explosive was excessive and that lives might well have been lost.
It is a serious accusation,' Cesario retaliated.

Elliot leaned forward. 'One that you will find impossible
to substantiate! And you know it. Your client's wife thinks
she is going to be widowed and wants compensation. *If* you
can prove what you allege, and *if* Senor Juan Cardoso dies,
she would receive compensation.'

Jay gave Elliot a warning look. He had a strategy prepared
and he didn't want Grosvenor to confuse matters. He smiled
thinly at the young lawyer. 'I don't blame you for trying
but it really is a no-starter. You could save us all a lot of
time if you accept the fact that even if what you allege *were*
to be true, you could never prove it satisfactorily in a court
of law.'

Unabashed, the young man thumbed through his papers
and produced one which he handed to Jay. 'A list of men
who will swear to it that excessive explosive was used.'

93

'Hearsay!' Jay sat back in his chair. 'They weren't present at the time. They might guess but they saw nothing.'

'They experienced the blast.'

Elliot leaned forward again. 'If you were in the mining business, you would know that many conditions affect a blasting. You'll never convince a jury and the judge will throw it out.' Elliot ignored Jay's warning cough. 'Your list is worthless!' he said. 'Not one of those men can prove it. None of them would have been near enough to the setting of the explosives to know how much was being used. Most of them have no idea how much should be used.' His face had reddened and he mopped his face.

The door opened to admit Hugh with a tray of tea. He set it down and withdrew without a word. Neither Jay nor Elliot made a move towards it.

Jay said, 'I also have a list – of people who have volunteered to give evidence to Shreiker's reliability. What we call character witnesses in England.'

'I am unimpressed.'

Grosvenor's eyes narrowed. 'I also have the names of miners who recently have been reported to the management for attempted sabotage of one kind or another.' He reached for it. 'Refusing to obey an order – Carlo Cortes. Pretending deafness in order to avoid accepting an order – Mario Vitoria. Moving or hiding essential items . . . Interfering with the handling of the pit ponies . . . Working more slowly than necessary . . . claiming to be sick when fit . . . Fighting with colleagues . . .'

'These have no connection to the . . .'

'Oh but they do. These allegations are also impossible to prove but all could be prosecuted and most would lose their jobs.'

'But that is hearsay. You can't . . .' He frowned then muttered to himself in Portuguese.

Jay said, 'I have a letter here from Doctor Lourdes

containing a medical report on the patient.' He handed it over and sat back.

Elliot poured tea and added milk. He placed a cup and saucer on the desk in front of Manuel Cesario who ignored it and continued to read.

Jay sipped his tea. Elliot added three sugars to his cup and stirred.

At last the young lawyer looked up. 'So he is making a good recovery. I'm pleased to hear it. None of this, however, alters the fact that my client is unlikely to return to his work below ground. His wife has four children to support and . . .'

Jay handed him another sheet of paper. 'This is the job we have arranged for your client as soon as he is fully recovered. He will stay above ground and work in the station office where he will be retrained. No more dirty, dangerous work. No more risks.'

'And if he refuses?'

'He'd be a fool to refuse. Why should he? We are assuming he wants to work. Surely he wants to support his wife and family.'

'Yes. Naturally he does.' He sounded uncertain.

'He has until the end of the week to accept the offer. Do please visit him in the hospital before you return to Lisbon. He'll be pleased to see you, I'm sure, and you will find him in great spirits and far from death's door. He has benefited, as all our workers do, from the free hospital treatment.'

'Ah! Yes.'

There was a long silence.

Jay said, 'I assume he was arrested on your information? Naturally, in the circumstances, you will now contact the Chief of Police and tell him the charges have been withdrawn and insist that Mr Shreiker is immediately released.'

There was a long, pained silence.

Manuel Cesario shrugged expressive shoulders. His disappointment was obvious. 'Then that is what I must do. I will explain the situation to my client. In view of his remarkable recovery I think he will be reasonable.'

Grosvenor rose to his feet. 'Then I'll bid you a good day. I'm glad the matter has been satisfactorily dealt with.'

They all stood, there was more handshaking and then Elliot Grosvenor began to shuffle the papers on his desk.

Reluctantly the young lawyer repacked his briefcase, clicked it shut and rose to his feet.

Grosvenor said, 'My secretary will show you out.' He rang the small handbell and Hugh Stafford ushered the visitor out.

When he had gone the two remaining men looked at each other for a moment in triumph.

Jay said, 'Poor chap. Obviously hoping to make his mark at our expense.'

Grosvenor pursed his lips in annoyance. 'A damned waste of everybody's time and energy,' he said. 'I shall have something to say to young Shreiker when I get hold of him. He's put us on the defensive and I hate that. He'll have a lot of explaining to do.'

Andrew Shreiker was sitting in his cell anxiously rehearsing what he was going to say to his employer when he was finally released. He had no real fear that he would go to trial but the humiliation of being arrested, shut away in a small grim room with a barred window and locked door was doing nothing for his self-esteem. The overriding smell was of damp mixed with stale sweat. The furniture consisted of a mattress on a trestle bed, a hook on the wall in lieu of a wardrobe, and a rusty, unsavoury-looking bucket. The food was adequate but basic – garlic, bread and cheese or olives, bread and salt pork.

But he was not being ill-treated. He seemed to be regarded

more as a curiosity than a prisoner. For a few hours he had shared the cell with a young Portuguese man who had been caught stealing his neighbour's chickens. They sat together on the mattress and talked, after a fashion, and it helped pass the time but the man was soon removed and Andrew missed the company.

The worst of it was the amount of time he had to reflect on his recent mistakes and to marvel at the fact that Lucy still appeared to be willing to marry him. The sooner he was gone from San Domingos, the better it would be, he thought and groaned aloud as he imagined the varied reactions there would be to his present predicament. Hugh Stafford would no doubt be enjoying his downfall but Lucy would be upset and ashamed. Jane would think it was no more than he deserved and Elliot Grosvenor would be absolutely livid. The publicity would be damaging for the reputation of the mine and the whole sorry business would probably feature in Mertola's weekly newspaper with Cardoso as the hero and Andrew as the villain of the piece. He prayed his parents would never hear of the incident. They would be seriously mortified.

Thursday evening, just before seven, there were footsteps in the passage outside, a key turned in the lock and the heavy door swung open.

'Time you go, senor!'

Andrew regarded the man balefully. For a moment he did not respond. Let him wait, he thought irritably.

'You want stay here?'

The door began to close and Andrew was forced to scrabble ignominiously to his feet. 'Wait!' You idiot, he told himself. You're your own worst enemy.

Minutes later after signing several forms he was free to go. He understood that the man originally responsible for his incarceration had made a good recovery.

'Thank you, Doctor Lourdes!' he muttered, blinking in

the evening sun. The young doctor's skill had saved him. It had been a close call – he realized that – and knew he ought to be thankful. Instead he was full of resentment. The next few days would be a nightmare and he feared that Grosvenor would feel it necessary to notify the Australian mining firm to whom he had previously sent a glowing report of his senior engineer. With a deep sigh Andrew set off towards the English compound. At least in prison he had been removed from all unpleasant meetings. Now he was free and there was no way he could any longer delay the evil hour.

Jane Stafford had just visited Doctor Lourdes at the hospital – not as a volunteer auxiliary nurse but as a prospective patient. She had steeled herself for the ordeal and now walked out of the main doors with her head unnaturally high and her back ramrod straight. She walked with an unusual stiffness and stared straight ahead, seeing almost nothing. The fact was she was rigid with shock. After a quiet discussion with Doctor Lourdes he had confirmed her growing suspicion, she was expecting a child.

For her this was a monumental disaster because she knew the child was Hugh's and she didn't want it. She wanted Andrew's child and couldn't have it. Despite her best endeavours, Andrew had refused to go further than a fervent embrace and a few passionate kisses. She should have known then that he was a coward. He was afraid to face the world and confess that he was making a mistake with Lucy Barratt. She, Jane, would have sacrificed everything to live with Andrew and bear his children. Now, Andrew would hear the news with a sigh of relief knowing that he was safe. He would expect her to settle with Hugh for the sake of the child.

Hugh, of course, would overcome his present despair when he knew she was pregnant and would, in his naïve way, expect the child to make everything right again. A miracle. One big happy family!

With her eyes full of unshed tears, Jane passed Mrs Garsey who was walking her poodle. Flossie barked and the woman spoke to her but Jane marched on, deaf to the world, unaware of anything but the rage simmering within her.

She had behaved badly in the consulting room but it was too late for regrets. The doctor had been taken aback by her reaction to the news.

'Most young wives are delighted to hear this news,' he had told her, puzzled.

'I'm not most young wives!' She swallowed hard. 'I don't want to be . . . to have . . .' She closed her eyes then snapped them open. 'What can I do to . . . to undo this?'

His expression changed. He looked at her sharply. 'Nothing, Mrs Stafford. The deed is done, as they say in your country. But you will become reconciled to the idea. It's come as a shock but . . .'

'I don't want this child.'

'May I ask why? You are young. You are married. You have a secure future.'

'I can't explain. Isn't there a way?' She stared at him directly. 'You know what I mean.'

'That is illegal, Mrs Stafford. It is also dangerous.' She sensed his change of attitude. He had been surprised before but sympathetic. Now he was wary. Her suggestion had offended him.

After a few moments he said gently, 'Go home and talk to your husband, Mrs Stafford. He will help you come to terms with the idea. Believe me, when the child comes you will love it. That is always the way. You will wish to forget what you have said to me and I will forget it for your sake.'

Now she kept walking. Someone else passed her. 'Good evening, Mrs Stafford. Hasn't the weather been . . .'

Nodding, Jane walked straight on.

'Well, *really*!'

Jane wondered how long she could keep the baby's existence a secret. If she started to feel sick in the mornings, Hugh would guess. What on earth was she going to do?

The answer came to her in the middle of that night. She would tell Hugh the child was Andrew's. Andrew would deny it, naturally, but who would believe him? If Hugh believed it he would probably insist on a divorce and then Andrew might come to his senses and abandon Lucy . . . For a moment she was full of hope. It was so simple. She smiled up into the darkness. Andrew would have tickets for two for Australia. She could travel with him. By the time people missed them they would be on their way.

Moments later the truth struck her. Andrew would know it was not his child. Why would he want to raise Hugh's child?

'Oh my *God*!' she whispered, plunged into despair. The fall from the dizzy heights was like a physical blow. Whatever happened now, Andrew would never want her as his wife. The baby had removed every last hope. As realization filled her she felt a sudden chill. This was the end. She could see no future worth living for and it was Andrew's fault. He had charmed her deliberately, making her fall in love with him. Spoiling for ever what she once had with a man she loved – a marriage and a future. She had followed Andrew's lead and this is where he had taken her. If only she had resisted but it had been so exciting. She had been flattered. Instead of a married woman she had seen herself as an object of secret desire. Forbidden fruit. Their occasional glances and coded remarks had thrilled her. The shared whispers, the fantasies and, above all, the risks – had all delighted her. Then she had fallen in love with him and the romance had come to an abrupt end.

Lucy had been hurt. Hugh had been betrayed. Andrew

had been revealed as a philanderer and she, Jane, was left totally bereft.

One thing was certain. Baby or no baby, there was no way back to the relaxed relationship she and Hugh had once shared. Dry eyed she slipped from the bed. For a long moment she stared down at the form of her sleeping husband and was moved to pity. He had no idea of the further revelations in store for him – revelations that could shatter his hopes of a happy family life.

'If I could turn back the clock, I would!' she whispered. He murmured in his sleep and turned over. She moved to the window and stared out over the moonlit scene with growing awareness. She had sinned, she told herself, and the baby was her punishment.

Lucy was up early the next day and in a cheerful mood. Word had come the previous evening that the meeting at the Palacio had gone well and charges against Andrew were to be withdrawn. He would be released from prison and she knew he would come at once to see her. But, eager as she was to see him again, she had promised to meet Leo Grosvenor from the boat at Pomerao and she must be ready and waiting beside the jetty by nine thirty. The train at the nearby station consisted of a small steam locomotive with sixteen small iron tubs which carried copper ore from the mine. Attached to the rear of the train was a small passenger carriage which was easily hitched on to the rear of the train and used to transport visitors from Pomerao to the mine, whether for business or pleasure.

As Lucy waited in the sunshine in the railway yard, she provided an elegant splash of colour in her pale green skirt and blouse and the small straw hat banded with matching green ribbon lent her a certain maturity – or so she hoped. This outfit was not for Leo's benefit but for Andrew's. She expected him to be waiting for her when she returned and wanted to look her best. Ignoring the glances from the railway men, she thought about Andrew. She was curious as to his mood. How had he survived the ordeal? At least while he was incarcerated he was free from prying eyes but since his release he must have attracted a great deal of curious attention which would have mortified him.

Was he bitter and resentful at his treatment, she wondered, or shamed by the whole sorry incident? Perhaps he would treat it as a bit of a joke – play himself up as a kind of hero – but she doubted it. Andrew's pride must surely have been badly dented and he would need her loyal support. Well, she decided, she would give it and he would be in her debt. She would ask no awkward questions. He could tell her the details in his own time and she would be sympathetic.

A long-drawn-out whistle from the engine made her hurry up the step into the carriage and take her seat in solitary splendour. With a screech and a jolt the train got under way and quickly settled down into a familiar rhythm which Lucy found soothing and she watched the barren landscape slipping past with pleasure. The grass had dried to a brittle fawn colour but thirty or more goats still grazed hopefully across it, watched over by the goatherd and his lean dog. She listened to the goats' tinkling bells and felt very much at peace with the land. Australia would have to be very beautiful to match Portugal, she thought wistfully.

A lone horseman came into view, a rifle slung across his back, and for a moment her hopes rose. Was it Doctor Lourdes? If so, she would lower the window and wave to him. But that was unlikely because he was tied up at the hospital and unlikely to be wandering far from the town. Disappointed she watched a hare bounding along beside the ponderous train. Later she saw a wolf. It was crouched down, watching something she couldn't see, and every now and then it inched slowly forward – then sprang! Lucy gasped as it straightened up with a bird in its mouth and loped away until it was hidden by some boulders.

'Poor thing!' she muttered. Probably a grey partridge. Goodbye partridge! Not much chance against a wolf. She shuddered.

The railway ran for 17 kilometres but it took its time and Lucy was almost disappointed when she saw Pomerao coming into view, its small white dwellings clustered thickly against the steep sides of the river bank. When the train reached its destination it ran out on to a raised track that extended over the river. This way the ore could be tipped straight into the holds of the waiting lighters that would take the ore downstream. Fascinated, Lucy had watched the procedure on a previous occasion, but as the ore had fallen, the dust had risen high into the air and she'd had to step down from the carriage carefully shielding her eyes.

Today, a small steamboat had tied up at the jetty below and this was the *Roda* which had brought Leo to Pomerao from Vila Real. But where was Leo, Lucy wondered. She walked slowly along the street, smiling at a woman with a basket of washing on her head. She patted a tabby cat and avoided a mean-looking dog. She had no intention of being bitten. A young miner had contracted rabies the previous year and even her uncle's best endeavours had failed to save him. News of his death had shocked everyone. Lucy was taking no chances.

A crashing sound alerted her to the beginning of the business of emptying the tubs of their ore. She stared across the river to the small ships' chandler on the other side of the river. The Guardiana river ran fast and deep and for much of the day was cast into shadow by the steepness of the banks. This gave it a sombre air and Lucy remembered with a shudder that Elliot Grosvenor's wife had fallen into the water here and had been drowned.

Pushing the thought firmly from her mind she walked

further towards a man and his son who were fishing from the lower edge of the bank. She watched them for a moment as the boy flicked the rod clumsily to and fro and the man laughed. A moment later she realized that the boy was in fact Elliot Grosvenor's son. He wore a Norfolk jacket, short trousers and knee-length socks.

'Leo!' she called and they turned.

Leo looked up at her in surprise. 'You're not Aunt Agatha or Joanna.'

'They're both busy. I've come instead,' she told him.

'That's jolly decent of you. I've been here for hours and hours! I thought I might as well learn to fish while I was waiting. I nearly caught a grass snake which was swimming in the water. Do we have to go now?'

'As soon as the ore has all been transferred.'

The man spoke to Leo in Portuguese and he nodded and with some reluctance handed back the rod and clambered up the steep bank towards her. His face was flushed and his hair tousled. She smiled at him, touched as always by his youthful eagerness.

'Are you Lucy Barratt?' he asked. 'I remember you from last time I was home. You play a lot of tennis, don't you? I hate the game because I'm no good at it but I like cricket. I'm a useful bat. Women don't understand it, though. Cricket, I mean. Mama told me that. I offered to teach her once but she said she'd rather not because women have the wrong sort of brain.' He frowned. 'But there must be exceptions. Do you think you're one?'

'I'm afraid not, Leo. It's all about googlies, isn't it, and silly mid-off and leg-before-wicket. It's like another language.'

'I could explain it to you,' he offered, 'but I think it might take a long time.'

'Maybe not then,' she said with a laugh. 'I'm only a frail woman and I might have a brainstorm!'

They made their way back towards the train. A cloud of

dust now rose from the barges in the river. Leo told her
about the chicken pox and the new teacher who was from
Scotland. Apparently his accent was so extreme that nobody
could understand him. He also explained a dare that they
had to prove you are brave.

'You have to climb out of a window and along a ledge
and down a drainpipe in the middle of the night,' he told
her. 'I did it all right but it wasn't much fun. Poor old
Franks Minor slipped and broke his leg and so the teachers
found out and so did his parents and now anybody else who
tries it will get expelled.'

'Does your Aunt Agatha know about this?' Lucy asked,
appalled.

'No. It only happened a few weeks ago.'

'I shouldn't mention it if I were you, Leo!' she advised.

They arrived back at San Domingos just after eleven but
when Lucy went in search of Andrew he was nowhere to
be found.

Instead she found Eduardo Lourdes on the patio with her
aunt and Marion, enjoying a cup of lemon tea and talking
earnestly. He half rose when she appeared and offered her
his chair but Marion said, 'There's no need, we have plenty
more. I'll fetch one.'

Her aunt said, 'We're discussing John. He's being very
stubborn. He wants to go back to work and it's much too
early. Quite ridiculous and anyway, I like having him at
home for a change.'

The chair arrived and Lucy fetched another cup and saucer
and topped up the teapot.

Lucy said, 'But he must know the risks. Why is he in
such a hurry?'

Eduardo smiled. 'I think the hospital is his life and he
probably thinks I am doing all the wrong things. I hope I'm
not but I cannot convince him.'

Marion squeezed lemon into her tea. 'He wants to go back to his office and he promises he'll just deal with the administration and not spend time in the operating room or doing rounds. But will he?'

Sarah said, 'Of course he won't! At the first opportunity he'll find an excuse and off he'll go. I know him. The question is, how can we stop him, apart from tying him to the bed?'

'I suspect that his frailty would prevent him from even spending a few hours in the office,' Eduardo answered her. 'He has no idea how weak he is because we are not allowing him to do anything. I doubt he could walk more than a few hundred yards. Have no worries on that score, Mrs Barratt.'

Marion changed the subject, turning to her sister, and asking 'How is young Leo? I'm sure he's happy to be home with his family.'

'He seems in good spirits,' Lucy told them. 'He's very independent.'

Marion nodded. 'But when he's at school, Portugal must seem a long way for him. I've always thought boarding schools should be a last resort.'

Lucy stared at her. 'But we were happy enough at boarding school.'

'We were less than a hundred miles from our parents. They weren't abroad.'

'I, too, was sent away to school in England,' Eduardo reminded them. 'Mr Grosvenor was very generous to me. I wasn't unhappy even though I did not speak the language at first. I learned to cope. Children are very resilient.'

'Poor you,' said Lucy. 'All those miles away and you couldn't converse.'

'I learned quickly. You have to.'

There was a moment's silence broken by Lucy, who said, 'I was expecting to find Andrew here. They have released him, haven't they?'

Her aunt nodded. 'He was around first thing. Mrs Garsey saw him talking to Hugh. She said they were arguing about something and sounded really angry but when they caught sight of her they stopped. Flossie was off her lead and went for Andrew's ankle and he kicked her. Mrs Garsey was very upset. She dotes on that silly dog.'

Lucy said nothing but her heart thudded uncomfortably. Hugh and Andrew arguing in public. What had that been about, she wondered, and hoped there was going to be no more unpleasantness.

Marion was saying, 'With animals it's all a matter of training. A dog that bites should never be off the lead. Suppose that had been a child's ankle. The poor little mite would have been frightened of dogs for life.'

Sarah shook her head. 'I think it's a question of temperament with dogs. Our dear old Tapper never bit anyone. Do you remember him, Marion? He was very docile. Spaniels are usually rather . . .'

'He did fight other dogs, though,' Marion recalled. 'There was that big Labrador and . . .'

Sarah bridled. 'We were talking about *people,* not other dogs! Of course he would fight another dog if the dog attacked him first. He would have to defend himself! Tapper was never aggressive but he would have to defend himself.'

Eduardo caught Lucy's gaze and she thought he was hiding a smile. He pushed back his chair and stood reluctantly. 'I must go back to the hospital or your husband will be quite sure I am not looking after his patients properly and then he will have a good reason to leave his sick bed.'

Sarah smiled. 'I doubt if Sister will let him put a foot out of the bed. She can be very fierce!'

They all laughed and Eduardo made his excuses and left them.

Lucy watched him go. 'I had better go and find Andrew,' she said with a sigh.

Marion said, 'Let him find you!'

Ignoring this sisterly advice Lucy made her way to Andrew's house but received no answer to her knock. After a moment's indecision she tapped on the window then walked round to the rear of the house. Maybe he had been unable to sleep in prison and was now catching up on his sleep. He wouldn't be very happy if she woke him. She was peering through the back door when she heard the knocker go on the front door and hurried round again. To her dismay she met Jane halfway round. At once fear and anger made her shrill. 'What do you want, Jane? Haven't you done enough harm? Andrew's finished with you so don't come snooping round here . . .'

'Keep your voice down, you stupid woman!'

'I will not! And don't you dare call me stupid!'

'Don't you think it's bad enough to have the two of *them* arguing in public? Do we have to stoop to their level?'

Lucy now saw that she had recently been crying and felt a moment's compassion but quickly fought it down. Jane had only herself to blame. Neither spoke and Lucy was desperate to get away from her but she had no intention of leaving first. This was where her fiancé lived and if she surrendered it to Jane there was no knowing what would come of it.

'So what *are* you doing here?' she demanded, lowering her tone. 'Your home is on the other side of the *praca*.'

'I want to know what was said. When they argued. Don't you? You should.'

'Then ask Hugh. He's your husband.'

'I have asked him. He won't tell me. Do *you* know?'

'I haven't seen Andrew since he was released. I thought he'd be here but he isn't. So if that's all you want to know you can go now.'

'I don't need your permission!' Jane made no move away from her. Instead she gave Lucy a strange look. 'So you haven't heard the news – that I'm expecting a baby.'

It took a second for the words to sink into Lucy's conscious mind. When it did her immediate thought was how pleased they would be after waiting so long but then awareness of the present estrangement returned. It took another moment for the deeper significance to dawn on her. Hastily averting her eyes she struggled to hide her shock and the awful suspicions that suddenly overwhelmed her. At last she forced herself to speak. 'Congratulations. It's what you wanted, isn't it?'

'Is it?' Jane's expression was enigmatic.

Lucy longed to shake her. She shrugged although her heart was thumping. 'Don't ask me. It's your child.'

Jane watched her through narrowed eyes. 'I'm certainly the mother,' she said.

The question uppermost in Lucy's mind was now so overpowering that it seemed to hang in the air, echoing around them although no words had been spoken. She forced a thin smile. 'Hugh must be very pleased.'

'He isn't, as a matter of fact. He thinks it's Andrew's child. I've told him it isn't but he doesn't believe me.' With that she turned on her heel and strode away leaving Lucy weak with shock. Her heart was racing, her legs felt weak and her mouth and throat were dry. In a few seconds Jane had utterly shattered her renewed faith in Andrew. She had thought the worst was over, it was not so.

Andrew had promised her that nothing physical had happened between him and Jane but had he lied? Or was Jane lying now? Or was she trying to unsettle her so that she would quarrel with Andrew? Desperately, Lucy struggled to overcome the trembling fear within her. Somehow she must continue to trust Andrew.

'Don't let Jane poison your mind,' she told herself.

But her good intentions were not enough. The damage had been done. Suddenly she could no longer bear to

continue the search for her husband-to-be. She didn't want
to see him while she was so confused and emotional. She
certainly didn't want to have to ask him about Jane's child.
Instead she wanted to run off into the surrounding vastness
and never come back. Where could she hide away, alone
with her thoughts?

She walked up the hill, to the little English cemetery,
on legs that barely functioned. She pulled open the high
wooden gate, stumbled inside and, in the nearest corner,
collapsed sobbing. The cemetery had high walls and very
few people visited it for the gravestones were few and far
between. Here she felt safe from prying eyes.

After a while she sat up and composed herself and looked
around. She saw the two Grosvenor graves, Elliot's mother
and his wife. Also Charles Warren, who had been Agatha's
husband. There were three other graves but they were older
and she knew nothing about them.

A sound caught her attention and she saw Flossie peering
in at her and instinctively wrapped her skirt around her
ankles.

'So you bit Andrew's ankle!' she muttered. 'Good girl!'
She held out her hand but the white poodle eyed her suspiciously. 'I won't hurt you, you silly thing!'

Andrew had said that when they were in Australia he
would buy her a puppy. Not that she would ever choose
a dog like Flossie. Lucy had always wanted a golden
retriever.

'What are you doing up here, anyway, all on your own?'
she asked. 'Your mistress will be looking for you.' She
could imagine Mrs Garsey's distress. She hated to let Flossie
out of her sight. Sighing, Lucy decided she would take the
dog down with her when she left her refuge and return her
to Mrs Garsey.

'Come here, then, Flossie!' She patted her lap invitingly.
Flossie began to bark.

'Ssh! Stop that!' The silly creature would draw attention to her hiding place.

Flossie barked again and began to jump about.

'Stop your noise, Flossie!'

When she realized that the dog was not going to be silenced but was going to lurk in the gateway making a lot of noise, Lucy abruptly lost patience. She clapped her hands.

'Go away then! Shoo! Silly animal!'

To her surprise Flossie obeyed. She stopped barking and put her head on one side as though considering Lucy's suggestion. Then she sprang backwards, turned and ran off leaving Lucy feeling guilty. It wasn't the dog's fault that it had been hopelessly spoiled and had a spiteful nature. After another ten minutes had passed, she stood up and brushed down her skirt. The time she had spent alone had helped her and she felt marginally stronger. As she tidied her hair she realized that she no longer felt entirely happy about marrying Andrew. Marion had laughed at her reservations but Marion wasn't going to spend the rest of her life with him. It was time she learned to trust her own judgement. She would have to do some serious thinking and come to a decision about her future.

Six

L ess than a mile from the fringes of the town a wolf raised its head and sniffed the air enquiringly. The scent carried to it on the warm air was not sheep nor was it goat. The puzzled wolf was a large male with a damaged right ear. It was old and had been in many fights but it was tough and very knowing. Slowly the wolf followed the unfamiliar scent, turning his head this way and that. It didn't think it was man. The wolf knew that smell from the goatherds it had tracked in the past, waiting for the chance to steal a lame goat or a kid. If it were man it would be very wary for man carried a noisy weapon and it had seen wolves killed by the sound of it.

From the corner of its eye the wolf saw a plump bird race across the parched grass and then take off into the air in a desperate flurry of wing beats. Ignoring it, the wolf moved on, closer to the town. Much closer than it had ever been before. It could hear the strange sounds and could feel the tremors through the earth. The wolf's ears flattened. Creeping nearer, it suddenly recognized the scent. It was dog. He knew dog from those that accompanied the goats and sheep – but where was it? The wolf stood a little higher, searching the terrain with cold grey eyes, then the wolf saw it. A small white animal that might have been mistaken for a lamb. It was half-hidden behind a patch of cistus. Staring straight at the wolf, the animal was frozen with an instinctive fear. The wolf smelled of a mix of dog and fear, and the hairs on the back of its neck rose in anticipation. Dog! Saliva filled the wolf's mouth and its tongue lolled as it gathered speed and launched itself forward . . .

A second or two later a shot rang out. The bullet missed the moving target and the wolf, with the limp dog trapped firmly in its jaws, sped on and out of sight.

An hour later, just under a mile away, propped against a large outcrop of rock, Andrew awoke and found himself in gathering shadows, his head a confused mass of swirling thoughts and fears. His stomach cried out for food and his mouth was parched. The remains of the whisky bottle still circulated in his bloodstream and his head ached abominably. Hearing the distant shot, he opened his eyes, blinked and sat up carefully. Peering round through bloodshot eyes he saw the vast Alentejo plain stretching out into the distance – and saw nothing at all to alarm him. Reassured he set about unravelling his woolly mind. Vaguely he remembered feeling unable to face anyone after his meeting with Hugh. Feeling sorry for himself and at odds with the world in general he had decided to come up here with only whisky for company. Now it was all coming back sharply into focus and he groaned in frustration. He had never made love to Jane so she could not possibly be having his child and he had told Hugh so in an embarrassingly loud voice. Why had he flown into such a rage?

'Damn you, Andrew!' he told himself. 'You're such a fool!'

Hugh obviously didn't believe him. So what exactly had Jane told her husband about the child? As he massaged his aching head Andrew wondered whether Jane was deliberately sowing the seeds of doubt in Hugh's mind for her own purposes.

Somehow he was going to have to convince Hugh but how? No-one could determine the father of a child. There was no way to know for sure – unless the likeness from father to child was irrefutable and even if that were the case it was months away and time was slipping by. Long before the child was born he would be in Australia and Lucy would be his wife. Or should be. In spite of his misgivings he would be pleased to be away from San Domingos.

He groaned. Ahead of him there was the meeting with Elliot Grosvenor and an inevitable stormy meeting with Lucy . . . He was so sick and tired of it all.

'God in heaven!' he muttered as he struggled upright and stood swaying, his eyes half closed.

'Heh! Senor!'

Andrew turned quickly but instantly regretted his haste for his head swam painfully. A swarthy man on horseback had appeared, apparently from thin air, and was staring down at him. Two rabbits and a grey partridge dangled from his saddle.

Andrew said, 'Yes? *Si!*' To head off a stream of incomprehensible Portuguese he added, 'I'm English. *No tengo Portuguese.*'

The man rolled disapproving eyes. 'You hear this, no?' He raised his rifle.

'Ah! The shot! Yes. I hear – I mean, I heard!'

'I shoot but no good. Dog is gone. Pouf!' He shrugged. 'Plenty more dogs.'

'Gone where? Which dog?' This conversation, Andrew thought, was requiring a great deal of effort. He had no idea what the man was talking about.

The man drew his hand across his throat.

Andrew felt vaguely alarmed. He swayed slightly and wished he had remained sitting down.

'Senor is sick?' The man's eyes narrowed.

'No . . . At least . . . Not really.'

'My son Eduardo is doctor.'

'Doctor. Is he? That's good. That is very, very . . . good.'

Horse and rider were silhouetted against the setting sun and Andrew had to squint to see the man properly. He put up a hand to protect his eyes.

'Ah!' The man pointed to the whisky bottle which lay on the grass, and grinned broadly. *'Muito vinho!'* He roared with laughter which made his horse skitter uneasily. 'Much wine! Too much!' He tapped his own head and grimaced then slapped his horse and trotted away in the direction of the town, still laughing loudly at Andrew's predicament.

Andrew watched him go with as much resentment as he was capable of, which wasn't much at all in his state. All he wanted was to go home, drink some water, eat a sandwich, maybe, and go back to sleep. He didn't want to see or speak to any living soul. With a determined effort he turned to examine the huddled white buildings below.

'San Domingos!' he muttered waspishly.

Slowly he began to make his way back down the hill. Back to what, exactly, he wondered miserably and almost wished he were dead.

Friday, 27th June. It is now nearly midnight and I have spent the past hour praying for guidance and trying to decide what to do. Jane has made me lose what little confidence I had. The longer I leave matters, if I am going to break off the engagement, the more problems I will create for everyone. Everyone will be furious with me, including Andrew. Or will he? If he really is in love with Jane perhaps he would be grateful to be released from the commitment.

I'd like the chance to talk to Mama although I think she would expect me to go ahead with the wedding and make the marriage work. I would accept the risks if it weren't for the children we may have together. If we have a family I could never contemplate the stigma of a divorce and I would stay with Andrew no matter what.

I ask myself the question, Do I love him? Yes, I do. Do

I trust him? I don't think so. Does he love me? I no longer know. If only we were not booked to go to Australia we could delay the wedding by a year and see how we feel about each other at the end of that time. Now, of course, we have no time. Perhaps the reason why I don't want to say 'No' is that I dread the consequences and that is cowardly. I think I must find the courage to tell Andrew I've changed my mind. Yes. In my heart I think that is the safest, most sensible, course of action. I shall just announce it and wait for the fur to fly. Please God, give me the courage to do that.

Saturday morning saw Lucy back on duty at the hospital. She was becoming used to the routine and found it less strenuous than at first. She still marvelled at the nurse's caring attitude which survived both the most difficult circumstances and the most awkward patients. Although she had learned enough to know that she was probably too impatient ever to make a good nurse, she found the work kept her mind away from personal problems and was grateful for the distraction.

She was trying to spoon-feed an elderly Portuguese woman who found it difficult to swallow. She had been bitten by a venomous snake and the consequent swelling had partially closed her throat.

'Try another spoonful, Senora,' Lucy urged, holding a spoonful of milky porridge to the woman's lips.

Obligingly the patient did so but Lucy could see how painful it was for her and finally gave up.

'Time enough,' said a familiar voice, 'for nourishment when the swelling has gone down, Miss Barratt. We have given her the antidote and she will recover in a day or two. She won't starve in the meantime.'

It was Eduardo Lourdes and Lucy turned towards him with pleasure. She hadn't heard him approach. She wiped the woman's mouth with a clean cloth and straightened up to face him.

He said, 'I haven't seen your fiancé yet, not since he was released. Was he treated reasonably well, do you know?'

'I believe so but he wasn't freed until Thursday and I haven't seen him yet.'

'He is probably sleeping. Sleep is good for emotional shock. It allows the mind to relax and be restored.'

Lucy wondered how he would react when he heard that the wedding was off. She said nothing, however. No-one, not even Andrew, knew yet that she had made her decision.

He said, 'I have to tell you some bad news, Miss Barratt.' Her face must have betrayed her, for he smiled and rested his hand lightly on her arm. 'No, no! It doesn't concern you. It is sad news for Mrs Garsey.'

'Not her husband? Oh no!'

He shook his head and explained that the previous day his father had seen Mrs Garsey's dog taken by a wolf. A small white dog. A dog that closely resembled a small poodle.

Lucy's eyes widened. 'Oh! Not Flossie!' A hand flew up to her mouth as she gasped. 'Mrs Garsey will be heart-broken! A *wolf*, did you say?'

He nodded. 'My father tried to shoot it but it was on the move and he missed and then the chance was gone.'

'Did he follow it? Did he find . . . anything?'

'There would have been no point in trying to return the body. A wolf snaps through the neck. They take lambs and young goats with ease. I've heard tales that they will take a small infant if they find one – which they rarely do but it is not unknown.'

Lucy looked stricken. 'Poor Mrs Garsey will be looking everywhere for her dog.'

'Yes. This is why I have to speak with you. Who is to

tell her? Or is it better for Mrs Garsey not to know his fate? I cannot say.'

'*Her* fate,' Lucy corrected him. 'Flossie was a female dog. Oh dear! What a dreadful way to die! It's too horrible!'

'But it would have been very quick, Miss Barratt. No pain. Just . . . snap! All over.'

'Don't you think it would be kinder not to tell her? That way she can go on hoping.'

He raised his eyebrows. 'But is that kind? She will fret for weeks and never really know. That might be agony for her. Searching and waiting. If I were in her place I would rather know the truth and deal with it. She can grieve, recover and eventually buy herself another dog.'

Lucy looked doubtful. 'I wonder how I would feel.'

'Better than imaging a long slow death by starvation, lost and wandering far from home.' He shrugged.

'I suppose so.'

'Would you like *me* to tell her?' he offered. 'Doctors are trained in the art of breaking bad news to relatives.'

Lucy was about to jump at the offer when she paused. Mrs Garsey hardly knew the doctor. Maybe it would be kinder for her to hear it from a woman friend. She thought of the way she had chased Flossie away up at the English cemetery and bitterly regretted her behaviour. If only she had persevered. If only she had carried the dog back down the hill and returned her safe and sound to Mrs Garsey. She gave a deep sigh.

'It's my fault, so I think I should be the one to tell her,' she confessed and explained to Eduardo what had happened.

He regarded her curiously. 'Why would you be hiding in the English cemetery?' he asked. 'If you will forgive the question.'

Somehow Lucy resisted the urge to tell him everything. 'I needed a little space,' she said, adding defensively, 'We all have our problems.'

'Indeed we do.'

He looked as if he were going to say more but then he shook his head. 'I must go about my work. Don't let me keep you from your patients.' He turned to go then turned back. 'I nearly forgot. I know that your uncle was going to give you away at your wedding. He will definitely not be fit enough, Miss Barratt, although both he and your aunt refuse to accept my verdict. Doctor Barratt has to stay in bed and not be worried or excited by anything. I don't wish to alarm Mrs Barratt but he is far from well and his heart is still very weak. As to the wedding, I am happy to offer my own services in his place if it helps you.'

Lucy stared at him in dismay. 'Give me away? Oh! Well. That is very kind. I will . . . That is, the wedding . . . I might not . . .' What could she say, she wondered. She could hardly tell Eduardo that she was not going to marry Andrew since her fiancé himself was still unaware of her change of heart.

He smiled at her confusion. 'There is no hurry. The offer stands. Tell me nearer the time.'

Before she could think about his offer she was joined by Nurse Robbins who had arrived with a trolley full of pills and potions and reminded her volunteer that her least favourite task was upon her. With a deeply martyred expression Lucy began to hand out the bedpans.

Later that afternoon she waited until Marion had gone to her work at the hospital. Lucy persuaded her aunt to sit with her and broke the bad news as gently as she could, telling her everything after extracting a promise that the details would go no further.

'. . . So you see, Aunt, I simply cannot go through with it.'

She waited fearfully for her aunt's face to crumple into

tears and was ready with a supply of handkerchiefs. Sarah said nothing but continued to stare at her.

'You do understand, Aunt, don't you? The wedding will have to be . . .'

'No dear! I don't understand. It's much too late to change your mind! Whatever are you thinking of, Lucy? This is not like you.' She frowned, dry-eyed. 'Of course you will marry Andrew. Of course the wedding will go ahead. Everything has been arranged and it is most unkind of you to . . .'

'Aunt! Have you been listening to me? Didn't you hear what I told you about Jane and Andrew? It's been going on for simply ages. How can you expect me to marry the man when . . .'

'But you said he denies it. That there was no chance it could be his child.' She looked at Lucy with indignation. 'If he wanted to marry Jane he would make the child his excuse, wouldn't he? If he thought it could be his child he would say so. He doesn't. So he doesn't want to marry Jane. Think about it sensibly, Lucy. For better, for worse, dear!'

'But that's *after* you're married.'

Sarah fiddled with her beads, a sure sign she was upset. 'I'm only telling you what your mother would tell you. And your poor ailing father. Do you really want to cause them unnecessary anguish? I'm sure you don't, Lucy dear. You simply can't see the wood for the trees!' She patted Lucy's hand. 'Don't give it another thought. It will all turn out for the best, believe me.'

Confused by her aunt's unexpected reaction, Lucy stared at her helplessly. What could she say to convince her? 'I don't love him any more. How could I?'

Sarah's mouth tightened in exasperation. She shook her head. 'I don't want to hear another word on the subject, Lucy! It's all arranged. You know it is. The marquee, the flowers, the beautiful dress! And what about Andrew? Have you told him that you've changed your mind?'

'Not yet. I can't find him.'

'Then you'll say nothing to him, dear. He's been through such a lot. Just fancy – first he's blown up and then he's thrown into prison. That must have been terrifying for him, poor man. You should be there now, supporting him, promising loyalty and affection. Not turning on him for no good reason.'

'No good reason!' Lucy made a last attempt. 'For heaven's sake! He's been flirting with another woman. Telling me lies!'

'He's been very, very silly, that's all. You're making a mountain out of a molehill.' Another thought struck her. 'Do you know how many wedding presents the postman has brought over the last four weeks, from friends and loved ones in England?'

'I don't care about the presents. I don't . . .'

'Well you should care, you ungrateful girl! Nine presents! One said "Fragile" so I expect that's glass of some kind.' Her face had brightened. 'Two were from Heals and one of them felt like linen so it may be a tablecloth. No doubt more will arrive next Monday. I've kept them hidden and I shall arrange them on the morning of the wedding . . . What was I saying? Oh yes! Don't forget Andrew's parents are on their way. They'll arrive the day before the wedding. Who is going to tell them the wedding is off? Don't look at me, Lucy, for I won't help you.'

Totally baffled, Lucy regarded her aunt with growing consternation and struggled for words that would convince her aunt of the rightness of her stand but before she found any Sarah continued.

'And what about your poor uncle? How do you think John will feel if you suddenly change your mind? He will be so upset and you know what the doctor said about quiet and rest. It will most likely bring on another heart attack! I'm sure you don't want that on your conscience.' She stood up, her face set in implacable lines. 'I don't want to hear another word on this subject, Lucy. It's pure selfishness on your part. I'm truly shocked and disappointed. I thought you would show more consideration for others . . . And your poor parents!' Her eyes widened. 'Imagine what *they* would go through if they could hear us now. They'd be utterly distraught! Poor Marion already a widow and you throwing away the chance of a wonderful marriage to a charming young man!'

'Charming? How can you say that? He does have charm but he has been unfaithful and we aren't even married!'

'Lucy Barratt! You are trying my patience!' Her face, usually so colourless, now boasted two bright patches of red, one in either cheek. 'Andrew is no better and no worse than any other man of my acquaintance. Men can be fickle as well as women. Look at Jane! She has behaved very foolishly but you don't see Hugh tossing her out of the marriage bed.'

'Perhaps he will! We don't know . . .'

'Oh don't talk in that wild manner!' Sarah almost snorted with disapproval. 'Let's hear no more about cancelling the wedding because I won't tolerate it. In a year's time you'll be settled in Australia with a new baby and will look back on this episode and thank me for what I've said.'

'And if I don't? You may be wrong and then I shall blame you!'

'I shan't be wrong. Rely on it.'

Lucy searched for any argument that would change her aunt's mind. 'You forget, Aunt Sarah, that your marriage was apparently made in heaven!' she suggested. 'I'm sure Uncle John has been a wonderful husband and you have never wanted to . . .' She couldn't put the rest into words.

Her aunt's expression changed. 'Never strayed. That's what you mean, isn't it? Well, you might be surprised at what John and I have survived.' She sighed. 'No marriage is without its trials, Lucy. I was once very much in . . .' She faltered. 'I once met a man . . .' She stopped again as Lucy stared at her then gave her a challenging look. 'You needn't look so surprised, Lucy. Yes. I was in love with someone else – or rather I thought I was. Your uncle was marvellous. He forgave me and we've been happy together . . .' Her eyes clouded with something that might have been regret. 'I had Paul a year later and looking back I am so thankful that John and I stayed together. We survived a very difficult time.'

'I'm sorry . . .' Lucy stammered. 'I had no idea.'

'And neither has anyone else.' She swallowed hard. 'I've only told you to help you understand that you and Andrew can weather this storm if you really love each other. Pray for God's help and he will give you strength. Forget Jane and Hugh. They have to solve things in their own way. I mean what I say. It's for your own good . . . Right, I must get on.'

Lucy, speechless, watched her leave the room. Stunned, she replayed the entire conversation in her mind, unable to believe what had happened. 'So Andrew is whiter than white,' she muttered to herself. 'Prince Charming, no less! I suppose that makes me the bad fairy!'

For some time she sat without moving as her mind raced. When she finally stood up she was utterly confused and certainly no wiser than before. Her talk with Aunt Sarah had not ended the way she had hoped but perhaps she *was* right. Perhaps, after all, Lucy had magnified the problems and her aunt had seen everything more clearly. In a way, if that were so, life would be a little easier. No need to disrupt the plans. It would take a leap of faith on her own part but her future was at stake and she would seriously consider giving Andrew the benefit of the doubt. She would need to be strong for both of them.

Later that afternoon she and her aunt were together in the sitting room drinking tea and saying little. Sarah was working on the seating list for the wedding breakfast and trying to involve Lucy.

'I thought we'd put the Garseys on the same table as Joanna and Leo Grosvenor. What do you think?'

'If you think so.'

'Because then Elliot Grosvenor and Agatha could sit with Andrew's parents . . . Is that a good idea?'

'I'm sure you know best, Aunt Sarah.' Lucy took another biscuit and munched it thoughtfully.

Her aunt gave her a sharp look but said nothing. There was a knock at the front door and Lucy jumped. 'Oh! That might be Mrs Garsey!' She had told Sarah about Flossie and so they exchanged startled glances.

Sarah said hastily, 'I'll sit in the patio until she's gone. I don't think my nerves will stand it.' She made a hasty exit leaving Lucy to make her way towards the front door with a sinking heart.

Mrs Garsey stood on the doorstep wringing her hands. 'I wondered if you'd seen Flossie any time today?' she began. 'I'm asking everyone because I can't seem to find her.'

Lucy had put a hand on her arm and was drawing her gently inside. Closing the door firmly she led her into the sitting room and seated her on the sofa while she quickly poured a small glass of sherry for her. Mrs Garsey, fussing with her scarf, was so busy explaining about Flossie's 'naughtiness' that she simply nodded when the drink was placed on the coffee table in front of her.

'She's never run away before and she knows how much I worry,' she told Lucy. 'It really is too bad of her. Naughty little thing! Unless, of course, someone's taken her. She's such a sweet creature and I've heard of people stealing dogs and . . . She's so trusting. She'd go with anyone.'

Lucy swallowed hard as she looked into Mrs Garsey's anxious face. She took a breath and said, 'Mrs Garsey, Doctor Lourdes has some news of Flossie . . . but it isn't good, I'm afraid.'

Mrs Garsey brightened. 'He's seen her? Oh, thank goodness! I was so worried. I'll ask him . . .'

She half rose but Lucy steadied her with a hand. 'I'm afraid it is bad news, Mrs Garsey. Very bad news.'

'Bad? Not . . . How bad?' She clutched at her scarf. 'You don't mean . . .' Her voice rose.

Lucy nodded. 'Yes I do. Flossie has been killed, Mrs Garsey. The doctor's father . . .'

'He's killed my dog? Oh no!'

'No, but he saw it happen. He says it was very quick. Flossie wouldn't have . . .'

Before she could finish Mrs Garsey let out a scream that made the hairs rise on Lucy's neck. Lucy tried to take hold of her hands but she snatched them away, threw back her head and went on screaming – long, anguished animal sounds, full of pain and shock. They echoed through the house and beyond. Lucy was helpless to console her; she tried to put an arm round Mrs Garsey's thin shoulders but was pushed roughly away.

'Mrs Garsey, I'm so sorry,' she began, kneeling on the floor beside the distraught woman. 'But you must take comfort from the fact that Flossie didn't feel any pain. None at all! It was very sudden and . . .'

'Flossie! *Flossie!* Oh my darling little dog!' She rocked to and fro, her face white, her eyes glazed with despair. Lucy remembered the sherry and offered it. 'Take a sip, Mrs Garsey. It will steady you. Just a sip!'

But the poor woman knocked it aside and the liquid was

spilled. Lucy bitterly regretted allowing the doctor to persuade her that the truth was best for the patient. Why hadn't she let *him* do the telling since he was so sure of his diagnosis and treatment.

Abruptly, Mrs Garsey fell silent and after all her screams the contrast was unnerving. Lucy thought that perhaps she was going to faint but instead Mrs Garsey made a huge effort to control her grief. Dry-eyed, she looked at Lucy.

'How did it happen?'

Lucy sat next to her and held one of her hands. Stroking her fingers she said gently, 'It was a wolf. Flossie had run up on to the plain, beyond San Domingos. She was probably lost. The doctor's father thought she was a small white lamb. When he saw the wolf pounce, he tried to shoot it but he was too late. The wolf had Flossie in its jaws and that meant her neck was broken.'

'So . . . So where is Flossie now?'

'The wolf ran away with her. I'm so deeply sorry, Mrs Garsey, but you must tell yourself that Flossie had a wonderful life and she didn't even see the wolf. It was all over in a . . .'

She paused as she heard sounds in the passage and her uncle's voice.

'What in God's name is happening here? I heard screams. Is anyone hurt?'

Lucy's eyes widened. Her uncle had left his sick bed! That was strictly against the doctor's advice. Jumping to her feet as the door opened. John Barratt was stood in the doorway clutching at the door jamb for support. He wore nothing but his pyjamas, his hair was dishevelled and he was breathing heavily. His face was white, his expression full of alarm.

Mrs Garsey hardly noticed his entrance, so wrapped up was she with the details of Flossie's death. She crouched forward on the sofa, her head in her hands and began to sob.

Now all Lucy's concern was for her uncle. 'It's nothing to worry about,' she told him, grabbing him around the waist and trying to support him. 'You must get back to bed at once!'

'But who was that screaming? Not Mrs Garsey, surely!'

'It was her but she's recovered,' Lucy told him. 'Now hold on to me while we get you back to bed and then I'll explain properly.'

Reluctantly he allowed her to steer him back into the bedroom but they made slow progress. Lucy clutched him fearfully, well aware of what this might be doing to his heart.

'I thought someone was being murdered,' he grumbled. 'All that noise. I was asleep and it woke me up. I thought it was Sarah . . . or one of you two girls.'

Lucy had just managed to get him back into bed when Sarah appeared. To Lucy she said, 'Has she gone?'

'I don't think so. I'm afraid the noise woke Uncle John and . . .'

'I'm not surprised.' She tutted. 'The poor woman's had a shock but there was no need for all that!' She glanced at her husband who now lay back against the pillows, his mouth open, his lips grey. Lucy saw that his face was covered in a sheen of perspiration and felt a flutter of alarm.

Lowering her voice, she said, 'Perhaps we should fetch Doctor Lourdes . . .'

Her uncle opened his eyes. 'No! He'll take me back into hospital and I'd rather be at home. I can rest better here.'

Sarah stepped forward and patted his hand. 'We won't let him take you away, dear, but he could take a look at you. As for resting better here, we had hardly expected such a display from Mrs Garsey. Carrying on like a hysterical child at her age!'

Reminded about Mrs Garsey, Lucy slipped away and found her still in the corner of the sofa but the tears had lessened. Probably they had relieved some of the shock. She hoped so. She helped the woman to her feet and walked with her to her house. Her husband came out at once and Lucy explained that she had had sad news and needed a drink or a cup of sweet tea.

Returning home she found her aunt reading to her husband from *Gulliver's Travels* in soothing tones and decided thankfully that she was no longer needed.

Back in her own room she settled down to write the second of two letters.

> '*Dearest Andrew,*
>
> *I have talked with my aunt who has persuaded me that you and I were meant to be together and that what's happened should be put firmly in the past. She is convinced that I must forgive and forget and I will do my best.*
>
> *I know you have returned from prison (and know you were wrongly accused) . . .*'

Did she know that, she wondered briefly, then despised herself for even allowing such a doubt to enter her mind.

> '*. . . so you are obviously too ashamed to call on us but we must meet and talk and find a way to be happy again. If you don't respond to this letter I shall be deeply worried and all my doubts will return.*
>
> *On a happier note, Aunt Sarah tells me that she is keeping wedding presents for us and that all the arrangements are now made. And your parents are coming so we must present a united front and not cause them any alarm or dismay. They must never know what happened between you and Jane . . .*'

She reread it and nodded approvingly. She wanted to sound confident and in control of her emotions. Andrew, no doubt, was seriously unhappy about his incarceration and fearful of what Elliot Grosvenor would think of him. She had to restore him in some way and she hoped that her letter would boost his morale which must surely be at a low ebb. This period might well be the lowest of his life and she wanted him to feel positive about the future. She found a better nib and carried on.

'. . . *In your continued absence I have written to Jane and Hugh to say that my cousin Paul will act as your best man (I could not bear Hugh to do it and I hope that neither will come to the ceremony) – I hope you agree with this.*

Uncle John is very unwell and we are worried. He will not be able to give me away but Doctor Lourdes has offered to do so. I will accept unless I hear from you that you do not wish it for any reason. I consider it a kind offer.

I shall be waiting to hear from you either by letter or in person as soon as possible.

Your loving Lucy'

Reading it through for the last time, she was rather pleased with the tone of it and slipped it into an envelope. Feeling rather drained emotionally, she kissed the envelope which held Andrew's letter. Later she would walk round and push it through his letterbox.

Soon after breakfast on the following day, which was Sunday, Mrs Garsey sat in the sitting room, alone with her grief. Her husband had tried unwisely to console her with the promise of another puppy but she had seen this as a terrible betrayal and cried even harder. He had then patted her on the head, murmured, 'Do cheer up, dear!' and hurried back to work with obvious relief. Her head ached abominably.

When the front door bell rang she muttered, 'Go away!' Whoever it was had staying power however and on the third ring she dragged herself to her feet and moved unwillingly towards the front door. When she opened it she found Leo Grosvenor on the doorstep. Unable to face anyone and aware that she looked a mess with unbrushed hair and reddened eyes, she could find nothing to say to him and at once began to close the door but he quickly put his foot in the way.

'Please, Mrs Garsey, I want to talk to you about Flossie. I know . . .'

Tears filled her eyes. 'Flossie's dead,' she whispered. 'Didn't you know? She was killed! *Murdered!*'

'I heard,' said Leo. 'It was a most terrible thing. That's why I'm here. Can I come in?'

Mrs Garsey hesitated. She had seen the boy from time to time when he came home for the holidays and had watched him grow up. Her husband had tried to teach him to play football but apparently the boy had no co-ordination and showed no real commitment to the game.

'I don't really want to talk about it . . .' she began, but even as she looked at him she was aware of the familiar yearning. She had always wanted children. Two boys. That's what she had ordered, jokingly, before they were married. Fourteen years later and she had never even conceived. Over the years several small dogs had joined the household and she had lavished her love and attention on Flossie and her predecessors. The latter had obligingly died in more acceptable ways. Flossie's death was made so much worse by the manner of her passing.

Leo appeared undeterred by her reluctance so she said, 'I don't feel like company, Leo. I'm sorry but . . .'

'That's because you're bereaved,' Leo explained. 'I know about bereavement.'

'You do?' She stared at him, startled by his claim.

He said, 'My mother was drowned last year.'

'Oh dear!' She clapped a hand to her mouth. 'Yes of course! You poor boy! I remember now.' She felt guilty about forgetting his loss. 'Such a tragedy!' She had never liked Catherine Grosvenor but felt obliged to add, 'Your mother was a very sweet person.'

'Yes, she was. She didn't take to Joanna but I think that was understandable. It must have been upsetting for Mama to find out that Joanna was Papa's illegitimate daughter.'

Mrs Garsey felt herself becoming rather flustered by the direction of their conversation. 'Er . . . Yes . . . I daresay . . .' she began, wondering how to change the subject. Feeling rather hot, she took out her handkerchief and dabbed at her neck.

Leo leaned towards her, his manner confidential. 'It's pretty dreadful, isn't it, being bereaved. Nobody understands.'

'We-ell, yes it is.' Her mouth quivered. He gazed hopefully past her into the house and she wavered. 'I don't know . . .' she said.

He looked crestfallen. 'If it's not convenient I could come back some other time but . . . I've brought something for you.'

'Brought something?' She looked into the earnest young face and knew she hadn't the heart to refuse him. Without a word she opened the door wider, closed it behind him and led the way into her sitting room.

She sat down and he sat opposite. Unused to children, she was at rather a loss. She said, 'Can I offer you some refreshment, Leo?'

'That would be nice.'

Before she could follow up on this offer, however, Leo pulled a small object from his pocket and handed it to her. It was a wooden photograph frame. It had been roughly polished and one of the corners had not been properly mitred.

There was glass but no photograph in it. Puzzled, she turned it over.

'I made it last night,' he explained. 'It's not awfully good because woodwork is not my best subject. Mr Banks at school says I have little or no idea how to handle tools but he doesn't blame me. He says it's not my fault because I really do try.'

'It's . . . very nice.' She nodded. 'Very nice, Leo.'

'It's for you. I thought you could put a photograph of Flossie in there and keep it on the mantelpiece or by your bed so you would always remember her. I have a photograph of my mother and it's really quite comforting. The boys at school tease me but I don't care. They have mothers and I don't.' He was looking round with interest while he talked. 'I punched Berris Minor on the nose when he laughed at it and then he said he was sorry for my loss. I'm sorry for yours. Did I say that?'

'Did you? I expect so.' She swallowed. 'I'm touched, Leo. You're a very kind boy.'

He was staring at a stuffed owl in a glass case. 'Is that a real owl? I mean was it once a real owl? Did Mr Garsey shoot it?'

'Shoot it? Good heavens, no!'

'Papa shot a stag once, a long time ago, and he had the head mounted and . . .'

Mrs Garsey said quickly, 'Mr Garsey and I disapprove of shooting innocent creatures. The owl was given to us by a friend.'

The boy jumped up from the sofa and took a closer look at it. He tapped the glass and said, 'I think it blinked!' then laughed as he returned to his seat. 'Not really. It was a joke!' Catching sight of the photograph frame he was reminded of his mission. 'I don't know if you have a photograph of Flossie but if not I have a birthday card with a picture of a fluffy white dog. You could have that if you like. I was nine at the time but the number isn't on the card. Joanna says the dog looks more like a Sealyham than a poodle but . . .'

'I do have some photographs.' She looked at him, resisting the sudden urge to stroke his hair. 'I wonder, if we look through them together sometime, would you help me find the best one? If it is too big we could trim it with the scissors.'

His face brightened. 'Right now would be a good time because I'm not doing anything special. No-one will miss me.'

Blinking back sudden tears Mrs Garsey said, 'Wait here then. I'll find the box of photographs and – what do you think about some orange juice and a slice of caraway cake?'

Leo's smile lit up his face. 'That's a splendid idea, Mrs Garsey. It might take some time to find the best photograph and we could get rather hungry.'

Seven

A fter church on Sunday, Lucy returned home to find Doctor Lourdes sitting out on the patio in consultation with her aunt and Marion. She soon learned that there was concern for her uncle whose condition had been worsened by the unfortunate incident with Mrs Garsey.

Aunt Sarah looked at Lucy, her lips quivering. 'Your uncle has to go back into hospital so that he can be kept under observation twenty-four hours a day. He's going to be very upset and that will do him no good at all.'

Marion shrugged. 'It's swings and roundabouts, Lucy. Stay here or go back to hospital – either could make his condition deteriorate.'

Lucy looked at Eduardo.

'It's true,' he agreed. 'Either way is a risk. If we take him in, he may have a second attack anyway. But if it happens in hospital, medical help will be on hand. If it happens here we may have to rush him into hospital. I have to leave the decision with your aunt and uncle. I cannot make the decision for them.'

Lucy sighed.

Marion said, 'For what it's worth my vote is with Doctor Lourdes. I'd hate to be responsible for him having an attack at home. We wouldn't know how to cope.'

They all looked at Sarah who slowly nodded.

Lucy said, 'The best place has to be in the hospital – but who's going to tell him?'

The doctor steepled his fingers. 'I think I'll give him a mild sedative and then we'll break the news. He should be half-asleep by then so any extreme reaction should be reduced.'

Lucy said, 'We could appeal to his better nature by saying the responsibility of him staying at home would be an unfair burden for Aunt Sarah to bear!' She looked round eagerly. 'So he would be doing the decent thing by agreeing to go into hospital.'

'Very clever, Miss Barratt!' Eduardo said. 'You have missed your vocation. A position in the diplomatic corps would suit you.'

The laughter broke the tension and they relaxed a little, relieved that they had reached a decision.

An hour later the manoeuvre had been successfully accomplished and they congratulated themselves. Marion made a pot of tea for herself, Lucy and Sarah and the household settled down again. Mentally, Lucy ticked it off in her mind. Next on the list was a talk with Andrew and, knowing that he had had time to read her letter, she set off for his house with her fingers crossed that this time she would find him and not Jane.

Andrew was at home. As she heard footsteps within, she breathed a sigh of relief. He came to the door looking better than she had expected; shaved and in clean clothes. Before she could say a word, he pulled her inside, shut the door and kissed her. Then he held her close, whispering her name over and over.

'I don't deserve you, my sweet Lucy!' he murmured. 'Your letter has given me new hope. I promise you from the bottom of my heart that I shall spend the rest of my life trying to make it up to you. No man could ever love you the way I will. Oh Lucy! My darling girl!'

He finally released her and led the way inside and they

sat in the untidy kitchen while he unburdened himself, describing his shame and fear and the hazy wandering he had undertaken in an effort to rationalize all his anger.

'I was drunk,' he confessed. 'I won't lie about it. I thought the whisky would dull my thoughts and it did to some extent. I slept out under the sky, hardly knowing where I was or what I was doing.' He regarded her anxiously. 'I don't want you to think ill of me, Lucy, on that account. The shame and the horror was physical as well as mental. The cell was small and dark and I had no idea how long they would keep me there. I tried to convince myself that they would never take me to trial but . . .' He ran fingers through his hair.

'My poor dear!'

'You can never understand what that arrest did to me.' His eyes were dark with the recent memories. 'I felt such rage! And yet I was helpless. Locked up and treated like a criminal! I was so humiliated . . . so frightened. My God, Lucy. You have no idea what I went through – and now I have to face Grosvenor and he is going to be very, *very* angry. I can't blame him. It all reflected badly on the mine and he is so proud of the achievements and its good reputation. Anything that tarnishes that . . .' He shook his head and swallowed nervously. 'He will never forgive me.'

Lucy listened unhappily. 'But he must believe you, Andrew – that it was an accident! You *didn't* do it deliberately although some of them said you did! Stephen Benbridge says that *that's* what has upset Mr Grosvenor. The idea that one of his English staff might wantonly endanger the men working under him. It would be unforgivable.'

'But *how* do I convince him?'

'Tell him the truth, then he *cannot* blame you. He *won't!*' She squeezed his hand. 'You'll see, darling. He'll come round. It was a mistake and . . . Well, nobody's perfect.

Everyone's allowed one mistake. Isn't that what they say?'
He closed his eyes, groaned softly then reopened them.
'Some of the men were hurt. I didn't intend that, I swear
it!'

'Of course you didn't!' She hugged him fiercely. 'You
didn't intend any of it. And the men are recovering. They've
found the worst injured man a new job above ground with
no risks.'

Andrew pursed his lips. 'It's not quite that simple . . .
Lucy, I need to tell you the truth – I have to tell someone
– but you must never tell a soul. You must promise. Not a
soul. Not even Marion.'

Surprised, she looked at him and the expression on his
face frightened her. 'I . . . I promise, Andrew.' Her insides
lurched. 'It's about Jane, isn't it? The baby!' She covered
her mouth with her hand. 'I don't think I want to hear it,
Andrew! I don't know if I could bear it.'

'Jane?' He stared at her with a hint of impatience. 'It's
nothing to do with Jane. That's over and done with.'

She felt a wave of relief which was followed quickly by
apprehension. If it wasn't about Jane what *was* it about?

He took hold of her hands. 'It's about the explosion.
Darling, I know this will sound perfectly frightful but I did
do it . . . I *was* trying to . . . to kill myself!'

Lucy was aware of a tightening in her throat. She tried
to breathe but failed and finally gulped for air. Andrew had
intended to kill himself? Was she hearing him correctly?
'No!' she stammered. 'You didn't! You couldn't have wanted
that. Oh God, Andrew!' She stared at him, hypnotized. How
could he say such a terrible thing and look so much like
the man she had loved for the past year?

'I was in such a state over everything, Lucy. You and
Jane and Hugh. It all seemed so hopeless and I didn't see
how it could ever come right. I felt so ashamed of the way
I'd behaved and I knew you would never forgive me. It

was . . . Just for a few seconds I wanted to get away from it all for ever.'

Lucy was imagining the scene deep underground. Andrew setting explosives which were much too large for safety. 'But all those men! Didn't you ever think that you might kill them too?'

'I don't know what I thought and that's the truth. I was full of anger and self-loathing and I – I was desperate.'

Lucy put a hand to her heart which was racing uncomfortably. 'You tried to cause a big explosion so you would be killed? That's what you're saying, isn't it?'

He looked at her reproachfully. 'I thought you'd understand.'

'I'm trying to but . . .' She wanted to be sympathetic but the enormity of what he had done sent cold shivers along her spine.

'It was a spur of the moment thing. Not planned at all – or I might have succeeded. I used too much but not enough.' She stared at him in horror as he continued, 'I told you, it was a spur of the moment thing. One of those crazy thoughts. I can see what a fool I was now. A dangerous fool! But at the time . . .' He drew a long breath.

She whispered, 'So the men told the truth.'

'But I can't admit to it, Lucy. If I do I shall most certainly go to prison for a long time. Attempted murder, probably. Dangerous negligence at the very least. You do see, don't you, darling?'

Slowly she nodded. Yes, she could see that. 'But the men were accused of lying!'

Andrew shrugged. 'I regret that but what can I do?'

Lucy wished with all her heart that he had kept the truth from her. Hadn't he known what it would do to her? Why hadn't he felt determined to protect her from the burden of knowledge? Carefully, she withdrew her hands from his as she considered the options. He could confess and ask forgiveness but it would never be that simple. They would have to sack him and where could he find another job as a mining engineer without a decent reference? If he confessed, they could never stay on in San Domingos even though the new life in Australia would no longer be possible . . . For better or for worse! She saw with a heavy heart that they would both live out their lives with the secret of his guilt.

He put a finger under her chin and lifted her face towards his. 'You're very quiet, Lucy Barratt.'

'I'm trying to see a way out for us. A way for you to be honest but . . .'

'To be honest?' He frowned. 'You did promise, darling. I know I can trust you.'

She nodded but the air seemed to have been squeezed out of her lungs. She felt frightened and very alone. There was no way she could ask anyone for advice without betraying Andrew. It was obviously better that everyone thought it was an accident but if the miners knew . . .

'But the men,' she said suddenly. 'They know the truth. How can they work for you? They won't respect you.'

'I'll fight that battle when it comes. We'll be going to Australia soon, in any case.' He sighed. 'Tomorrow at nine o'clock sharp I'll be face to face with Grosvenor. You'd better pray for me, Lucy!' He managed a thin smile.

Lucy remained silent. It seemed certain to her that no amount of praying could persuade God to take up Andrew's cause. Her husband-to-be would have no one but her. She would have to play her part in the deception but the prospect appalled her.

Across the *praca*, Jane and Hugh were also face to face. Jane had spent a restless night, torn by indecision. Maintaining a high level of anger was sapping her energy, and grief at Andrew's betrayal was adding to her distress.

She felt ill with unhappiness and was constantly trying to hold back tears. The effort required to deal with Hugh's bitterness was also a factor in her deteriorating condition and the idea had entered her mind that this could not be good for the child she was carrying. All the women's magazines insisted that a mother-to-be should aim for a calm and happy existence. Hers was far from that and she was beginning to worry.

She dreaded an outburst from Hugh for he was waving Lucy's letter in her face while she was pretending to polish the furniture in the sitting room.

Hugh was trying to convince her that they should respect Lucy's wishes.

'They don't want us in the church and who can blame them,' he insisted. 'I certainly don't want to be his best man after the way he's behaved with you.'

'For heaven's sake, Hugh!' Jane snapped. 'You simply cannot let it go, can you!'

'Of course I can't. You're expecting a baby and you don't know whose child it is but you want to believe it's his but you expect me to bring it up as my own. Can't you stop that damned polishing? We have to talk, Jane. This is important.'

'Someone has to keep the place clean. We can't all mope about.' She hesitated. 'So if I told you it couldn't be Andrew's child? What then?'

'I wouldn't know whether or not you were lying. I can see why Lucy wouldn't want you at the wedding. You'd be like a spectre at the feast.'

The words stung but Jane would never let him see that. She tossed her head. 'Well, I want to be there. I shall go with or without you. I'm not afraid of Lucy Barratt! If we don't go it will look very odd. People know we've been good friends and they don't know what's been happening.'

'Some of them probably do. I bet Sarah Barratt knows

and you know what a gossip she is. Agatha has probably found out by now.'

Jane pushed past him and turned her attention to the sideboard. She dabbed the cloth in the polish tin. 'I'm surprised that Lucy is still willing to marry him. If it were not for Elliot Grosvenor he'd still be in prison. If I were her I'd walk away from him. He's going to drag her down. You can see that.'

'So he's no longer your knight in shining armour?' Hugh made no effort to hide his surprise.

Jane heard it in his voice. She stopped polishing for a moment and regarded him with irritation. 'I can't see him making a success of that marriage. Lucy is too young and too naïve. He's in trouble and needs someone with more courage to see him through this period in his life.'

'And you'd like that person to be you! Is that it?'

She applied more polish to the sideboard. She hated housework but at least this gave her a chance to avoid looking into Hugh's anguished face. She was becoming slowly resigned to the idea of Hugh's baby and saw that she could enjoy motherhood. She could even enjoy being a family with Hugh – but had she ruined her chances with him? How could she convince him of the truth – that he *was* the baby's father?

'Would I like that person to be me? Not any more,' she told him, tight-lipped. 'Not since he turned his back on me. I'll never forgive him for that.'

And not since he had been arrested, she thought. Not since his integrity had been questioned. She moved across the room and bent down to polish the table-legs, glad that her husband could no longer see her face. In fact, she didn't want to go to the wedding but pride wouldn't allow her to stay away.

If her words gave him any hope he gave no sign. Defiantly she went on. 'I shall go to annoy Lucy,' she said. 'I may even say something when we are asked to "speak up or for ever hold your peace"!'

'Jane!' Hugh was horrified. 'You will do no such thing! God's name! What's got into you? You've successfully ruined our marriage and now you seem determined to ruin theirs. You are such a – a *bitch,* Jane. I can't believe you're the same person I married and that's the truth!'

For a moment neither spoke. Jane was stricken by his attack and his choice of words. *Bitch.* She had never heard any man use such a word to any woman and it shook her to the core. When she finally risked a look at her husband, he was white-faced and furious. Abruptly he spun on his heel and bolted for the door.

As soon as he had gone Jane stopped polishing and sank down on to the floor. She was trembling. Had she gone too far, she wondered frantically. Was he going to pack some clothes and walk out? Was he going to abandon her? Would the whole community know that he had left her? In that dreadful moment, Jane knew she deserved nothing else but she bitterly regretted the self-destructive emotions that had driven her to such wild behaviour. She listened, trying to guess what her husband was doing. She heard him go down the passage slamming the front door behind him.

Jumping to her feet she ran to the window to see if he was carrying anything. He wasn't. So perhaps he hadn't left her. Perhaps he was going to talk to Stephen Benbridge. Stephen had been married once and might be able to advise him. She felt hot and then cold at the thought of the two of them discussing her faults but she had brought it on herself. There was no denying that.

Fighting down a growing sense of panic, she longed for her mother. At least she could give up all pretence, cry on her shoulder and receive some words of comfort even though she had been such a fool and her mother would tell her so. Of course Jane had no intention of spoiling the wedding.

She wouldn't even lower herself to attend. She would tell Hugh that when he returned. If he returned.

In an attempt to ward off further panic, Jane thought about her baby and had a bright idea. She would write to tell her parents the good news. She would not mention Lucy's wedding but fill the pages with possible names and preparations they were making for the arrival of the child – even though they were making none. Another idea struck her. She would write a similar letter to Hugh's parents. Hopefully that would make it more difficult for him to leave her and give her time to somehow turn the situation around. One fact was gradually taking precedence over everything else – she didn't want to bring up her child without a father.

Recovering slightly, with a positive plan in mind, Jane laid a hand over that part of her body where new life was growing.

'It will be all right,' she whispered. 'I promise you I will make it all right.'

Monday morning dawned and promptly at ten o'clock Andrew presented himself at Grosvenor's office and waited in deep trepidation for the summons. Hugh, in his role as secretary to the great man, treated Andrew with studied indifference and Andrew was relieved when he was at last called into the inner sanctum.

Grosvenor kept him standing while he looked him up and down. Andrew had made a great effort to look smart and efficient and to hide any sign of the torment he had so recently undergone. His suit was pressed, his shirt clean, the collar starched, the tie properly knotted. He wanted to remind his employer of the way he was before the disaster had overtaken him. There was no way, Andrew had told himself, that he must appear a victim. Grosvenor despised weakness.

'Sit down, Shreiker.' His tone was not encouraging. 'I hope you have a good explanation.'

143

'Yes sir, I have.'

'Let's hear it.'

Andrew leaned forward and adopted what he hoped was an earnest expression. 'I have a confession to make, sir,' he began. 'I – that is, my fiancée and I – have had some troubles recently. Personal troubles . . . of a marital nature.'

Grosvenor's expression hardened. 'What the hell's that supposed to mean? And what's it got to do with me?'

'I mean, sir, that I have to confess that my . . . my concentration suffered. That's the only thing I can think of to account for . . .' He realized too late that this was the wrong approach.

Elliot Grosvenor's expression had darkened ominously. 'I hope you're not telling me that a squabble with your fiancée led to what might have been a major disaster for the San Domingos mine?'

'What I'm trying to say is . . . if there is a reason for my first ever lapse, that must be it. I'm deeply sorry for what happened.'

'It didn't just *happen,* Shreiker. Accidents *happen.* You caused it. An act of criminal carelessness.' He stabbed a finger in Andrew's direction. 'And I don't accept this nonsense about a domestic argument. I know you better. It's not easy to use too many explosives especially when you're as experienced as you are. I told the lawyers what I believed – that the miners must have sabotaged the work. Undermined you in some way. God knows how.'

'Sir! As a matter of fact they had no . . .' He hesitated. What was Grosvenor implying? That this explanation would exonerate him? Or did he really believe the men were to blame? If so he could hardly go along with it . . . but that would suggest a lack of respect for Grosvenor's authority and that would hardly improve his chances. Damn.

'Damned lucky for you I was able to convince them of

your integrity or you'd still be in prison.' He leaned back in his chair and drew a deep breath. 'Why should the men deliberately monkey with the work when their own lives were on the line? Of course they wouldn't. No, there's more to it than meets the eye and we need to get to the bottom of it.'

Andrew decided to revert to his original plan. 'I'm sorry, sir, if . . . Well, if it was a mistake on my part. I'm very glad that no-one died. What I mean is, if my being distracted momentarily, a lapse of concentration . . .'

'*You're* glad no one died! *I'm* damn well glad. It was touch and go, you know, for a time. That man could have died. Doctor Lourdes did a good job. But the chap will never be fit enough for his old job so we've had to find him another above ground. Crisis averted.' He frowned. 'Not exactly averted but resolved satisfactorily. I've got the police off your back so think yourself lucky.'

'Indeed I do, sir, and thank you for all you've done. I know . . .'

'I didn't do it for you, Shreiker.' He rolled his eyes. 'So when you see Doctor Lourdes, you shake him by the hand.'

'Yes sir. I will. I'm very grateful for everybody who has helped me. Truly I am.'

Grosvenor stared at him, brows beetled. 'If I thought you'd been less than honest with me, Shreiker . . . If you've been holding something back.'

'I swear to it, sir. On my word. It was a lapse of concentration and I wish I could explain it.'

'So how do I know you won't have another little lapse and bring down the whole bloody lot!'

Andrew recoiled slightly. His employer was known for his gentlemanly behaviour and his present language was unexpected. 'You have my word on it, sir!' he said stiffly. 'I've learned my lesson and I'll be on my guard.'

'I don't want to have to amend your reference. I ought

to warn them that I may have overestimated your reliability but I know doing that would ruin you.'

Andrew felt sweat breaking out all over his body. 'I think I deserve a second chance, Mr Grosvenor. I swear I'll be on my guard from now on. I'll take an oath on the Bible if it . . .' He heard the whine in his voice and faltered. He mustn't look weak.

Abruptly Grosvenor stood up. 'I'll think about it but don't take anything for granted. If I'm not happy I'll be forced to let them know. I have my own integrity to protect and that matters more to me than anything.' He fussed with papers on his desk and then glanced up. 'Are you fit to return to work?'

'Absolutely, sir. Trust me. You won't regret it.'

'That's it, then. Take the rest of the week off. Sort your problems out and for God's sake pull yourself together. Start next Monday. Let feelings cool a little all round. The men can be very unforgiving, Shreiker, especially when their lives are at stake.' He indicated the door with a nod of his head. 'Oh by the way, we have two new engineers due, coming up river any day now. Your replacement – a single chap called Sutton – and an older man, Betts I think it is. You can give them the usual tour once they arrive. Show them the ropes.'

'Up river, sir?'

'Yes. Sutton's wife will be travelling that way with a very young child and he wanted to satisfy himself that she'd be able to cope. He paid the extra himself.'

'Certainly, sir. Sutton and Betts.'

'Betts came with him. They've been friends for a long time.'

'Right, sir.'

Weak at the knees, Andrew walked from the office. He took a few steps along the passage then sagged against the wall. Had he made it? Grosvenor had made him crawl.

Damn him! But at least he *seemed* to have accepted his story. If so it meant Grosvenor was prepared to trust him. But if not . . . It should have been a moment of triumph but Andrew didn't feel at all euphoric. He felt uncertain, adrift somewhere in limbo. Plus he'd lied his way out of trouble and it didn't feel good.

Jorge glanced up from polishing his shoes as his son came into the house and they exchanged smiles.

Jorge said, 'How's that horse of yours? It was looking good a week ago. You should get a good price for it.'

Eduardo nodded, deliberately vague. What he wanted to do was make a gift of the horse to Lucy Barratt but she was about to depart for Australia where there would be plenty of horses for her to choose from if she ever did learn to ride. She could have it shipped out, of course, but her husband would surely take a dim view of such a gift.

He smiled at his mother. 'Where's Mariana?'

'She's taken the small washing down to the river.'

Jorge examined the shoe and, satisfied, laid it aside and took up its fellow. He said, 'All they do down there is gossip! I know why she offers to take it. She sees that stupid Anna and they talk about the menfolk!' He shook his head despairingly. 'How's Doctor Barratt?'

'Very low. I've tried to tell his wife just how serious it is but she's a nervous creature and the son thinks it should be kept from her. I talked to his niece – Marion. She has a sensible head on her shoulders.' Half-heartedly he cut himself a slice of bread from the loaf.

His father asked, 'Heard anything about Shreiker? I understand he's out of prison but face to face with the big boss man,' he said laughing. 'Wouldn't like to be in his shoes!'

'The secretary, Stafford, would know if anyone does but I've heard nothing. No doubt he's got away with it. I could have told you that would happen. Mason and Barry have big lawyers.' He spread butter on to the bread. 'Did you hear that Carlos is dead? Carlos Modesto?'

His father shrugged. 'He didn't last long once he was home. You could have bought him some more time.'

'The man wanted to die at home, I can understand that. We could only have given him a few more days. His were numbered. Doctor Barratt's son is back at work, I hear. Another bout of malaria. He seems to have very little resistance.'

'Assaying seems a strange career for a doctor's son, don't you think?'

Eduardo shrugged. 'This Paul – he's very shy. Diffident. Takes after his timid mother. I doubt he would have the social skills to be a doctor. You need to be able to gain the patient's trust. He's probably happier tucked away in a laboratory, testing the ore.'

'Too highly strung. Many of the English are like that.'

Eduardo grinned. 'If you say so!'

'You don't think so?'

Eduardo paused thoughtfully. 'I like some of them very much.'

Jorge gave him a long look. 'Don't get too fond of them, Eduardo!'

The doctor got quickly to his feet. Jorge Lourdes had a very disconcerting stare. As a boy, Eduardo had been convinced his father could see right into his heart.

Eight

Tuesday morning was not one of Lucy's duty days at the hospital but she made her way there around nine thirty in lieu of her aunt who had woken with a bad headache. In a small basket Lucy carried a book on angling which Aunt Sarah had found on the shelves in the library.

'This will make interesting reading for your uncle,' she had told Lucy. 'I want to give him some ideas for his retirement and fishing is very restful – if you go by the illustrations. You can sit beside the river for hours just waiting for a fish. It can't be very exciting, can it?'

'It sounds dull enough – until you catch something. Then it might become more interesting.'

'Not *fish* dear, surely. They don't do anything. If John cannot be a doctor he will go mad unless he can embrace something else. I did wonder about fretwork – my cousin used to do that – but then he'd be at home all day and I think he would get under my feet.'

'Maybe Paul could interest him in collecting stamps.'

Sarah shook her head. 'They'd argue over them . . . A pity.'

The basket also contained a small goat's cheese and some cracked olives. Lucy walked with a light step because she anticipated seeing Eduardo Lourdes and discussing her uncle's progress. She liked the way he looked at her and had dressed with extra care in a pale cream dress and shoes and a string of blue beads.

On entering the hospital she made her way to the bed in which she had last seen him but it was empty. At first this did not alarm her. She imagined he had been moved. Maybe he was greatly improved and had been allowed to lie outside in a reclining chair to enjoy the fresh air. On the long patio she found two women and one man. No sign of her uncle. She went back inside. Could he have recovered so quickly that he had been sent home and they had somehow missed each other? It seemed unlikely.

Still unaware that anything was seriously wrong Lucy caught sight of Paul. He was sitting on a chair in the corridor, his thin shoulders hunched forward, his head in his hands. At that moment she felt a frisson of apprehension and hurried forward.

'Paul! What are you doing here?'

He looked up and she saw the shocked expression on his thin face. 'I came to – to collect my prescription,' he stammered. 'For the malaria. They always . . . they give me a tonic after one of my bouts . . .'

'Where's Uncle John? I've brought some . . .' She narrowed her eyes, alarmed by his appearance. He was very pale and his eyes were wide. 'Paul? What's the matter? He's worse, isn't he? Something's happened. Oh! Don't say he's had another attack!' As the suspicion dawned, she sat down on the next chair and put her arm round her cousin's shoulder. Her insides churned. Nothing *that* bad could happen to her uncle, surely. It was unbelievable. She clung desperately to hope. 'He can't be . . . I mean, he's doing so well. Isn't he?'

He sighed. 'He never was doing well, Lucy. We simply dared not tell Mama how bad he was. You know what she's like. So easily upset. I thought the shock would be too much for her.'

A cold fear was taking hold of her. 'So . . . he's . . . dead?'

He ran slim fingers through his fair hair but could only nod. Lucy drew in a sharp breath then pressed a hand to her heart. She felt a wave of shock run through her and fought against fainting. Her throat was tight with overwhelming grief. Her uncle was dead. Dear Uncle John. She would never speak with him again. He would be gone from their lives completely. No, she couldn't accept it. She opened her mouth to say 'Are you sure?' but realized how ridiculous that would sound. Of course he was dead. This was a hospital. They would know. Tears sprang into her eyes and she wept and now it was Paul's turn to slip an arm around *her* shoulder. He waited until she had her grief under control.

He said, 'It happened during the night apparently. They found him this morning soon after six. Poor Papa. They said it was very peaceful. Not another attack – nothing violent or painful. He wouldn't have known anything about it. He just died in his sleep.'

'Oh, I do hope so!' She swallowed hard and wiped her eyes.

'They would say that, naturally,' he agreed, understanding her suspicions, 'but it may be true. I shall tell it that way to Mama.' His voice shook. 'I've been here for some time. I had to wait for Doctor Lourdes . . .' He covered his face again and Lucy saw that his shoulders were shaking.

Lucy stared down at the cheese, the olives and the book on fishing. There would be no retirement after all. She searched desperately for something positive to say.

'Maybe, Paul, he would have preferred it this way. He would have hated being a semi-invalid. He would never have enjoyed retirement.'

'Maybe. But he's gone and now Mama is all alone.'

'No! She's got *you*, Paul.'

'Me?' He gave her a despairing look. 'What good am I?'

'Paul! Don't talk like that! She's going to need you now. She'll rely on you.'

Before he could answer, Doctor Lourdes appeared at the end of the corridor and strode towards them. Lucy slowly rose to her feet but Paul remained sitting, apparently sunk in a shocked apathy.

Eduardo said, 'I'm so sorry, Miss Barratt. Your uncle was a very good man. Very dedicated. I'm afraid it was inevitable. Nothing else we could have done, I promise you.'

'I'm sure you did all you could.'

He glanced down at Paul's bent head. 'Who is going to tell his wife?'

Lucy opened her mouth to suggest Marion as the elder of the two nieces but to her surprise Paul looked up sharply and said, 'I am! There is no one else. I'm his son.'

Lucy blinked. 'Are you sure, Paul? Marion might . . .'

'No. It has to be me.' He stared up at them and then forced himself to his feet. 'I expect there are forms to be filled. Arrangements to make. I don't want my mother to worry about anything.'

Lucy remembered her wedding and wondered if finally it would be delayed. Or cancelled. Did she even care, she wondered wildly. The events of the last few weeks had left her feeling that her fate had been stolen from her and handed over to others.

Lucy said gently, 'Have you seen your father, Paul? His body, I mean. Would you like me to come with you?'

Eduardo answered her. 'Your cousin has been very helpful. He has identified his father already but there are one or two formalities waiting in my office for his signature.'

Paul said, 'You go home, Lucy, and I'll come as soon . . .'

'I can't!' she cried. 'Your mother will take one look at my face and know what has happened.'

The doctor nodded. 'Miss Barratt is right. Perhaps she should wait and go with you, Mr Barratt.'

Lucy saw the expression on her cousin's face. He wanted

to deal with things alone and in his own way. Much to her surprise, he didn't need her help and she accepted that with mingled relief and disappointment.

'I'll go and find Andrew,' she compromised. 'I haven't seen him since his meeting with Mr Grosvenor. I'll tell him, of course, and say you are dealing with the arrangements.'

She watched him walk away with the doctor and marvelled at her quiet cousin. It had taken a crisis to bring out his resolve.

Lucy knocked on the door of Andrew's house and was quickly drawn inside. Before he could say anything about his meeting with Elliot Grosvenor, she broke the news about John Barratt's death.

'Dead? Good God! I'm so sorry.' He led the way outside and they sat either side of a small table while he poured her a glass of lemon barley water. 'I thought he was on the mend.' His expression changed again. 'What on earth . . . Does this mean that our wedding's off?'

'I don't know yet. It seemed too early to be worrying about our problems before Aunt Sarah has heard the news. Paul is being an absolute rock! I'm astonished. He's taken charge of everything. He's telling his mother as we speak.'

'But there'll be the funeral to think about as well as the wedding, which is only eleven days away. I don't see how we can do it all in the time without rushing everything. And if you and I aren't married we shan't be able to share the cabin we've booked.'

Lucy had not thought that far ahead. She was reflecting on the small English cemetery where her uncle would be laid to rest. If that happened she could not believe that her aunt would ever agree to return to England.

She said, 'I wonder if they will take Uncle John's body back to England for burial.' The thought brought fresh tears to her eyes and she dabbed at them ineffectually for some minutes.

Andrew patted her hand awkwardly. When she had recovered, busy with his own thoughts, he said, 'That might mean Paul would have to give up his job here. There can't be many assaying jobs in England. Would he leave your aunt there and come back here alone?'

They were both silent for a while wrestling with all the new problems that now arose.

Lucy said, 'I haven't had a chance to speak to Marion about it . . . and I haven't asked you about the meeting with Mr Grosvenor. Was he very angry?'

Andrew hesitated. 'Not angry so much as . . . disappointed in me. Shocked that I could be so careless. Embarrassed by the whole episode and blaming me – quite rightly.'

'So he did believe your story – that you lost concentration.'

'I wish I could be sure. I don't know. I don't think he guessed the real reason but he wouldn't commit himself. Couldn't quite bring himself to say he has confidence in me. To tell you the truth I don't know where I stand with him. He hasn't actually *sacked* me!'

'Well, that's something to be thankful for.' She squeezed his hand but her words did nothing to cheer him.

'I felt an absolute cad!' he told her. 'Still do. Probably always will.'

'No, darling,' she protested. 'We'll put it behind us and make a new start.'

He wasn't listening. 'Part of me wanted to confess but then he said that if I *had* done it deliberately he would have to contact the Australians.'

'And *tell* them?'

'Yes. I couldn't risk it, Lucy. I know you don't think much of me but . . . Oh God! I wish I could undo the last few weeks!'

Lucy hid her despair. Her husband-to-be, the wedding and their wonderful future together had all been tarnished but she could do nothing to restore their hopes. Her uncle's death seemed like one more shadow over their happiness. Nothing was going to go their way and she must try and prepare herself for the worst while hoping for a gleam of light in the darkness.

'Whatever happens, we'll be married,' she told him. 'Your parents will be here and Aunt Sarah and Marion. Even if we have to cancel the festivities we can still go to the church for the ceremony. Just a small group if necessary. We'll be husband and wife, Andrew. That's what we've been waiting for this last year – ever since we met.'

He gave her a weak smile. 'Let's hope Paul knows what he's doing. Let's hope the funeral goes ahead promptly and gives us all a chance to recover from the loss. Your poor aunt. What can we do to help her?'

'I don't know. If she wants to cancel the reception we'll agree. And I'll have to borrow something black – I didn't expect to have to go into mourning. It really won't be right to marry so soon but I don't see that we have any option.'

'Should you go to her now?'

'Yes, I will.' She stood up.

Andrew followed her to the door. 'You do think . . .' he began. 'I mean, you do still want to go ahead with us. You haven't had second thoughts?'

'No, Andrew, I haven't. Have you? You must tell me.'

It seemed an eternity until he shook his head. 'No, I haven't. We still love each other, don't we?'

Lucy found her throat was dry and could only nod. She reached up, planted a small kiss on his cheek and hurried away.

Eduardo Lourdes was at the house when she returned. The curtains had been closed as a mark of death and to encourage people to pass the house quietly. Her aunt was lying on the bed upstairs with Marion beside her. Paul had broken the bad news and had then gone to the Palacio to notify Elliot Grosvenor of the death of his senior doctor.

Eduardo and Lucy spoke together in hushed tones at the bottom of the stairs. He repeated his offer to give her away at the wedding and this time she accepted. Marion came down the stairs looking tired and stressed. She smiled at the doctor and put an arm round Lucy's shoulders but at that moment Paul Barratt returned and said that Elliot Grosvenor wanted to speak to Eduardo. 'I suspect it's about a replacement for my father,' he told him. 'I said I'd pass on the message.'

Lucy said, 'Is it urgent?'

'Everything's urgent with Grosvenor. How's Mama?'

'She's resting,' Marion told him. 'Probably asleep by now.'

Eduardo made his farewells and headed across the *praca* in the direction of the Palacio. Once there, Hugh notified his employer of the young doctor's arrival and Eduardo was shown into Grosvenor's office.

'Sit down, Lourdes. I expect you've guessed why I've sent for you.'

'Indeed I have, sir. The hospital cannot remain under-staffed any longer?'

'Exactly. For a start the novelty will wear off and the volunteer ladies will falter!' He smiled briefly. 'We do need two doctors. I'm wondering whether you would be happy to take over the senior position left by John Barratt? The alternative would be to find another senior man – I would have to approach Barts in London and see if they can . . .'

Eduardo hid his excitement. 'I'd be pleased to take over Dr Barratt's position and work with a new junior man.'

Grosvenor eyed him carefully. 'You're very young for

the responsibility but . . . Do *you* feel confident you can do it?'

'I do, sir.' Eduardo had been wondering whether this opportunity would come his way and had decided what to say if it did. 'I had anticipated a longish period before Dr Barratt returned to full-time work and the prospect didn't alarm me. Would *you* have confidence in me, sir?'

'I wouldn't have offered you the job otherwise.' He fished a wooden ruler from the top drawer and began absent-mindedly to tap it on the desk. 'What I was going to suggest was six months as a sort of probationary period. Then if we're still both happy about it, it becomes permanent.'

There was a long pause while Grosvenor, apparently deep in thought, tapped away. Suddenly he tossed down the ruler. 'I was trying to remember how old Barratt was when he first came to us. Still . . .'

Eduardo waited. Was an answer expected?

Grosvenor said, 'We're agreed then?'

He suddenly smiled and Eduardo momentarily realized how much younger he would look if all his cares and responsibilities were shrugged off. Not that he could ever shake the responsibility for long. The mine was the largest copper mine in Europe and the past year had been their most productive ever. Making a success of a business was never a matter of luck. It required wholehearted commitment and Eduardo guessed it could never be far from Grosvenor's thoughts. Twenty-four hours a day, fifty-two weeks of the year. Is this what had ruined Grosvenor's marriage? Had his beautiful wife felt neglected?

'I'm happy with that, sir,' he said.

'You'll get an increase in salary and you can help me select a junior. We'll advertise the post in Lisbon. Any questions?'

He seemed pleased to have reached a conclusion. Probably relieved to have solved yet another problem. Eduardo studied him curiously. Still a good-looking man if somewhat austere in manner. His face had acquired stern lines over the years but a woman would see past that. Would any woman ever see him as a potential husband? He wondered. Grosvenor's words interrupted his train of thought.

'Bad business about Doctor Barratt,' he was saying. 'I hadn't realized quite how serious it was.'

'He would never have returned full-time, sir. Part-time maybe. He could have lived longer but he was still very frail when the woman screaming over the dog set him back. He wasn't supposed to get out of bed but he did. Then he came down the stairs – God knows how – and . . .'

'Business with the dog?'

Eduardo explained about Flossie's untimely end and Mrs Garsey's reaction.

'And you think that finished him off? Good God!' Grosvenor's eyes widened. 'So that was what my son was talking about yesterday evening. I was busy and Leo was prattling on.' He shook his head, frowning. 'Damned wolves! There was a time they kept away from all signs of civilization but they get bolder every year. I daresay they become accustomed to us being here. I wouldn't want to wander about out there after dark without the means to defend myself. One, yes. Two or more would be a different matter.' He looked bemused. 'A man would have no chance against wolves. Makes you realize how vulnerable we all are to chance, doesn't it.' He had lost the thread of the conversation. 'What was I saying?'

'About Doctor Barratt – coming down the stairs because he heard Mrs Garsey screaming.'

'Ah, yes. The dog and the wolves. So that made him forget your warnings. Poor old devil, he was a very decent chap and he deserved better.'

He stood up abruptly, held out his hand and Eduardo realized that the meeting was at an end.

*　　*　　*

That evening Sarah called Marion and Lucy to her and they sat one on either side of her in the sitting room. Sarah had dressed with great care and had spent time on her hair. She seemed to be in an unnaturally buoyant mood, sitting up straight and no longer twisting her hands in her lap.

Seeing Lucy's surprise she said, 'Now don't fuss over me, dear. I'm fine.'

'Are you sure? You . . .'

'I tell you I'm fine! Don't I look fine?'

Marion said, 'Yes, of course you do, but . . .'

'No buts, Marion, please. John wouldn't have wanted to me to go to pieces, you see. I suddenly realized that as I lay on my bed this afternoon. I knew he was there with me, I knew he was urging me to make an effort.' She paused and looked from one to the other of her nieces with an almost triumphant expression. 'I didn't only feel his presence, I saw it.' She nodded, apparently pleased by the effect of her words. 'I saw a sort of glow like . . . like a column of energy, about so high.' She held her right hand four feet from the floor. 'It was John!'

Marion and Lucy exchanged startled glances.

Marion said soothingly, 'I'm sure he *is* with you, Aunt Sarah . . . in spirit.'

Their aunt looked at her. 'I've heard it said by others and now I know it's true. Our loved ones are never far away. It's a comfort to know that. I feel he's helping me. Guiding my thoughts.'

Lucy said, 'I'm sure he is.' She knew her voice lacked conviction.

Lucy was wondering what this meeting with her aunt was about. She suspected that her aunt would suggest postponing the wedding and, to her shame, she didn't immediately object.

'If it's about the wedding . . .' she began.

'No dear, it's not. It's about the future. Mine. I've decided

I want to go home – back to England. I'll move closer to your parents and we can look out for each other as we grow older.' She looked from one to the other of her nieces.

Marion said slowly, 'But what about Paul?'

'He doesn't need me, Marion. He's old enough to be independent. I don't intend to stay here and blight his future. He needs to marry and settle down and he won't be inclined to look for a wife while he's got me to fuss over.'

Lucy resisted the urge to roll her eyes at her sister. 'Does he know . . . I mean, has he heard this plan?'

'Not yet but he soon will. I'm telling you two girls first because my plans affect you, Marion. If you are willing I should like to travel home with you when you return to England. I don't fancy making the trip alone.'

Marion nodded, trying to hide her surprise. 'That would be splendid. It's a tiring, sometimes tedious journey and I'd enjoy your company.' She turned to Lucy. 'You'll be on your way to Australia, Lucy, unless . . .'

Taking her cue, Lucy asked, 'Shouldn't we delay the wedding, Aunt Sarah? In deference to Uncle John. To his funeral, I mean? There's the mourning period.'

Sarah gave a satisfied nod. 'I knew you'd say that, Lucy, and I'm touched by your concern but I'm sure my poor husband would hate to think he had spoiled your big day. If you delayed the wedding and Marion and I had left for England, you would be here on your own and that would never do. No, the funeral will take place tomorrow and your wedding will go ahead on the twelfth.'

'But whatever will people think?' cried Lucy. She was watching her aunt uneasily, hardly able to recognize the erstwhile timid woman who now seemed determined to wrest control from the younger generation. Was this a result of the shock she had suffered – an irrational reaction of some kind to the loss of her husband? Or had her 'vision' of her husband's spirit energy given her a false sense of confidence?

Seeing her expression and reading her mind, Sarah smiled. 'No, I haven't gone mad, Lucy. But I saw how bravely Paul took over the reins when his father died and I was so proud of him. It wasn't easy for him but he didn't falter for a moment. I was inspired to follow his example and think for myself.' She smiled breathlessly from one to the other.

Marion said gently, 'We didn't think you'd want to leave Uncle John.'

Lucy added, 'His body. Unless you were thinking of taking him home.'

For a moment Sarah's control faltered but she quickly squared her shoulders. 'I think he'd want what's best for me, dear.'

Lucy was trying to understand this unexpected development. If her aunt stayed, what could she do in San Domingos? How would Aunt Sarah live without Uncle John's salary? Was she afraid to stay or was it financially impossible for her to do so? Maybe the bright and exciting plans hid a fear of humiliation. It all depended how much she had in the way of savings . . . if any.

Sarah said, 'So let's not talk about me any more, dears. I'm sure your mother will be pleased to have me back in England and able to help her care for your father.'

Marion said, 'But she has me. I'll be home again within a few weeks.'

Sarah raised her eyebrows. 'And are you planning to stay a widow for the rest of your life, Marion? If I were in your shoes I should hope to wed again and have a family before it's too late. Oh! Don't look at me that way, Marion. Too many daughters throw their lives away on ageing parents and it's very commendable but a sad waste of a life. You think about it, Marion. If I'm there you won't be needed.' She gave a satisfied nod as both young women stared helplessly at her. 'Now I shall have a small sherry and play Solitaire.'

For a few seconds her newfound confidence seemed to waver but then she smiled briskly and they felt they had been dismissed and instinctively made their way along the passage and out of the door in the direction of the *praca*.

Outside, beyond their aunt's hearing, Lucy and Marion were speechless for a while as they walked but eventually came to a stop beneath the eucalyptus tree.

Marion shook her head. 'It's probably a question of money,' she suggested.

Lucy, frowning, drew a long breath. 'Maybe we should talk to Paul. Try and make him understand the situation.'

It seemed the best thing to do in the circumstances.

On Thursday, 3rd, the suns ray's slanted through the windows of the small white church as the coffin was carried in. The church was full and all heads turned as it was laid on the trestles to one side of the altar and the accompanying wreaths were respectfully laid around it. The padre was officiating at the service which by arrangement was held in the Roman Catholic church of San Domingos. Lucy, Marion, Paul and Sarah sat together in the front row and behind and around them the pews were filled by many of the English community.

Andrew sat in the second row, nervously aware of the Grosvenors sitting on the opposite side of the church. Joanna Grosvenor sat with her fiancé, Stephen Benbridge, and Lucy wished that she and Andrew were together. Sarah had wished it otherwise, however. She had insisted that only family should occupy the first row and they had all agreed to her wish.

Lucy had seen Mr and Mrs Garsey and various other people she knew well and many that she knew only slightly. She was painfully aware that Hugh and Jane Stafford were seated at the back of the congregation and was surprised to discover how sad that made her. The sight of Jane had moved her inexplicably to remember all the happy times they had shared during the past year when they were a foursome. No doubt the news of their broken friendship was common gossip, she thought regretfully. How much did anyone else know, she wondered, and how much had they guessed? Had Jane told anyone yet that she was expecting a child? Her *husband's* child. Lucy was now entirely satisfied that Andrew was not the father because he had sworn an oath to that effect with his hand on the Holy Bible and Lucy finally believed him. The relief was enormous – but did Hugh know it?

'Let us pray.'

They all knelt while the padre began the familiar, well-loved phrases and dozens of voices rose and fell in response. Lucy stared ahead at her uncle's coffin and thought about happier times. Before he came out to San Domingos with Sarah and Paul many years ago, the Barratts had owned a small farm, just outside Sidmouth in Devon, and Lucy and Marion had enjoyed wonderful holidays with them – helping to milk the cows, collecting hens' eggs, feeding the pigs. And, of course, vying with one another for the attention of their shy cousin, who in their eyes was almost grown up. The young Paul had seemed to be without friends of his own age and had pretended to have no interest in girls but he *had* condescended to show them his stamps, to play board games with them in the evenings or accompany them on picnics to the riverside where they would swim before devouring the piles of sandwiches Aunt Sarah had made for them. Always potted shrimps, Lucy recalled, and fish paste of an indeterminate flavour. There was gingerbread, too, and slices of caraway cake.

Now she glanced at Paul's face set in sad lines and wondered how his father's death would change his life. She hoped he would one day marry and have a family of his own but it had never seemed likely.

'Now let us raise our voices to the Lord in song. Please turn to hymn number . . .'

As one, they rose obediently to their feet.

Across the aisle young Leo Grosvenor caught her eye and smiled. What would his future be, she wondered. Would his father expect him to follow him into the mining industry? Did Leo have the skill or the inclination? She thought of him as an odd, sensitive child. How would he cope underground in what was a demanding life at the best of times? Maybe Andrew should have studied something else. It seemed that if you were born a man in or near Redruth in Cornwall you automatically considered mining engineering as one of your main options. For the right men it was a good career, very sought after.

Marion whispered something to her. 'Aunt Sarah is feeling the heat. Should we take her outside?'

Lucy hesitated. 'Ask Paul.'

Sarah sat down in the middle of the hymn and began to cool herself with a black lace fan. 'I shall be all right!' she hissed.

Seeing her sit, the padre indicated that they should omit the last two verses and everyone sat down.

It was cooler inside the church than outside but the temperature was in the high nineties and the mourners, crammed uncomfortably together, were longing for the service to end. Regardless, the padre began his address and Lucy made an effort to pay attention. Andrew tapped her on the shoulder and she turned round.

'Hugh and Jane are at the back,' he whispered. 'Are you going to speak to them?'

'I shall be polite, that's all. What do you think?'

'I agree . . . Suppose they come back to the house.'

She shrugged. 'I doubt if Aunt Sarah has invited them.'

At that moment she caught the padre's reproachful gaze upon her and felt herself blush guiltily.

When the sermon was at an end, Paul went up to the lectern and spoke about his father's life and the devotion he held for his calling. He was nervous and kept it short but his words were sincere and his grief very visible. When he sat down again his mother patted his knee and smiled at him and for the first time Lucy could see a likeness between Paul and his father.

When the service ended they followed the coffin up the hill to the English cemetery where a grave had been prepared. John Barratt was laid to rest beside Elliot Grosvenor's wife and the flowers were heaped upon it in silence. As they walked away they heard the earth falling on to the coffin lid and Sarah could hold back the tears no longer.

Back at the house a few close friends gathered for the simple meal which had been arranged by Agatha and Joanna. Elliot Grosvenor had returned to the Palacio and business, Hugh and Jane had disappeared, Leo was present and enjoying himself hugely but Eduardo stayed for only a few minutes before returning to the hospital.

For Lucy, it had not proved to be the ordeal she had expected but surprisingly the funeral helped her, later that day, to come to a decision. She was going to try and resurrect the friendship with Hugh and Jane. The truth was their friendship had been important to her and she missed the easy camaraderie the four of them had shared. Seeing them at the back of the church had been a shock. They looked so defensive, as though they thought they had no right to be there and were fearful of being considered intruders. She knew this was because of the letter she had sent asking them to stay away from the wedding. Jane looked pale and unhappy – maybe she was suffering morning sickness. Lucy had felt an illogical urge to rush to her and offer help and advice. Hugh had looked miserable and quickly averted his eyes. With the summer evolving in such a negative way,

Lucy longed to make something positive happen.

Also, if she was going to say 'Goodbye' to San Domingos, she didn't want to leave any bitterness. She had forgiven Andrew whose betrayal had been the worst, so it should be possible to forgive Jane also.

The day after the funeral, Agatha studied the calendar. As ever she found it difficult to keep track of the days in San Domingos. Sundays were easy because they all went to church but the weekdays sometimes became confused.

'Friday the fifth of July,' she muttered. 'Just over a week to go to the wedding. After all the alarms it is actually almost upon us.'

Only to herself would she admit that she would be glad when it was over. Not that she minded the preparations – she had enjoyed those. It was good to have something purposeful to do. 'The devil finds work . . .' had been drummed into her as a girl. No, it was not the preparations that irked her but the summer itself. It had been an unsettling period, blighted by vague rumours that rumbled round the English compound and a number of disasters both large and small, which struck indiscriminately. Agatha felt, somewhat illogically, that Lucy Barratt and her husband-to-be were somehow attracting these in the way a church spire attracts lightning. She had the uncomfortable feeling that a storm was brewing and didn't know whether to be pleased or sorry. A summer storm often cleared the air. At other times it started a grass fire which could linger for days, filling the sky with acrid smoke and scarring the landscape. Perhaps when Andrew and Lucy were safely on the way to Australia, the town might settle down again. Agatha certainly hoped so.

The tragic death of the doctor had been unexpected but she was sure Doctor Lourdes would make a good replacement even though he had much less experience. That would come. John Barratt had been much younger when he first arrived. She knew from her brother that there had also been three applications from the hospital in Lisbon for the position of junior doctor and one of them had been selected for interview later in the week.

'But now I must talk to Sarah Barratt,' she said with a sigh. She had discussed the woman's situation with Elliot and she now had a proposition to put to her. 'And now's as good a time as any,' she decided. She selected one of her many straw hats – a black one – jammed it on her head and set off.

She spotted Sarah sitting alone on a seat in the *praca*.

'Mrs Barratt! Good morning to you!' she smiled cheerfully. 'Just the person I wanted to see. May I sit with you?'

Sarah nodded but she didn't return the smile. 'I used to sit here when John was alive,' she said. 'Always alone, of course, unless one of the girls was with me. John was always so busy at the hospital. He hated to sit about when there were things to be done. He was never able to delegate. "You're too conscientious, dear," I used to say . . .' Sighing, she changed the subject. 'Sometimes there's a game of tennis going on but not this morning.'

Agatha settled herself beside her. 'I suppose Lucy's getting very excited,' she said. 'Only seven more days.'

Sarah nodded. Inevitably her hands began to toy with her bead necklace as she lowered her voice. 'Between you and me, I shall be pleased to hand over the responsibility, if the truth be told. I always think girls are more difficult to bring up than boys. My niece is a sweet girl but such a scatter-brain – and impulsive. Her mother always says how unpredictable she is. Her husband will have to be firm with her . . . My son Paul was never any trouble.'

'He's a charming young man,' Agatha agreed. 'I'm afraid he'll miss you if you go back to England.' She took a deep

167

breath. 'Which brings me to the reason I'm here. It's not purely by chance, you see. I'm rather hoping to persuade you to stay in San Domingos. My brother feels that . . .'

Sarah turned to her quickly, a bleak expression flitted briefly across her face. 'Oh no! I must go back!'

'My brother feels that, having already lost your husband, to lose you, also, would be a great loss to our community.' Sarah was staring at her but she hurried on. 'You've been here longer than any of the others and Mr Grosvenor has always believed that you and your husband – and son, of course – have been a steadying influence all these years. So many of our people are young and inexperienced. They look up to you.'

Sarah looked astonished but pleased. 'That is most kind of you, most kind. I'm sure we've always tried to be a good influence. My husband was totally wrapped up in his work here. For him there was nowhere on earth quite like San Domingos and I have been very happy here.'

Before she could explain why she must go back to England, Agatha continued. 'The point is we were developing certain plans for the benefit of the community and we do need your help.' Now she held Sarah's attention. 'My brother is so impressed with the work you do at the library he wants to expand it. He was planning to find some money to invest in it. He wants longer hours and he is prepared to pay someone to manage it,' she told Sarah. 'He was, of course, expecting it to be you. He was also going to set aside some funds to buy new books and thought you might send for English publishers' catalogues and order from them. Foyles, I suppose, would be a good place to start.'

Sarah was regarding her wide-eyed. 'Expand the library? Oh, that would be wonderful. *Wonderful!*'

'We couldn't expand the room, obviously, but could make better use of it, perhaps. He had thought of asking Mr Garsey if he would make two free-standing bookshelves. He's very talented and I'm sure he would help us out. It could be very successful but I don't see anyone else but you who has the necessary experience.'

She gave a rueful smile and paused to stare out across the tennis court where four young men were beginning to knock up prior to a game.

After a long pause, Sarah said, 'I see!'

Agatha waited a little longer then said, 'I don't suppose it's of interest but the remuneration would be very fair because it would also include another project which I have dreamed up.' She leaned forward. 'I've thought for some time now that we need a social club of some kind for the ladies. The men have their work to keep them occupied – and their football and tennis – but we ladies are left very much to our own devices. I thought we might connect it to the library. I was hoping you might come up with an idea or two for us.'

She could almost see the idea taking root in Sarah Barratt's brain and felt immediately hopeful. Say nothing more, she cautioned herself, let it come from Sarah herself.

'I suppose . . . Well, that really is an excellent idea.' Sarah stopped fiddling with her beads, leaned back and stared thoughtfully upwards as though awaiting inspiration from above. 'A reading group, perhaps . . . or a discussion group.'

'Maybe a combination of the two. There's no need to limit the ideas.'

Sarah sat up. 'We could invite those among us who have anything interesting to say to give a talk.' She turned towards Agatha.

'Excellent. I think we're getting to the nub of it, don't you?'

Sarah nodded. 'Maybe "The Library Group" . . . or "The Ladies Group"!' She frowned in concentration. 'Should we exclude the men altogether? Could we perhaps allow them to be speakers occasionally? But not be members. Would that work, do you think?'

'Absolutely! Your son might give a talk on assaying the ore. How many women know anything about that subject? You could talk about being a doctor's wife!'

Sarah's small brown eyes glistened with excitement. 'There could be a small membership fee – an annual one – to cover the cost of tea and biscuits. Members could give book reviews. Maybe we could have a folder into which members put the reviews of the books they've read . . .'

Agatha smiled broadly. 'I knew I could rely on you.'

'Oh no! It was your idea.'

'But it needed someone to put flesh on the bones, so to speak. Do I see a chance that you might reconsider your plan to return to England?'

Sarah looked puzzled for a moment, then she laughed and said, 'I'm certainly very tempted by your offer.'

'Perhaps you could think it over and let me know.'

There was a short silence. 'I'd much rather stay . . . near John.'

'Of course you would. You'd also be helping us. We do rather need your expertise.'

Sarah closed her eyes, gave a deep sigh and reopened them. 'I'd certainly like to stay,' she said. 'It would depend on certain circumstances. I haven't spoken to our solicitor yet. But I know John would like me to be near him . . . and he'd like me to be useful to the community. San Domingos was his life.'

'Well said, Mrs Barratt. If you do stay we'll make a start as soon as you feel up to it. We seem to work well together, don't we?'

They stared at each other.

'I . . . I wish you'd call me Sarah.'

'Thank you. I'd love to. And I'll be Agatha.'

They both laughed. Agatha hid her growing sense of

triumph. 'Oh!' she said. 'I forgot to say you could stay in your present home. That would be part of the financial arrangement.'

'Stay, oh,' Sarah put a hand to her mouth as she struggled with her emotions, 'that would be wonderful. Your brother is very generous.'

'He is, isn't he? People don't really understand him but ...' She shrugged. 'I must go home. Joanna is out for the day and Leo will want his tea. He has a huge appetite.' She stood up and smoothed down her skirts.

Sarah also rose. 'I'll walk back with you,' she said eagerly. 'There's a lot still to talk about.'

As they walked Agatha congratulated herself on a job well done.

Nine

The next morning Lucy caught Marion before she departed for the hospital to do her voluntary work and told her of her decision. Marion approved and Lucy hurried to finish her hair and rub a hint of colour into her lips. She prepared a light breakfast for her aunt and took it in to her. While she propped Sarah up on the pillows and settled the tray, she told her she wanted to bring about a reconciliation with Jane and Hugh. 'I'm on my way to see them now,' she told her.

Sarah smiled. 'Very sensible, Lucy dear. I knew you'd see reason. This way they can come to the wedding but Paul will still be Andrew's best man.'

'Certainly.' She had forgotten about the switch.

'I do know he is working very hard on his little speech. It will do him good to be the centre of attention once again.'

'He was very good at the funeral. Very nervous but he overcame it. And so sincere. You must have been proud of him.'

'Oh, I was proud, Lucy. And I know his father would have applauded his efforts. Poor John was there, you know, in the church and at the graveside. I felt his presence. It was such a comfort to know I am not really alone.'

Lucy hesitated. Her aunt seemed in surprisingly good spirits but how would she feel back in England, she wondered uneasily. With Uncle John buried in San Domingos, would she still feel that his presence was with

172

her? Better to say nothing for the time being, she decided. Maybe she would speak with Paul about it. She was halfway to the front door when someone rang the bell. She opened it to find Jane standing there.

'Jane! I was on my way to see you . . .'

To her dismay, Jane's eyes filled with tears and instinctively Lucy threw her arms around her. 'Don't cry!' she begged. 'It's going to be all right. Truly it is!' She led her friend into the sitting room and they sat down on the sofa.

Jane said, 'I'm so sorry about everything. Your poor uncle, too! It's been a perfectly beastly summer for all of us and it's all my fault. I don't know what to say. I don't know how to put things right – or even if I can.'

Lucy offered her a handkerchief. 'It wasn't all your fault. Some of it was Andrew's.' Instinctively she steered clear from their own problem. 'A lot of it was chance. Chance that Mrs Garsey heard about Flossie and brought Uncle John from his bed when he wasn't fit.'

'How is your aunt?' Jane struggled to quell the tears and went on without waiting for an answer. 'Then there was the accident in the mine . . .'

Lucy said nothing.

'And Andrew being arrested. Hugh said the world's gone mad. At least our corner of it. Stephen Benbridge said that he can't recall San Domingos ever having such a stormy summer.'

Lucy listened in silence, simply smiling encouragement. How wonderful, she thought, that Jane had been the one to make the first move. 'I was coming to your house to suggest that we forget the past few weeks and make a fresh start. I haven't said anything to Andrew in case Hugh didn't want to be friends again but I know he'll be pleased if we can. To tell the truth he's in a bit of a state as you can imagine. Nothing is going right for him although Mr Grosvenor is giving him another chance.'

'Hugh wondered if he'd be suspended.'

'Not so far but I suspect it came close. Andrew is so depressed – I think he's keeping out of my way although I've forgiven him. He's got . . . other things on his mind. Mr Grosvenor was rather rough on him about . . . everything. Andrew thinks he's lost confidence in him. It's a good thing we're moving on or . . .'

'Or what?'

'Andrew thinks someone's been speaking badly of him.' She stopped abruptly. 'I'm not supposed to discuss it with anyone so please forget I said that.'

'Of course I will.'

Lucy took a deep breath. 'I know this is a lot to ask but could you please tell me how it started. Your affair or whatever it was. I don't understand how it happened and I'd like to be aware in case . . .' In case it happened again with someone else, she thought, but couldn't finish the sentence aloud. For a moment she thought Jane was going to refuse but then she nodded.

Staring fixedly at the floor she began haltingly, 'It was all because of a quarrel I'd had with Hugh. We expected to start a baby as soon as we were married – that's what we'd planned. But it didn't happen and didn't happen and I began to worry that something was wrong but Hugh insisted it was early days. Men are like that. You'll find out for yourself soon enough!' She rolled her eyes. 'When I said perhaps I should see a doctor he was annoyed. I said he didn't seem very concerned and he said I was obsessed with the idea of having a child and . . .' She shrugged.

'Poor you. How awful.'

'He called me hysterical and neurotic!' Jane said, her voice trembling. 'The stupid thing is that even while we were quarrelling I was already expecting the baby but didn't know it. The sign . . . You know what I mean. Nothing had changed but now I know from Doctor Lourdes that that's quite normal for the first month or two. So we needn't have quarrelled and then I wouldn't have been angry with him and . . . flirted with Andrew.'

'So you did start it?'

Jane nodded, avoiding Lucy's gaze. 'That same evening we came to supper at Andrew's place and you were in the kitchen and Hugh was in the bathroom and I said something like "Marriage isn't a bed of roses". He said it depended who you were married to and I said that maybe I'd married the wrong man and he looked a bit surprised and didn't know how to react. Then Hugh came back. I didn't think anything of it until the next time we met for tennis and he winked at me. So stupid!'

'He told me you'd fallen in love with him.'

'I did. Or thought I did. Looking back I can't believe we were so naïve. He had you, and I had Hugh and we were all happy. Do you truly forgive us – me and Andrew?'

'Truly!' Lucy certainly hoped that was true. 'I know the baby's Hugh's child, Jane, and so do you, of course. Is Hugh convinced?'

'I think so but he's very miserable. Things aren't right between us and he won't talk about it any more. I suggested that he talk to Stephen Benbridge but he wouldn't consider it.'

'Why Stephen Benbridge? He's not even married.'

'But he was. His wife died. Stephen's a very sensible type of man and I thought he might put things in perspective for Hugh. He keeps saying there must be something lacking in him for me to turn to another man.' She turned a tear-stained face to Lucy. 'I've been such a fool. I don't suppose he will ever really trust me again and I've only myself to blame.'

'He will trust you! I trust Andrew.'

'Then why did you want to know how it all started?'

Lucy said quickly, 'Because I was being neurotic! Give

Hugh time. He's not one to bear a grudge. He's a very decent man. Once we're all friends again it will be easier for him. At the moment he probably blames you and Andrew for breaking up the friendship but if we solve that . . .' She took hold of Jane's hand and gave it a squeeze. 'We can do it, Jane. The menfolk will fall into line . . .'

'D'you think so?'

'Yes I do.' She leaned forward, gave Jane a kiss and settled back down. 'Now tell me about the baby. How are you in yourself? I can't imagine you expecting a baby. I'm quite envious, to tell you the truth!'

Jane managed a smile. 'Your turn will come.'

'It's a shame I'll be in Australia and I won't be able to share it with you. Of course we can write to each other. We must, Jane. Have you thought of names?'

Jane shook her head and her mouth trembled. 'We don't mention it.'

'Well, now you can,' Lucy said firmly. 'We all can. We've got a little time left and we'll make it especially happy. You'll come to the wedding, won't you? Forget that spiteful letter I sent. Though Paul will have to be the best man. He's determined to rise to the occasion and Aunt Sarah insists it will be good for him. I can't disappoint her.' She frowned. 'What? You look a bit . . .'

'I've done something dreadful,' Jane confessed. She stared down at the handkerchief in her hands. 'I've cut up your present. I've got nothing to give you.'

'Cut it up? What was it?'

'When we got your letter, Hugh was in despair and we had a row and I – I went a little mad. I snatched up the shears and hacked at it and . . .' She swallowed hard, jolted by the ugly memory. 'It *was* a collage I'd made for you – a wall hanging. I had put things in it about San Domingos to help you remember us all. I imagined it on your wall in Australia.' Her expression brightened as she visualized it. 'There was a sprig of purple heather, of course, and a wolf, although he did look rather like a big grey dog, birds, a blue rock thrush and a black eagle, and white cistus flowers. Along the bottom edge there were a few white villas.'

'How clever of you!'

'Oh and the tennis net – I worked that in – and the bandstand. That was just an outline in the background. Hugh thought it a bit confused but men don't appreciate artistic things, do they? I tried to explain it was symbolic of life in San Domingos but he didn't understand it.'

'Is it totally ruined?' Lucy asked wistfully.

'I'm afraid so . . . but I could make it again!' She leaned forward eagerly. 'I could send it to you. It might be even better the second time. Would you like me to?'

'I'd love to have it. Maybe you could embroider your name and Hugh's in a corner.'

Jane gave her a long look but her heart was too full and she said nothing. Then she gave her friend a fierce hug and smiled broadly. 'I'll start on it tonight,' she promised.

The same evening Paul sat alone in his bedroom working on the speech he was going to give at Lucy's wedding reception. Still dazed from his father's unexpected death he was nonetheless currently buoyed up by the congratulations he had received after the funeral. People had spoken kindly of his confident handling of the arrangements and the way he had given his address. For the first time in his life he had been placed centre stage and had, to his surprise, risen to the occasion. Flushed with the success he was now determined to make a great and memorable speech as best man at his cousin's wedding.

Outside on the patio his fellow tenant and two friends were drinking bottled beer and 'putting the world to rights' while he persevered at his latest challenge.

*'Ladies and Gentlemen, gathered here today to cele-
brate the marriage of my cousin Lucy Barratt and . . .'*

No need to use her surname, he corrected himself – and,
in fact, by the time he gave his speech she would be Mrs
Shreiker and not Lucy Barratt. This wasn't going to be as
easy as he'd expected.

*' . . . the marriage of my cousin Lucy who from hence-
forth shall be known as Mrs Andrew Shreiker . . .'*

A touch of humour would go down well, he thought. But
not too much. It was too soon after his father's death to
make many jokes. He knew that most best man speeches
produced loud hilarity, guffaws and whispers, but not this
time. This time they were still mourning his father's death.

*' . . . Today is a time of great rejoicing but we all know
that something – someone – is missing and that casts a
shadow over the proceedings. But not a dark shadow, for
my father would not have wished to spoil his young niece's
happiness or mar her special day. I'm sure my father is
sharing the moment with us . . .'*

He paused again. He did wish his mother had not spoken
about seeing a glowing spirit. It was nonsense, of course,
but if it helped her through the dark days of loss he could
overlook it. He would let her keep her illusions but he hoped
she would keep them to herself. His parents had brought
him up to be strictly religious but there had been a time
back in England when his mother had once dallied briefly
with spiritualism, urged on by a close friend who was a firm
believer. They had attended seances together until his father
put a stop to it. He pushed the thought away and tried to
concentrate.

'Throughout our childhood, Lucy was never far away. She and her sister Marion used to spend their holidays at our farm in Sidmouth in Devon . . .'

If he thought back he could still see Lucy, aged six or seven, coming to the back door, windswept but triumphant, carrying a basket of eggs she had collected from the hens. Or sitting on a stool, around eleven years old, her head pressed against the flank of a cow, trying to coax milk into the bucket. He wrote:

'. . . Andrew is a lucky man and I say that unreservedly.'

He certainly was, if the gossip was to be believed! It had come to Paul's ears that he and Jane Stafford had been a sight too friendly. That was why, at the last minute, he, Paul, and not Hugh Stafford, was preparing the best man's speech. Not that he had ever liked Andrew particularly but then he had hardly known him. The engineers had little to do with the assaying department and the two men had rarely met but recently he had heard about the explosion and the arrest and it seemed to him that Andrew was a very lucky man to have escaped unscathed.

'Will they be happy?' he murmured as he waited for further inspiration. Were they an ideal couple? Was there such a thing? 'Yes, of course!' His parents had, to his knowledge, been very happy together. If either of them had strayed he had never been aware of it. A devoted couple . . .

'. . . Soon the happy couple will be on their way to a new life in Australia and I know I speak for everyone here when I wish them Godspeed and every happiness in their new life.'

179

Paul laid down his pen and considered his handiwork. It could be improved, he felt, and he would fine tune it some other time. The basis was there, however, and he felt he could relax. He found himself wondering, not for the first time, about marriage. Would he ever take such a drastic step? He found the idea of courtship rather daunting. Perhaps he was not 'the marrying kind'. Living together with someone for the rest of your life and producing children. It seemed a huge responsibility and not everyone was suited to it. Not that he didn't enjoy women's company but he never knew quite how to approach them.

He thought about Elliot Grosvenor. He would probably never remarry. His history was a sad one. He'd fathered an illegitimate child by one of his Portuguese servants and had had a marriage to Catherine who had, by all accounts, led him a fine dance before her death. Was he embittered by his history? No-one knew. Grosvenor ran the mine with admirable efficiency and had never shown any desire to abandon his solitary state. Doctor Lourdes was another man who had so far escaped the trap. Paul felt he was in good company.

At that moment someone shouted to him that they were off to the tennis court. Paul abandoned his speech, reached for his tennis racquet and hurried to join them.

The following day the sky was mercifully overcast and there was a cool breeze blowing in from the sea as the crew of the small steamship *Roda* released the mooring ropes and tidied them away. The narrow gangway was drawn up as she increased her engine revs and was skilfully edged out into the deeper water in the middle of the river in preparation for her journey up the Guardiana river to the port of Pomerao. It was nine thirty in the morning and Thomas Betts and Philip Sutton stood together at the rail and watched the shoreline slip past.

Betts grinned. 'Nearly there!' He rolled his eyes. 'This journey's taking a lifetime. That train ride from Lisbon was a revelation. I can't even remember which day it is.'

He was nearly forty with dark hair and a ruddy complexion that would have looked more suitable on a farmer than an engineer.

'It's Sunday – not that it matters. The thing is we're nearly there!' Philip Sutton said as he pushed back the hair from his eyes. 'Too late to change our minds!' He was in his mid-twenties, thin with a nervous manner. The attempt at a joke didn't come easy to him. 'They were a nice couple, the Shreikers. Coming all this way to see their son get married. I can't see my parents being that keen. Not that I'm planning on getting married!'

'We'll need all our energies for San Domingos!'

'When's your family coming out to join you?'

Betts and Sutton, friends from the same town in Cornwall, had chosen the long route to the mine normally unavailable to the workforce. Betts had wanted to discover this alternative route because he had to convince his nervous wife that she would manage it with a young child in tow. The men were paying the difference in fare themselves and were enjoying the further glimpses into Portuguese life that it offered. Betts would also be able to reassure his wife that the trip, though protracted, was a pleasant one and a good introduction to life in a strange land.

He now turned away from the gathering wind which was blowing his hair into his face. 'Moyna will be here three months from now. I want time to get settled in and she wants time to get the baby on to solid foods before she makes the trip.'

Sutton nodded but he was still thinking about the Shreikers. 'They'll feel ghastly going back to England again after the wedding, knowing their son and his new bride will be on the way to Australia. But mining is full of partings.

Par for the course, as they say. They must have known that their son has to go where the work is.'

'Have to follow the prospects for preferment.' Betts nodded. 'Could have been South Africa. There's plenty of opportunity there, so they say. Personally I only plan to stay in San Domingos about five years.'

There was a shrill blast from the *Roda*'s whistle and they fell silent, content to watch the town of Vila Real fall away behind the wake from the ship. On either side the scorched sides of the riverbank passed slowly. A herd of goats of assorted colours and sizes grazed hopefully for tender green shoots among the withered foliage but ate whatever they could find. At the sound of the ship's engine, the animals raised their heads and watched them incuriously, showing no fear and quickly resuming their search for food. The swarthy faced goatherd, furled black umbrella strapped to his back, waved his hat and the ship's captain called out to him in Portuguese.

Sutton said, 'Do you ever wonder how simple life could be? No real cares. Follow your herd of goats and keep them safe at night. Day after day.'

Betts grinned. 'You'd be bored in no time!'

'Not necessarily. You'd have different problems, that's all. One of your goats gets sick . . . another goes missing or falls into the river or is taken by a wolf. It might be satisfying on a different level. Time to think . . .'

'Don't let Grosvenor hear you talk like that. You'll blot your copybook. You'll go down as a dreamer and he won't like that.'

Sutton shrugged and changed the subject. 'I wonder who'll meet us at Pomerao. I hear Grosvenor's daughter is very attractive.'

'It might be Grosvenor's elderly sister. Just our luck!'

The captain took out a chunk of ham and began to cut slivers from it with his knife. Seeing the Englishmen watching he held it up, offering them a share but they hastily declined.

'It's either a late breakfast,' Sutton suggested, 'or an early lunch.'

The two men had had a simple meal earlier in a small riverside bar – a small cup of very strong coffee and three stale cakes which tasted of orange and were not unpalatable. Their main luggage, the steamer trunks, would be transported from Mertola by mule to the mine, supposedly in a few days' time. All the two men had with them were their documents, references and a change of clothes. For both men, born and bred in the town of Redruth, their foray into the Portuguese hinterland was proving an interesting and somewhat daunting experience. Sutton's uncle and grandfather had both been miners in San Domingos years earlier. Betts had no such connections. Both were a little anxious.

Some hours later, the ship turned yet another bend in the river but by this time the water had deepened and the sides of the riverbanks had grown higher and the sun cast strong shadows across the town of Pomerao. To the two weary travellers it was a welcome sight – the end of the trip. Both were longing to be ashore and one step nearer to the mine which was to become their home. The ship's whistle alerted men on the bank who hurried forward to catch the mooring ropes which were thrown to them and which they then made fast to stanchions on the shore. The rows of whitewashed buildings which clung to the steep slopes were attractive enough but the railway which ran along the lower roadway rather spoiled the effect. It projected right over the river and would give access to the lighters that regularly collected the ore from the mine.

On the far side of the river there was a ship's chandlers which Sutton recalled being mentioned by his uncle and grandfather.

He glanced around in wonder. 'It's hardly changed from the photographs I've seen! Hardly changed at all!' He glanced up and down the landing area as one of the deckhands manhandled the gangway into place. 'No sign of a welcoming committee.'

Even as he spoke a train appeared round a bend in the narrow gauge track and drew slowly into place along the roadway and out over the river. The two lighters had yet to arrive, it seemed. The train consisted entirely of an engine and about twenty-five small tubs of ore but right at the end there was a small carriage.

Betts grinned. 'That looks like us,' he said. Both men thanked the captain for the journey and made their way down the gangway to the shore.

Sutton glanced up and saw the black and white eagle soaring slowly in the thermal of warm air. 'Bonelli.' he said.

'What's that?'

'A bonelli eagle. See the white under the wings? They warm up their bodies in the warm air currents.'

'Since when are you an expert on birds?'

'Since my wife bought a book on Portuguese wildlife.'

'I'm beginning to worry about you,' Betts told him as they waited for the carriage door to open. When it did, a boy stepped out and walked briskly towards them.

'Welcome to San Domingos. I'm Leo Grosvenor.' He gave them a brief smile. 'My father's sent me to meet you.' He looked at the small pieces of hand luggage each man carried. 'I suppose the rest of it is coming via Mertola?'

Sutton said, 'Yes.' In spite of the boy's rather odd charm he felt a little affronted that Grosvenor could find no one else to meet them.

Leo grinned. 'It'll come by mule train and it takes forever. But it will come. People over here are very honest. You'll like them.' He pointed suddenly downriver. 'See there!

Those are the lighters for the ore. They'll be loading shortly but it doesn't pay to watch because you get dust and grit in your eyes especially when the wind blows. Shall we sit in the carriage and wait or would you like to look round Pomerao. I can introduce you to a very nice man who is teaching me to fish.'

The two men glanced at each other. More delays. It seemed that actually arriving at the mine was becoming a fantasy. Overhead there was a distant rumble of thunder and all three glanced up to find the sky empty of real clouds.

The boy said, 'We get summer storms here sometimes. Thunder and lightning but no rain. Sometimes the lightning sets fire to the undergrowth and then it burns acres of the land. All the rabbits and hares and foxes run from it. Aunt Agatha saw it happen once many years ago. She said the smoke and ash hung in the air for days and it burned the bark from the trees but it all grew back again and so did the grass.' He looked at them for their reaction.

Obligingly, Sutton said, 'Good Lord. Must have been terrifying!'

'How long will they be emptying the trucks?' Betts asked, unimpressed. He was tired and hungry and eager to see the town and their new quarters. A bath would be welcome and a meal and then he would write the first of his promised letters to Moyna.

'Getting on for an hour,' Leo told them, 'but there's a little bar further up.' He pointed. 'You could get a drink. I'm not allowed in because Papa doesn't want me to start drinking alcohol in case it frazzles my brain but I expect your brains are past the frazzling stage. I can amuse myself and then I'll come and find you when the time's right.'

It seemed to be the only alternative to standing about, watching ore being tipped. They agreed to find something to drink and offered to fetch something non-alcoholic for Leo but he declined graciously and said he was going to fish.

185

As they turned to go he added, 'I know lots about what goes on in San Domingos so you can always ask me. What I don't know I can find out. Nobody takes any notice of me because I'm not grown up and I hear all sorts of things.'

He hurried away, presumably in search of the man who was teaching him to fish, and the two engineers, feeling decidedly put out, set off towards the bar and solace.

Ten

Later that evening, a few miles outside the town, a blue rock thrush swooped through the oppressively warm air of a darkening sky. Above it small wisps of cloud, tinged with pink, floated aimlessly like bunched muslin. The bird let out a short cry and changed direction. Down below the scene on the ground shifted slightly as one of the wolves crept closer to a dark shape which lay on the ground. There were three wolves, two heavy bodied and one younger and sleeker – this year's growing cub – which followed the lead of the other more mature animals. The bird flew lower, instinctively curious. A man lay on the ground, crumpled and still, one hand flung out. One of the wolves glanced up as the bird flew into a nearby tree and perched with a flurry of folding wings.

Below it the wolves crept closer, still very wary. The man lay still and seemed innocent enough but the old wolf knew that they sometimes brought death. The wolf raised its head, suspiciously searching the surrounding countryside in search of other men but saw nothing alarming. Yet another rumble of loud thunder made all three animals pause, frozen in their tracks. Distracted only momentarily, one of the wolves crept close enough to smell the hand of the man. The others closed in, jaws working in eager anticipation.

As soon as the wolf's teeth snapped around Hugh's hand, his eyes jerked open with pain and shock. He instinctively jerked his hand and the movement took the wolf by surprise so that he loosened his grip and sprang backwards. Hugh stared in disbelief at the teeth marks in the flesh of his injured hand then turned his head in horror. He saw the wolf at terrifyingly close quarters – the thick grey coat, the crooked ear, the thickset shoulders – and knew he was in deep trouble. The animal was so close he could see the colour of its eyes and smell its breath. Hugh's high-pitched scream echoed across the grassy plain and sent the startled wolves leaping and tumbling backwards in a short-lived retreat.

About this time Jane found Lucy on the patio of her aunt's house and slid into an empty seat beside her.

'I don't suppose you've seen Hugh, have you?' she asked. 'He's not with Andrew and he didn't come home after his shift. I've asked Will Hawks who was on shift with him but no-one seems to have seen him.'

Lucy frowned. 'You look worried. Are you?'

'In a way because he always comes straight home from the mine and the meal's waiting, getting cold.' She hugged herself as though she, too, were cold. 'He's been so down lately and . . . I can't make him understand that the trouble – *our* trouble – is over. I've told him we're all friends again but he's brooding about it. I know him. He takes everything so seriously.'

Lucy raised her eyebrows. 'But it *was* serious! Honestly Jane, you must see that. Hugh's had a most frightful shock, finding out about you and Andrew and then you tell him about the child and pretend it's Andrew's! For Hugh it must have been catastrophic! You have no idea but I do. I'm a victim too, remember. Hugh and I suffered most because you and Andrew were in control, so to speak. And poor Hugh's always been a soft-hearted soul.' She stared out across the small garden. 'You told me once about that injured fox he found once – years ago in England.'

'Which fox?'

'The one that had been in a trap and its back legs were both broken and he wanted to . . .'

'Oh! *That* fox!'

'. . . put it out of its misery . . .' Jane nodded. 'And he found a rock and then couldn't do it. Couldn't kill it although he knew it was an act of mercy! So he left it to die in agony.'

'Because he was too soft-hearted to do the deed.' Jane's tone was disapproving and she had the decency to look ashamed. 'I know. I don't deserve him. I didn't want to admit how worried I am but . . . Lucy, you don't think he'd do something rash, do you? I mean, really, seriously rash – like try to kill himself?' As soon as the words were out they were both shocked into wondering if that could be the reason for his disappearance.

Lucy said, 'Oh God! Oh no! He wouldn't, would he?'

Before Jane could answer, a loud peal of thunder broke overhead and made them jump.

Lucy said, 'It won't rain. There are no clouds.' Almost at once there was a bright flash of lightning followed by more thunder. 'Aunt Sarah calls it summer lightning and insists it's harmless. My father calls them electrical storms.'

Jane wasn't listening. 'If Hugh does . . . something to himself then I'll have killed him! It will be my fault!'

Lucy allowed the words to go unchallenged. She thought that if he died because of what had happened Jane and Andrew would both be to blame. Or partly so. 'Let's not think about it,' she said. 'I don't think he would do that. He couldn't kill the injured fox and to kill himself would be much worse.' She pushed aside the uncomfortable thought that in a desperate moment Andrew had meant to blow himself up. She said quickly, 'Let's think where he might be . . . or better still, let's go and look for him. A

189

discreet search.' She brightened as an idea struck her. 'He might have gone into church to pray.'

Jane appeared unconvinced. 'Shouldn't we tell someone he's missing?'

'We don't know for sure that he is. Did he leave you a note?'

'A note?' Jane looked shocked. 'Of course he didn't. Do you think I wouldn't have mentioned it!'

Lucy stiffened. 'No need to take that tone! I'm only trying to help.'

'Oh Lucy, I'm sorry, I know you are. We'll do what you suggested. Perhaps we should split up. I'll go and look in the church, you . . .'

'I'll go and sound out Stephen Benbridge. All the men like him. Hugh might have gone to him to confide.'

There was another flash of lightning and overhead the thunder rolled again, nearer than before. Lucy pushed back her chair. 'At least it might clear the air. It's so still. A breath of wind would help.'

'We'll meet back here and exchange our findings. There's sure to be a perfectly logical explanation to it. Don't you think?'

'I'm sure there will.'

And on that hopeful note they went their separate ways.

Not too far away on the plain the wolves had retreated but not for long. The sight of a moving figure excited them and they hovered only yards away, heads down, sensing the man's fear. One of them uttered a low growl, deep in its throat, and the sound was echoed by a rolling crack of thunder, much closer this time. Galvanized by the growl, Hugh scrambled to his feet, dishevelled and slightly disorientated. He stood and stared round him, aware that he was in serious danger and totally unprepared for it. He had no weapon with which to fight them off and he felt weak. How long had he been lying there? Had he been missed? His absence must have been noticed but was anybody looking for him? If he tried to run he didn't think his legs would carry him far or at any speed.

He saw one of the wolves creeping round behind him and his heart lurched with terror. All the stories of wolves came back to him. Three would be enough. They were pack animals. All he had was his voice and anything he could find to hurl at them. He glanced round but the parched grass which was within reach was bare of stones or rocks and the nearest tree, a stunted oak, was too far away. He would never make it and even if he did and could climb the tree, he could hardly stay there for ever. They would simply wait for him to fall asleep, lose his hold and tumble from the tree.

Why the hell had he come up here alone in the first place, he asked himself bitterly. To be alone and think? But there was no way he was going to save his marriage unless he sat down *with* Jane and talked. Walking up here to get away from everything had been a stupid, empty gesture and now he was going to pay for it – probably with his life. Thoughts of his parents flashed through his mind. They would never understand what had happened. They loved Jane. Always had from the first moment he'd taken her home to meet them.

In sudden desperation he ran stumbling towards the nearest animal, waving his arms and shouting at the top of his voice. The wolf backed away, turned and ran – but the other two moved closer. He screamed for help but his voice rang out over the empty plain and there was no reply. Overhead the storm intensified; around him the wolves flattened their ears at the sound but still dodged and circled.

Hugh's terror grew. 'Just let me survive this, God,' he begged silently, 'and I'll be a model husband and father for the rest of my life.' Why hadn't he accepted the peace offered by Lucy and Andrew? Why had he been unable to forgive and forget like Lucy? His stupid pride had been his undoing and now he was going to pay for it. He took off a shoe and threw it wildly at the nearest wolf and by some fluke it struck its head and sent it howling into a temporary retreat. He decided he would make for the tree and hopefully break off a branch with which to keep them at bay a little longer.

He shouted again. 'Help me, someone! Please help me!' The sound only mocked him.

Edging closer to the tree he threw the second shoe but missed. Perhaps he should have kept the shoes. Now his feet were vulnerable. He could still recall the feel of those teeth closing on his hand. The storm was now right over-head and the rumbles had turned to ear-splitting ripples of sound, each one of which halted the wolves momentarily and gave him precious time. The tree was less than twenty yards away now and a small but stubborn hope began to grow within him. As he stumbled forward on legs that threat-ened to fail him at any moment he cursed his stupidity. So close to possible death he saw only too clearly that he could have come to terms with Jane's mistake and built a life for the three of them. With a moment's clarity he saw that he shouldn't be wallowing in self-pity – he should be thinking of his child. His son or daughter. If this episode ended badly the child would have no father and Jane would be a widow like Marion. Somehow he must find a way to return to them.

'God help me!' he muttered. Did he deserve help? Had he ever deliberately done anything to displease Him? He attended church regularly. They had been married in church. The baby would be christened in church. Tears sprang into his eyes. 'Please God, let me be there to see it!'

As the largest wolf approached him once more, crouched low as if ready to spring, Hugh tried to think how he might counter such an attack. Ten yards from the tree, but as though reading his mind, the other two wolves were now waiting between him and the tree. Waiting to thwart him! But he could still use his hands. Perhaps he could . . . it was too late. The big wolf sprang! Hugh threw up his hands instinctively and went for the wolf's throat. For a moment he felt the thick rough fur slide through his hands, he had no grip. He fought helplessly, his blows making no impression and the animal's weight sent him crashing down on to his back. Now, winded, his ideas of self defence seemed ludicrous. One unarmed man against one wolf stood little real chance but against three . . .

He continued to fight off the snapping jaws and also to shout and kick to cause as much confusion in the animal as he could – anything to delay the end he now saw as inevitable. At any moment he expected the other two wolves to join in the attack.

Without warning, however, there was huge a crash that almost deafened him and a flash of blinding light. The wolf above him seemed to be sucked upwards and backwards. Hugh felt the edge of the blast but was able to scramble to his feet, his heart thudding painfully. Unable to believe his eyes he found himself staring at a blazing oak tree. It had been split at the top, and one side already looked like charcoal while on the other side the foliage still burned and crackled from the lightning strike.

'Jesus Christ!' he stammered, wide-eyed and trembling.

The wolf that attacked him had suffered least injury because of the distance from the tree. One of the others was dead and charred, its fur gone, its eyes dulled. The youngest one was limping away as fast as it could go which was not fast at all, shaking its head from side to side as though deafened from the shock. The big wolf recovered its footing, shook its head in confusion, staggered a few unsteady steps then turned and gave Hugh a last puzzled glance. Then, following the other surviving animal, it loped slowly away without a backward glance.

Hugh knelt on the parched grass and checked to see if he had sustained any real damage. His ears were ringing and he felt as though he had been punched in the solar plexus, he was winded and weak. His hand was stinging from the bite the wolf had inflicted but he kept telling himself it could have been much worse if he hadn't woken when he did.

'Hey there!'

The sound of a human voice *in English* was a wonderful relief. Turning he saw two horsemen approach and managed to stand up. 'Thank God!' he cried.

As they drew nearer he saw that one was the young doctor and the other was Leo Grosvenor. As soon as they reached him they dismounted and regarded Hugh with a kind of wonder.

Eduardo stared at the burning tree. 'How did you survive that? You are a lucky man!'

Leo, his face flushed with excitement, cried, 'There's a dead wolf – and see the tree! It's dropping burning leaves on to the grass.' He turned to the doctor. 'We should stamp it out or else it will spread.'

Without waiting, he thrust his horse's reins into Hugh's good hand and began to fit actions to words.

Hugh was shaking his head, unable to believe he was safe. 'There were three wolves . . .' he began, his voice shaking.

Eduardo caught sight of his injured hand which was oozing blood. 'I hope that's not what I think it is!'

'I'm afraid it is. One of them bit me. To tell you the truth I thought I was a goner.'

'We must get you back and give you a rabies injection. Nasty looking brutes, aren't they.' He tried to lead the horse nearer to the dead wolf but it shied away, whinnying in alarm. Glancing upward, he said, 'Amazing. The vultures are here already!'

Hugh saw two birds circling high above them, two black shapes against the deep orange of the setting sun. He shuddered. Later he would tell all the dreadful details to Jane but he did not want to show weakness before the young doctor. Nor could he bear to think back on the events that so nearly ended in his death.

For a moment they watched the oak. Fortunately it was very old and had few leaves so the worst was soon over. The trunk continued to smoulder but as Eduardo pointed out, without a wind to fan it, it would probably be out by morning. 'Not that we can do anything about it, there's no water nearby.'

Hugh took a long deep breath and felt his life return to him and uttered a silent prayer of thanks. Then he said, 'What are you two doing out here?'

'I promised to teach Leo to ride and this is his third lesson. He's very good. Very promising.' He smiled. 'He may be a duffer at tennis but he's going to make a very good rider.'

Leo came back to them, his face alight with excitement. 'A real lightning strike and we saw it!' he cried. 'Wait until I tell the chaps at school! And Joanna! I wish she'd been here to see it. And that wolf is all charred and horrible but it must have died very quickly.' He looked at Hugh. 'Lucky you weren't closer to the tree. Oh! What's that?' He dashed away again, picked something up from the ground and carried it back in triumph. 'A bird!' he said, 'Not burnt to a cinder but with all its feathers singed. See how blue it was? Slate blue with a bit of black. I bet it was just flying past or perched in the tree when the lightning struck. It's as dead as a dodo, poor thing.' He tossed it down beside the dead wolf and glanced up at the vultures. To Hugh he said earnestly, 'You mustn't mind these things, Mr Stafford.

It's nature's way. All creatures have to eat and you shouldn't blame the vultures for being born what they are.'

Hugh nodded vaguely. His head was beginning to ache.

'We'll get back now, Mr Stafford,' Eduardo said. 'You can ride behind me if Leo gives you a leg up.'

Leo did so with alacrity and as soon as they were ready they set off with Hugh clinging tightly round Eduardo's waist. He had never ridden a horse before and found it uncomfortable but at least he was alive.

Leo was full of the adventure. 'I wonder what sort of bird it was. I think it was too big to be a bluebird. Could it have been a blue jay? I've heard of those.'

Eduardo shook his head. 'It was a blue rock thrush.'

Two hours later Hugh had received treatment for his bitten hand and he and Jane had been tearfully reunited and all trespasses had been forgiven and promises made for a happier future. Lucy was with them at their house and all three were reliving the providential escape in minute detail. Hugh was recovering from his shock, Jane was aware how close she had been to becoming a widow with a fatherless child and Lucy was glad to see them happy once again.

'So . . .' Hugh told them slowly, beginning to enjoy the attention he was getting, 'one wolf is toast . . .' He managed a weak smile. 'But two are still out there as dangerous as ever. Doctor Lourdes said the men will get a shooting party together and try and track them down. The younger wolf will stay with the taggle-eared one so they should be able to recognize them. No-one understands why they have become so daring this summer but—' He spread his hands. 'Thank God for the lightning strike!'

Jane clutched his hand to her. 'Every time there's a storm we'll remember how lucky you were.'

Lucy nodded. 'It certainly puts things in perspective.'

The front doorbell rang, Hugh answered it and returned

with Andrew who listened to the story with amazement and eventually congratulated Hugh on his escape.

'But I've really come to show Lucy a letter from my parents.'

He pulled up a chair and sat down and Lucy thought gratefully that it was just like old times.

He handed it to her. 'Read it out if you like. It's not private in any way.'

Lucy opened it obediently.

'Dear Andrew,
This kind gentleman, Mr Sutton, who is on the way to San Domingos with his friend Mr Betts, has offered to bring this letter to you. Your father and I have arrived a few days earlier than we originally intended. It seems such a waste to come all this way and not have time to see some of Portugal . . .'

Lucy said, 'I suppose that makes sense.'

Andrew looked doubtful. 'They're not great walkers,' he said. 'I don't know how they expect to get around. They can't hop on a bus or train.'

Lucy read on.

'. . . We have found a small but comfortable hostel in Vila Real and will stay there until you come to collect us but wonder if you could spare the time to spend a whole day with us as we would love to have you all to ourselves so that we can talk and you can catch up on the news from home. If you can't arrange this we shall do some sight-seeing – if we can manage it in this heat. How do you bear it? I suppose you get used to it.
Looking forward to seeing you and meeting Lucy,
Your affectionate Mother and Father.
PS Friends send their love and best wishes'

They all looked at Andrew.

He said, 'It needn't alter our plans. If they want to spend a few days down there I'll go as planned two days before the wedding and bring them back the following day in time to settle them in. They'll be staying in the house the Maddens had before his contract finished.'

Jane looked at Lucy. 'I'd forgotten you haven't met them.'

Lucy smiled. 'The moment of truth for all of us. Mind you, we've exchanged photographs so we know what to expect. No nasty shocks!'

They shared the laughter.

Marion had agreed to accompany her aunt to the cemetery to look at John's grave and add a small posy of silk freesias to the flowers that were already there. It was four days since the funeral and Sarah hated the idea that the wreaths would be wilting in the heat. Sarah had brought a small pair of secateurs with her with the idea of making a few repairs. The silk freesias had once adorned her straw hat but she now wanted to think of them close to her husband – a small reminder.

As they made their way slowly up the slope, arm in arm, the strengthening breeze fluttering the fringe of their large white parasol, Sarah told Marion about Agatha's offer.

Marion cried, 'But that would be marvellous! You can't refuse, can you? The library has always been your responsibility and it would be sad to think that you hand it over to someone else just as the expansion is underway.' She gave her aunt a sideways glance. 'Unless you are determined to return to England?'

Her aunt laughed. 'I almost said "Yes" on the spot but then I thought I should weigh it up in my mind. This is a difficult time for me and I mustn't be too hasty. A little quiet reflection, I told myself. That's what my husband would have advised. I talked to Paul and he says the decision's mine. Wouldn't you stay if you were in my shoes?'

'Most certainly! It's a most exciting opportunity and tailor-made for you, Aunt Sarah. You would enjoy it and no-one else could do it as well. And the Ladies' Club as well.'

'Group, dear, not Club!' Sarah frowned. 'A club reminds one of men's smoking clubs and all that terrible snobbery. Or the Library Group. The name's not settled yet.'

'It would be good to work with Agatha.'

'I'm glad you think so, Marion. I must say financially it sounds a very attractive proposition. It would be exciting to earn my own money! I should feel quite independent. It would . . .' She broke off, staring at something up ahead.

Marion followed her gaze and said, 'Someone's sitting by the cemetery. I think it's Mrs Garsey . . .Yes, it is her.'

Sarah frowned. 'Sitting on the grass – at her age? How very unseemly. What is she thinking of?'

As they drew nearer Mrs Garsey raised a hand and waved.

When they reached her they saw that she was clutching a small framed photograph.

Marion said, 'Mrs Garsey! Are you all right? Where's your parasol?'

'It blew away, dear. It was windier than I expected but it's shady here.' She scrambled to her feet with a little help from Marion but made no attempt to brush down her skirt. 'I didn't have the energy to run after it. Catching sight of the freesias, she said, 'Oh! Are they for your husband's grave? What a lovely idea. I've been in to have a look at the wreaths and they're bearing up considering the heat. It's always shady in there because of the height of the walls.'

Sarah said, 'You have a photograph . . .?'

Mrs Garsey held it out eagerly. 'It's my darling Flossie. It feels so strange to have no grave for her. But I come up here because this is the last place she was seen alive.'

Sarah gazed at the photograph. 'She was a sweet little dog and she had a happy life with you.' She handed it on to Marion.

Mrs Garsey said, 'Lucy saw her up here just before she disappeared. Young Leo Grosvenor made the frame for me. He's such a thoughtful boy. He reminded me that he too was bereaved – when his mother was drowned. I've told him he's always welcome at our house. A glass of lemonade and a slice of cake. Boys do love cake, don't they. He's having riding lessons, you know, with Doctor Lourdes.' Her cheerful chatter stopped suddenly and Marion and Sarah saw through the pretence. Her mouth trembled and she drew a long breath. 'It's such a long day without her,' she whispered. 'I wake up in the morning and for a moment I forget she's . . . dead. I can't bear to throw away her dinner bowl. I used to plan the day round her walks and . . .' Her eyes filled with tears which she brushed away with a trembling hand.

While Marion hesitated, searching for something helpful to say, Sarah returned the photograph thoughtfully.

'I've been trying to find you all morning, Mrs Garsey,' she said, with a quick glance at Marion. 'I shall be staying on at San Domingos and I'm going to need help very soon.'

With a deep sigh, Mrs Garsey pressed Flossie's photograph to her chest. 'My help? Really, I don't see how . . .'

Sarah smiled. 'If you do have time on your hands you might be interested in a little proposition . . .'

Marion saw at once what her aunt intended. 'Oh yes, that would be perfect!'

Mrs Garsey looked from one to the other. 'A little proposition?'

'Yes. In a project which Agatha Grosvenor has dreamed up. If you don't mind waiting five minutes with Marion while I give John these freesias and tidy up I'll tell you all about it.'

*　　*　　*

Two days later, early on Wednesday morning, Andrew set off from San Domingos to meet his parents, leaving a tearful Lucy in the capable hands of Marion and Sarah and with a promise that she would love his parents and they would adore her. Once on the train to Pomerao, however, he took out his mother's letter and reread it. Knowing his mother as he did he could read between the lines and this made him nervous. *'Wanting you all to ourselves . . .'* meant needing to talk privately without Lucy. *'Friends send their love'* could only mean one person, Elenor. After he had written to Elenor last year, and to his parents, to explain about Lucy, he had hoped the matter was at an end but perhaps he was wrong. He suspected that this was his parents' last opportunity to persuade him that Elenor was, and always had been, the right wife for him.

He had torn up her photograph after falling in love with Lucy for fear she should ever come across it and he had made light of the affair, suggesting to Lucy that the passion was mostly on Elenor's side and that her parents had forced the match. In his heart, however, he knew that was not true. They had met at Marcus's eighteenth birthday party – a picnic by the river with champagne and strawberries and cream. Marcus had drunk too much and was sick behind some bushes. Only Elenor had felt any sympathy for him and that is when he had first noticed her. He smiled at the memory . . .

As soon as he reached his parents' hotel later that day and saw their faces he knew that Elenor was going to be the subject of the 'news' his mother had referred to and steeled himself for a difficult few hours. His mother began as soon as they had ordered their dinner.

'Elenor has given me this for you,' she told him, plunging her hand into her capacious handbag and handing him a letter. His heart lurched suddenly as he recognized the familiar handwriting.

His father said, 'He can't read it at the dinner table, Clarice! What are you thinking of? It can wait. Let's at least enjoy our meal in peace.' He was a tall, gangling man, greying at the temples, with piercing blue eyes that were still bright.

'No, Horace, it *can't* wait!' Clarice Shreiker was also tall but she was bulky with it and her well-powdered face was large and round and showed her age. The small grey eyes were magnified by her spectacles. 'It's important and I shan't enjoy a single mouthful until I know that Andrew has read the letter.'

Andrew took it but made no effort to open it. His father said, 'If you must read it now I suggest you go into the Gentlemen's and read it there.'

Andrew rolled his eyes. 'Father's right. The letter can wait until we've finished the meal.'

'No, Andrew! Now don't start arguing with me the minute we meet up. Go and read it.' Her lips set in a determined line and father and son exchanged helpless glances.

The waiter brought the wine to the table, Andrew thanked him in Portuguese, and he withdrew.

His father said, 'So you speak the lingo, eh, Andrew?'

Clarice glared at her son. 'Well?' She stared pointedly at the unopened letter and with an exaggerated sigh he removed himself from the table.

He went into the men's room, locked himself in a stall and read Elenor's letter.

'My dearest Andrew, I hope you will forgive this letter but it comes from my heart and I cannot let this chance pass me by to tell you how I feel. After this I shall abide by your decision. If you wish to marry Lucy Barratt I will accept that. I do want you to know, however, that I still love you dearly and always will. My feelings for you have never wavered, even when you refused to answer my letters.'

Andrew closed his eyes, ashamed by the mild reproof. He could picture her face as she wrote, not wanting to reproach him yet needing to get her message across to him in this last bid for his affection. Poor, sweet Elenor. He was sorry for her – desperately sorry – but Lucy had taken her place in his heart. He read on.

> *'I had no idea when you left England that I would never see you again and that knowledge has been like a deep pain in my heart ever since that terrible letter. The irony is that Marcus has fallen in love with me and has proposed . . .'*

Andrew blinked and reread the last sentence. Marcus! What a nerve. He felt affronted. Marcus came from a wealthy family and could have any woman he pleased so why had he chosen Andrew's girl?

'Damn you, Marcus!' he muttered.

> *'. . . has proposed to me. I have explained that my heart is still with you but he rightly points out that you are now about to be married to someone else. If fate smiled on me, I would be your wife, Andrew, but if that is impossible I would not choose to spend the rest of my life alone and Marcus and I are very close friends. If I do not hear from you that you still love me I shall accept Marcus's offer of marriage. I know he will do everything he can to make me happy and secure for the rest of my life and I trust him implicitly . . .'*

'Meaning that you don't quite trust *me!*' he muttered. 'Damn!'

> *' . . . I want a family, Andrew, before it is too late . . .'*

Andrew groaned. 'Oh God!' He thought about the way she had looked when she saw him off at the train station on his way to London. Smiling through her tears. He had watched her from the train window as she grew smaller and smaller and his heart had felt as heavy as lead at the loss. His last glimpse had been of a petite young woman with dark curls and a sweet, serious face. Was it possible to love two women at the same time, he wondered.

'I've told Marcus that I'm writing to you and although he isn't happy about it, he's prepared to give us one final chance to be reunited if that is what you want. After that, I shall devote myself to making him happy. I cannot say more. The rest is up to you.
Your loving Elenor.'

For a long moment Andrew sat staring at the letter then he slowly refolded it and stuffed it into his jacket pocket. He went outside and splashed water over his face and reached for the towel. Then he stared at himself in the cracked mirror. Is this the face of a man Elenor could still love? Had he changed in the past year since they had been apart? The answer to that was probably in the affirmative. He had come to San Domingos as an innocent abroad but life had changed him. Suppose he thought the unthinkable and went back to Elenor . . . would she still love him? He groaned. The advantage would be that she need never know all that had gone wrong in San Domingos so she would have nothing with which to reproach him. It was a sobering thought.

He walked back to the table and sat down.

His mother said, 'Well?'

His father shook his head. 'Leave him be, Clarice. The boy needs time to think. Putting pressure on him won't help.'

The waiter arrived with the gazpacho and they busied themselves in silence. Andrew's mind was in turmoil.

Suddenly he looked at his mother. 'So you don't even want to give Lucy a chance. You don't even want to meet her. You've made up your mind she's not the one for me!'

'Oh Andrew! That's not it at all!' she protested.

He said suddenly, 'Whose idea was it that Elenor should write that letter? Did you persuade her, Mother?'

His parents exchanged glances. Horace said, 'We knew how Elenor was suffering. Her mother has been so worried about her. As the date for your wedding drew closer the poor girl wouldn't eat, couldn't sleep . . .'

His mother laid down the spoon, her soup hardly touched. 'We've always loved Elenor, you know that, and we were looking forward to . . .'

'So you'd be happy for me to abandon Lucy! Just like that! To please you. Is that the sort of man you want me to be?'

There was a silence then his mother said, 'But isn't that exactly what you did to Elenor?'

Andrew pushed his soup plate away. 'I've never liked gazpacho,' he muttered.

'Then why did you choose it?' She gave him one of her withering looks.

Horace said, 'This is going to get us nowhere so let's stop bickering. It's up to you, Andrew. All we did was bring out the letter. You have to admit we haven't met this Lucy person so we . . .'

'This Lucy person?' Andrew snapped. 'She's the young woman I'm going to marry in three days' time!' He glared at his father. 'I'll thank you not to call her "a person"!'

Horace held up placatory hands. 'I'm sorry. That was rude of me. I expect she's a very nice per— I mean woman. I mean, young woman.' He looked flustered.

The soup dishes were removed with a dark look from the waiter and pork fillet and boiled potatoes were served with a separate dish of lettuce and tomato dressed with oil.

In spite of the troubled atmosphere, Andrew found he was hungry and he cut into the pork with gusto.

Horace said, 'Very tasty pork. I do like a bit of well-cooked pork.'

'The potatoes are rather yellow.' Clarice gave her son a challenging look.

'They're yellowish potatoes,' Andrew snapped. 'That's how they come out of the ground.'

His father looked around at the white walls, the tiled floor and the low ceiling. 'A nice place to eat,' he said, smiling at Andrew. 'We had a strange breakfast, though. Some sort of cake and honey and a glass of milk.'

Clarice said, 'It was cinnamon cake. Very dry.'

'Oh no, dear. It wasn't cinnamon. I thought it was . . .'

'And no butter!' she said. 'I would have given anything for some butter and a pot of tea!'

Andrew ignored them, his thoughts elsewhere. His mother's jibe about abandoning Elenor had affected him more than he chose to admit. Had he abandoned her? Was he such a brute? He had written a very nice letter explaining that it was best for both of them, that he recognized he had made a mistake. He had assured her she would be much happier with a man who was worthy of her . . . and now she had Marcus.

His father said, 'Anyway, Andrew, how are things going at the mine? Nice reference I expect from your governor – what's his name?'

'Grosvenor.' He hesitated fatally and his mother pounced.

'What is it? Something wrong?'

'No, no!' he began but his courage failed. He had intended to bluff his way through this part of the interrogation but his mother's eyes were upon him and he knew he would never hide anything from her. 'There's been a bit of . . . a hiccup . . . I've had a few difficult weeks.' He stared fixedly at his plate and his appetite suddenly deserted him. 'I – I'm really not hungry,' he mumbled.

Clarice said, 'There is something wrong! I knew it! I thought the moment I set eyes on you that . . .'

'Oh stop it, Clarice! You thought nothing of the sort.' His father eyed Andrew. 'Is there something we ought to know? You're not ill, are you, son?'

Andrew shook his head. 'It's not that. I . . . I was rather confused and depressed but . . . it was not illness. Rather . . . personal problems. I made a bit of a blunder actually . . .' They were both staring at him open mouthed. His mother had her hand on her heart, his father looked fearful. Suddenly Andrew positively wanted to tell them everything. He needed them to tell him he had nothing to be ashamed of so that he could jettison the guilt he was carrying. More than anything he wanted absolution but would he receive it? He decided to risk it. 'I might as well tell you – I became involved with another woman.'

'Oh my God!' His mother leaned back in her chair, all the colour gone from her face.

Horace said, '*Another* woman? You mean . . . not Lucy?'

Andrew nodded. Clarice began to fan herself with her hand and his father looked thoroughly confused.

'So, son,' he asked, 'which one are you marrying?'

'Lucy, of course. It was only a silly infatuation but Jane – that's her name – didn't see it that way. When I tried to finish it she refused and she told her husband she wanted to leave him. I was . . . I was trying to protect Lucy but of course she was dragged into it and we quarrelled. I became depressed and . . .' Dare he tell them about the explosion? No, he decided to gloss over that. 'I couldn't concentrate properly at work and . . .' He shrugged.

His father said, 'And your governor hauled you over the coals? Is that it?'

Andrew nodded.

He glanced at his mother who had closed her eyes. When she opened them again she turned to her husband. 'I knew he should never have come out here. Much too young. I said so at the time.'

'You said no such thing, Clarice!' He looked at Andrew. 'So what's happening now, son? Are you still going to this place in Australia or has the governor put an end to that promotion?'

'I think I'm – I mean I think *we're* – still going. As far as I know. Grosvenor was thinking it over. I think I convinced him.'

Clarice sat forward again and her eyes had narrowed slightly. 'Well, you haven't convinced me. That brings me nicely to something else I wanted to tell you.' She glanced at Harold. 'I know you don't want me to say anything but I'm going to. In view of what's happened.' She waited and slowly he nodded.

She reached a hand across the table to cover one of Andrew's.

The waiter removed the plates with a roll of his eyes.

'Listen, dear, what I think is this. You should give up this idea of Australia, give up Lucy and . . .'

'Mother!'

'No just hear me out. It sounds to me as though you and Lucy were a mistake. You and Jane were another mistake. Don't you see why? Because your heart is still with Elenor.'

'No, Mother, you're wrong,' he protested weakly.

'Hear me out, I said. I happened to meet Albert Rogers in church a few Sundays ago and learned that your old teacher at the School of Mining had died. No, not an accident but heart trouble. Mr Rogers said to me that it was a pity you had gone abroad because they could do with you. They need a new instructor. They're already advertising the position.' She regarded him meaningfully over her spectacles.

Horace said, 'What your mother's trying to say is the job's probably yours if you want it.'

Clarice gave him a cold look. 'I wasn't *trying* to say it, I *did* say it!'

They both looked at Andrew and then at the waiter.

'Do we want coffee?' Andrew asked.

His mother said, 'No, we don't.'

Andrew said, '*A conta, faz favor.*' To his parents he translated, 'The bill, please.'

His father said, 'He's certainly mastered the lingo!'

Clarice said, 'I don't care for coffee, especially late in the evening. It keeps me awake.'

No-one answered her. Andrew was considering this new piece of information. A job as instructor at the School of Mining? He had never thought of instructing.

His father said, 'So what do you think, eh son? About the job?'

'I don't think so,' he began. 'I'm really looking forward to Australia. Such an adventure.' They regarded him stonily. 'And so is Lucy! I don't think she'd want to come back to England. She loves it out here. The climate agrees with her. She's quite an adventurous young woman whereas Elenor . . .'

Clarice interrupted frostily, 'I wasn't suggesting you brought Lucy back with you. I was hoping you'd come back alone and make a fresh start with Elenor.'

He shook his head. 'You've never even seen Lucy – except in a photograph. You'd love her.'

Clarice said, 'I've never been keen on blondes. Scatterbrains, most of them. But it's your decision, dear. You can go back and marry her and if that's what you want we'll come to the church and give the marriage our blessing.'

'And we won't let on,' Horace promised, 'that you ever had any doubts.'

'But I haven't had any doubts! It's you and Mother that are having the doubts. You blame me for "abandoning"

Elenor then encourage me to do the same thing to poor Lucy. Really, you are amazing.'

Clarice drew herself up. 'So that's the thanks we get for trying to save you from a big mistake. I never thought to hear my own son . . .'

Horace stood up. 'That's quite enough. I can't stand any more of this shilly-shallying. We're going round in circles. I'm off to bed. Night, son. Thank you for the meal.'

Andrew had risen also. Horace glanced at his wife. 'Are you coming?' he asked.

Reluctantly and with great dignity she rose to her feet. She kissed Andrew on the cheek. 'Sleep on it, dear,' she said. 'Say your prayers and maybe God will guide you.'

Andrew sat down again and tried to rally his thoughts. As always, after an argument with his mother, he felt drained. Poor Lucy. He tried to imagine her and his mother spending time together. He remembered her comment about blondes and smiled. Scatterbrain. Well, Lucy certainly could be but her heart was in the right place. But would Cornwall be big enough for both of them? But then the children would come along and everyone said that made a difference. His mother and Lucy would be reconciled. A subtle change came over them, apparently, as though the children drew them closer.

The idea of the instructor's job was intriguing. He wondered how the salary would compare with that of a mining engineer in Australia. Poor Lucy would probably feel horribly cheated if they abandoned the new and exciting life in Australia and went home to England. He frowned. It would mean that he and Lucy lived fairly near to Marcus and Elenor who would undoubtedly have a better house and more money. He and Lucy would be the poor relations.

'Oh Lord!' he muttered.

Upstairs in his room he took out Elenor's letter and reread it. How incredible after the way he'd treated her, that she could still write such a letter. And Marcus knew she had written to him begging for another chance. He felt a frisson of pride. Marcus, wealthy and good-looking, wanted Elenor but knew she still wanted Andrew Shreiker. It made him feel ten feet tall.

Did he want Marcus to have Elenor, he wondered. Suppose he went home and swept her off her feet and married her. Marcus would never forgive him. He had probably been delighted to hear that Andrew was going to Australia and Elenor would possibly never set eyes on him again.

But had Elenor *really* forgiven him? Perhaps as the years passed she would remind him from time to time of his betrayal. He would never live it down. Suppose he went back to Cornwall and they met again and the spark that had been between them was missing. More than a year had passed and they would both have been changed. Elenor might decide that she wanted Marcus after all and he, Andrew, would have given up both women and ended up in a dreary teaching job. He would have lost his big opportunity in Australia and it wouldn't look so good on his application form if he ever wanted to resume his mining career abroad.

'Damn them!' he muttered. Meaning his parents for unsettling him. He went to bed and tried to sleep but the questions went round and round in his head and he had no answers to any of them.

Eleven

Leo wandered round his father's office, pretending to study the various photographs that hung on the walls. Groups of earlier officials and staff of the mine and pictures of his father shaking hands and smiling with various visitors. Some were from other countries eager to study the new techniques and modern applications which existed at San Domingos. Leo had seen them all before on countless such occasions when he had been desperate to know exactly what was going on in the adult world around him. It was the morning of the wedding and the whole place appeared to be in uproar but he was not sure why. No-one had time to talk to him. They rushed to and fro with anxious expressions and he couldn't find Joanna who was usually willing to spend time with him.

Now his father was on the telephone, his face like thunder, bellowing at whoever was unfortunate to be on the other end of the line.

'But someone must have some idea, Goddammit!' he roared. The man can't just disappear into thin air! Then find me someone who can! I'm trying to run a mine here and my patience is wearing thin ... No, I don't want to speak to the station master. I've already spoken to him and a fat lot of good it ... Hell and damnation! *Do* something useful, man, and ring me back!' He hung up the receiver and sat back in his chair with his eyes closed.

Leo said, 'Problems, Papa?'

'Damned right. That damned Shreiker. If I get my hands on him I'll ring his neck!'

Leo thought about it. Why wasn't Mr Shreiker here? He was supposed to be getting married. 'Where's Mr Shreiker?'

'God only knows! I don't.'

'Maybe he's been kidnapped.' Leo edged closer to the desk and, as if sensing the move, his father opened his eyes. 'Don't touch anything!'

'I wasn't going to, Papa.'

Elliot looked at him in some surprise. 'What are you doing in here anyway? Shouldn't you be getting togged up?'

'But if Mr Shreiker's not here . . .'

'We're all pretending that nothing's wrong!' He leaned forward, put his elbows on the table and buried his face in his hands. 'Lucy Barratt's insisting that we all go ahead. "He'll come!" she says.'

'Will he? I mean, how can the wedding go ahead if . . .'

'Exactly! You've hit the nail on the head, Leo. He should have been here yesterday with his parents but they didn't turn up and the train driver didn't see them. So where are they?' He pulled out his watch and studied it. 'One hour to go and no bridegroom. What a farce!'

'Yes, Papa! I suppose it is.' He thought about Lucy Barratt when she met him off the boat at Pomerao and wondered why Mr Shreiker didn't want to marry her. 'So has he changed his mind?'

The telephone rang and his father picked it up. 'Yes. Put him through . . . What? All three of them? What time was this? . . . I see. But no mention of what they planned to do next . . . Hmm . . . Right . . . Thank you.' He stood up and crossed to the window. Then he said, 'Fetch Mr Stafford, will you, Leo – and take your hands out of your pockets.'

Leo stared at him indignantly. 'Mr Gooch our biology master *always* has his hands in his pockets and the boys call him . . .'

'Leo!'

'Sorry, Papa!' Withdrawing the offending hands he bolted from the room and scurried importantly around the building until he found Hugh Stafford. Hugh hurried back to the office and Leo followed at a discreet distance.

Elliot glanced up as his secretary entered. 'It seems they are all right – at least they were last night. No-one remembers seeing them this morning so they could be on the steamer on their way here but if they are they're going to be hopelessly late. It seems a waiter heard them over dinner and they seemed to be arguing and left most of the food. So there was something being discussed but he doesn't know what because he doesn't speak much English.'

'Perhaps one of the parents has been taken ill in the night?'

'D'you really believe that?'

'No, sir . . . I wish I did.'

'I have a very bad feeling about all this, Stafford. I don't know what the hell to do. Do I pass on this information or do I keep quiet and wait and see what transpires?'

Neither man spoke. Leo, listening outside the open door, finally realized that, as he'd suspected, a crisis was definitely approaching. It was all very exciting but he felt sorry for Lucy Barratt.

He turned and crept away. Maybe if the wedding was off he needn't get togged up. He hated wearing his best suit. Joanna would know what to do. He would tell her what he had heard and ask her advice.

Marion, Sarah and Lucy sat in her bedroom. Lucy was crying, Marion was trying to comfort her and Sarah was praying hard that the nightmare would end. She was asking God for a miracle. She was also asking the spirit of her husband if he could somehow put in a good word for them. Her mouth moved silently, her hands were clasped in front of her chest and her head was bent. Like Lucy, she was still insisting that the groom would suddenly appear and all would be explained to their mutual satisfaction. The wedding dress was laid out on the bed and Lucy was partly dressed. She had on her petticoat, white stockings and white shoes and the tiara waited on the windowsill in its box.

Lucy sniffed hard and wiped her eyes for the third time. She looked at Marion and forced a smile. 'He'll come!' she said for the eighth time. 'I know Andrew. He'll get here somehow. We'll just go ahead and . . . and he'll turn up. He may not be in his best suit but it won't matter, will it? Everyone will understand that he had . . . whatever difficulties he's had. I expect he's worrying himself about me, poor lamb!' Her smile wavered.

There was a knock on the door and Joanna looked in. Sarah stopped praying.

Joanna said brightly, 'I've come to do the bride's hair as promised.'

Sarah smiled graciously. 'Come in, my dear. The bride is ready and waiting. The dress and the tiara will go on last because it's so hot.' She pointed to the dress on the bed.

'Oh! It's beautiful!' said Joanna. 'I didn't know . . .' she began. 'That is I did wonder if . . .'

'Oh everything's going according to plan,' Sarah told her. 'We're sure the bridegroom will make it to the church so we're going ahead as planned. It's the only thing we can do, isn't it?'

They all looked at Joanna. 'Yes. Probably you're right,' she agreed. She began to unpack her brushes and combs and the hairpins that would keep the elaborate hairstyle in place. 'I'm a little late. I was looking for Leo but goodness knows where he is. Trying to put off the evil moment when he has to put on his best suit, I expect!'

They laughed dutifully. Lucy took her place in front of

the oval mirror and for a few moments Joanna worked in silence brushing her soft blonde hair. Lucy watched the others watching her in the mirror and saw the agonized expressions they were trying to conceal. Abruptly she turned round. 'Look, I know he may not come . . . in time, I mean. We may have to have the actual ceremony another day, when he gets back. But we must go through with it, one way or the other.'

Sarah sat down heavily on the bed with a small gasp of fear. Marion and Joanna exchanged astonished glances.

Marion said, 'Oh Lucy, dear, don't give up hope!'

Lucy took a few deep breaths. 'What I mean is that everyone's gone to so much trouble for us – the reception . . . all the food and the guitarist coming to play for us and the photographer. Whether or not I am married today we must go ahead with the party. Everyone can enjoy the food and the dancing.' She put a faltering hand to her mouth. 'If something dreadful has happened to him . . . I mean if he never comes back . . .' Tears gathered again but she blinked them back with a fierce shake of her head. 'We'll return the presents and . . . Not that I think for a moment that will happen but . . .' She swallowed hard but her throat was dry. 'Well, that's it. What do you think?' She looked from one to the other. Sarah was rocking herself to and fro in an agony of indecision. Marion, forced to think the unthinkable, had started to cry. Joanna recovered from the shock and took Lucy's hands in hers.

'You are so sweet and brave!' she told her. 'You're right, Lucy. We don't know what's happened so we can't prejudge the situation. He may yet surprise us!' Ignoring the palpable air of disbelief she ploughed on. 'Knowing Andrew he'll *swim* here if he has to – if the engine of the boat's broken down. And I agree wholeheartedly with Lucy. We'll do our best to have a great day, with or without Andrew. Let the future take care of itself.' She leaned forward and hugged the trembling bride-to-be. 'So . . . Let's finish your hair and get you into that beautiful gown. Whatever happens, Lucy, you will be the star of the day.'

Quickly Marion brushed aside both tears and doubts and hurried outside to fetch the small spray of freesias which would go hand in hand with the small Bible Lucy would carry. Twenty-five minutes later they had all dressed hurriedly in their finery and Eduardo was waiting outside the house to walk with Lucy to the church. As the little procession set out Lucy thought incongruously that, if Andrew *didn't* reach the church in time, Paul would be unable to make his best-man's speech.

Inside the little church the congregation were squashed together on the pews and very thankful that the interior was cooler than outside. Everywhere hats blossomed with veils, feathers, beads and flowers. The men sat stiffly in their best suits, their eyes to the front. The women turned repeatedly to steal glances towards the rear of the church in the hope of seeing the arrival of the bridegroom.

In the front pew, Paul waited in a frenzy of despair that his young cousin was going to be jilted at the altar. At the rear of the church Lucy waited with her arm through Eduardo's. He could feel her trembling and wanted nothing more than the chance to strangle Andrew Shreiker with his bare hands. The man was utterly contemptible.

Outside the church, the clock reminded the waiting crowd that the groom was now half an hour late. Whispers began. Inside the church Lucy pretended not to notice.

Eduardo leant down to her and whispered, 'How long do you want to wait? The padre will be asking us before long.'

'I don't know. Should we say another quarter of an hour? Would that be reasonable?'

Her voice shook slightly and he was filled with compassion. Her eyes were reddened from tears, her blotchy complexion had been heavily powdered and a little colour had been carefully rubbed into her cheeks to relieve the pallor. She reminded him of a sad little doll who was no longer loved. He was not as calm as he appeared, however. He was actually struggling with his conscience and feeling a complete hypocrite because in his heart he was glad that Shreiker had let her down in this cruel way. He had envied the man who was going to marry her and had decided, rightly or wrongly, that he was not the right man for her. Not until now did he admit to himself that in his wildest dreams he hoped that *he* was the right man. The discovery shocked him. He had never had a serious girlfriend although his sisters had tried hard enough to interest him in various female friends of theirs but he had been truly immersed in his work and was only now shaken by the discovery that his career was not enough. Life should have more to offer than dedication to a noble cause.

The padre appeared near the altar of the little church looking worried. He spoke to Sarah and then made his way along the aisle, smiling politely at members of the congregation who were by now becoming agitated.

He said to Eduardo, 'I think we have a problem, Doctor Lourdes. There is no sign of the bridegroom. We could wait a little longer ...' He smiled nervously at Lucy. Before either of them could answer, Paul followed the padre up the aisle, his face flushed with humiliation, his mouth set in an angry line.

Paul said to Lucy, 'The blighter's not going to turn up! We have to face facts, Lucy. Shall we just announce that it's been cancelled but that the party will go ahead as planned?'

Eduardo felt her stiffen. Perhaps she had been hoping against hope.

Lucy looked at him. 'If you think so, Paul, I'm agreeable ... but who will tell them?'

The padre said, 'I'm used to this sort of thing. I can make a discreet announcement if you wish.'

'No, I'll do it!' Paul patted Lucy's shoulder. 'Don't worry. I won't make it sound like the end of the world.'

Fitting action to words he strode down the aisle to the front of the church and turned to face the congregation. The organist hesitated then stopped awkwardly in the middle of a phrase. The whispering stopped abruptly as all eyes fastened on Paul.

'Ladies and gentlemen, you will have realized, I'm sure, that the bridegroom has been unavoidably delayed. It seems sensible to cancel the ceremony for today but my cousin Lucy hates to disappoint you all and has insisted that we go ahead as planned with the reception so do please stay and enjoy the party. Thank you.'

After a surprised silence there was a ripple of applause from the congregation and someone shouted, 'Well done, Lucy!' and another said, 'Bless you, dear!'

Eduardo glanced down at Lucy and gave her arm a comforting squeeze. 'The worst is over for today,' he told her.

Together they turned and walked from the church and the congregation rose and followed.

As soon as the guests had assembled, Paul spoke with Lucy and agreed to make an impromptu speech in an attempt to minimize the murmurings that had been heard in the church. He felt aggrieved that his carefully honed speech had had to be abandoned but felt it his duty to protect his cousin from the worst of the rumours. He made his way to the raised dais on which the guitarist was settling himself and waited for the chatter to die down. The faces raised expectantly to him were those of the friends and relations and with them he felt able to add a few more details.

'Friends and loved ones,' he began. 'You deserve some

explanation of what has happened but I cannot be too specific because the fact is we know very little. Andrew was expected to return from Vila Real yesterday with his parents who have come from England especially to see their son married and, of course, to meet Lucy, their new daughter-in-law.'

People were exchanging knowing looks and he hurried on.

'They didn't return and we haven't heard from them. Hopefully there is nothing seriously wrong but Andrew's mother has suffered with her heart in the past and may have been affected by the heat. Obviously we would have expected to hear if she has been taken to hospital but we cannot guess why this has not happened. Mr Grosvenor is trying to reach his various contacts at Vila Real and we may have news at any moment.'

Leo said helpfully, 'The boat may have been struck by lightning.'

Joanna laughed. 'Thank you, Leo, for those comforting words.'

Fortunately everyone laughed including Leo and the tension was broken.

Paul continued. 'So, to help Lucy enjoy her very special day, do help yourself to a glass of champagne from the table in the corner and we will drink to the young couple. They will marry later in a brief private ceremony as soon as the bridegroom and his parents reach San Domingos. Our thanks to Agatha and Joanna Grosvenor, Mrs Garsey, and my mother and all the others who have helped prepare the wonderful meal we are about to enjoy.'

There was a cheerful murmur of appreciation from the guests and Leo started the applause. Paul was pleased to see that the frowns of concern had left many of the faces. As soon as everyone had a drink in their hand Paul spoke again. 'After the wedding breakfast the guitarist will take a well-earned rest and have his meal. Stephen Benbridge has kindly offered us the use of his gramophone and there will be dancing throughout the afternoon.'

Leo was heard to say that Mr Benbridge had taught him to dance the waltz and the foxtrot and there was a ripple of laughter as heads turned in his direction.

Paul said, 'Well, at least we have one dancer among us! Watch out, you lucky ladies!' and winked at Leo. 'Now will you all join me in a toast . . . to Lucy and Andrew. May God bless them and grant them many happy years together.'

Glasses were raised and Paul smiled round, exuding a confidence in the future which he did not feel. He turned to Lucy who gave him a quick kiss.

'That was just right, Paul,' she told him. The colour had returned to her face and if her eyes were a little too bright everyone would expect her to have shed a few tears. She looked for Eduardo but he was nowhere to be seen and Marion said he had had to return to the hospital as a pregnant woman had gone into an early labour.

Marion hugged her carefully, afraid to crumple her dress. 'You look wonderful,' she said. 'The photographer is wondering what he should do. He didn't take any at the church. Do you want some photos here?'

Lucy hesitated. In her heart she was convinced that Andrew had abandoned her and she didn't know whether to be glad or sorry. After the way he had behaved over the summer months she didn't know whether she truly wanted to be Mrs Shreiker. If he *had* jilted her deliberately then she was well out of that particular union even if circumstances had prevented him from reaching the church . . . She sighed. Maybe fate was intervening on her behalf. Giving her a last way out. A final opportunity to break off the engagement.

'Yes,' she told Marion. 'Tell him to take plenty of photographs of the happy occasion. I'll be available whenever he's ready. A pity Eduardo had to leave. We won't have a picture of the man who gave me away!'

'Or tried to!' Marion raised her eyebrows and they both laughed. Lucy's laugh was a little shaky but she was recovering from the shock. Andrew had jilted her in front of all their friends and relations but she was determined to see the day through to the bitter end.

When they sat down for the meal she rose to her feet and thanked the guests for all the presents they had sent. These were arranged on a trestle table at the far end of the room.

'I shall open them during the dancing but this is a "thank you" in advance. I know I speak for Andrew when I say how grateful we are for your generosity.'

The meal Agatha had planned turned out well and soon everyone was enjoying the food, wine and congenial company and nobody mentioned the absent groom. The guitarist played a selection of hauntingly beautiful Portuguese ballads until it was time for the dancing to begin. Lucy found she was never short of partners. Paul, Will Hawks, Stephen Benbridge, and Hugh saw to it that she was never alone.

Jane went home early because she had backache but insisted that Hugh remain to make sure that Lucy was not allowed to dwell on Andrew's non-appearance.

At a quarter to four a message had come to Paul from Elliot Grosvenor to say that Andrew and his parents had been seen boarding a train for Lisbon but the news was kept from Lucy until the last of the guests had left and the celebrations were officially at an end.

Marion, Lucy and Sarah forced themselves to attend church next morning as usual even though they knew that Lucy had indeed been abandoned by Andrew. At that stage nobody else knew except the three of them, Paul and Elliot

Grosvenor. Lucy sat through the service with her head held high and smiled and waved as usual to the people she knew. After the service she met all the enquiries with a slight shake of the head and the suggestion that as soon as Andrew returned all would be revealed. In fact she was waiting to hear from him. Instinct told her that he would write, if only to try and explain his actions to her and to convince himself that his behaviour sprang from a desire to save her from future disappointment. Somehow, she felt sure, he would want to be forgiven so that he could slough off the guilt and start again.

Marion linked her arm through Lucy's as the three women walked across the *praca* back to the house.

Marion said, 'I didn't see Hugh and Jane in church, did you?'

Sarah said, 'She left the party early yesterday with a backache. Maybe she's still suffering. Or it could be something worse. Women in her condition can suffer a variety of aches and pains. I remember being quite poorly when I was expecting Paul.' Her face brightened. 'I thought he was marvellous yesterday, didn't you?'

They agreed wholeheartedly. Lucy slipped her arm from Marion's.

'I think I'll call in at Jane's,' she said, 'to see how she is.'

Sarah nodded her approval. 'I'm so pleased that you two are friends again,' she said. 'I expect she is thanking her stars that she is no longer infatuated with Andrew. Now she can see just how shallow he is, she will value her own husband that much more.' Sighing, she shook her head. 'I can still hardly credit that we were all taken in by him. And your uncle also. John thought very highly of him, you know. Poor dear John.' Her eyes misted over and Marion took her arm as Lucy turned away in the direction of Jane and Hugh's home.

As soon as Hugh opened the door, she could see the concern in his eyes. He led the way inside and they sat together in the small sitting room. 'We had rather a bad night,' he told her, 'but I think she's rallying a bit. Just tiredness and over-excitement. She's sleeping now, thank goodness, but the baby's not making things any easier. She's rather lost her appetite and is feeling the heat more than usual.'

Lucy nodded. 'And are you completely recovered after your "ordeal by wolf"?'

He shrugged. 'What can I say? I'm so lucky to be alive. Without that lightning strike I know I'd be dead by now. Those animals meant business. I should never have gone so far from the town. It was my own fault but I needed to get right away.'

'To be by yourself and think?'

'Yes. I was in rather a mess emotionally. Pathetic, really.' He looked a little shamefaced. 'Still, it brought me to my senses and showed me what mattered in my life. Jane and the baby.' He smiled. 'You know, she's so thrilled about it now everything has calmed down. We all make stupid mistakes . . .'

'I nearly made one!'

'You mean Andrew?'

She nodded and then passed on what she knew – that Andrew and his parents, both apparently in excellent health, had been seen heading back to Lisbon on the train.

'Unbelievable!' he gasped. 'You must be beside yourself! What has happened to the man? I always thought him very level-headed.'

Lucy hesitated, wondering whether to share her suspicions with him. She needed to talk to Jane but she was asleep. Slowly she said, 'I think his parents unsettled him. I think maybe they came all this way to turn him against me. In all the time I've known him they have never written to me. I thought it odd but I thought I was being melodramatic so I said nothing to Andrew.'

'But why should they dislike you if they'd never met you? It doesn't make sense.'

She sighed. 'There was a woman named Elenor. He thought he was going to marry her until he met me. She was the daughter of his mother's best friend. I suspect they all wanted the marriage and I spoiled it for them.'

'It's possible. Jane thought that maybe he wanted an excuse not to go to Australia and couldn't think of anything else than to sneak away. Naturally she hasn't a good word to say for him after . . . Well, you know what I mean.'

Lucy rubbed her forehead tiredly. 'He hasn't been good for any of us but I don't think he meant it. I think his life got out of control somehow.' She glanced up. 'Or maybe not!'

'You shouldn't be making excuses for him. Do you still love him, Lucy? Tell me you don't!'

For a long moment she closed her eyes. 'Do I love him? That's a good question. If he came back – if he walked in through that door – would I throw myself into his arms? I honestly don't know. I think I'm preparing myself for the worst.'

Hugh leaned across and took her hand in his. 'The doctor was here earlier to see Jane and set my mind at ease. He said . . .' He drew back. 'No, perhaps I shouldn't repeat it. Very indiscreet.'

She looked up eagerly. 'Tell me!'

'He said that Andrew had done you a big favour by failing to turn up and . . . and if you have any sense you will never take him back. He thinks you are totally unsuited. That you need someone more responsible. His exact words were "Lucy Barratt deserves better."' He regarded her anxiously. 'I'm sorry. Perhaps I shouldn't have told you.'

'I'm glad you did.' She looked startled.

Hugh came to a decision. 'There's something else I have to confess but you might never forgive me. At one stage Grosvenor asked in confidence for my honest opinion of Andrew – regarding his work and his relations with the miners. He was very unhappy with the way things were going and especially about that explosion . . .'

'I know. Go on.' She had a hand over her mouth and was looking at him wide-eyed.

'I was very angry with him at the time because of . . .' He faltered.

'Understandably.' She nodded impatiently.

'I told him exactly what I thought. That he was unreliable and that the men didn't respect him. It was a rotten thing to do. I made things worse for him.'

'What he did to *you* was rotten. Don't blame yourself.' She was beginning to see that Andrew had been hedged in on every side. His mistakes had returned to haunt him. What had her grandmother said on so many occasions? That chickens come home to roost! Suddenly she could bear it no longer. Jumping to her feet she said, 'Give Jane my love. I'll call in again sometime. I'll see myself out.' Even as Hugh protested, she was hurrying away, desperate to be alone with her thoughts..

Outside, she hesitated. Where should she go and what should she do now? She made her way to the *praca* and sat alone, deep in thought. She had the rest of her life to think about. She looked around at the flowers and watched the gardener clipping one of his bushes. Mrs Garsey sat dozing on one of the seats beside the bandstand. Four men, including the new man Sutton, were playing tennis and Leo was acting as ballboy for them. When he saw her he withdrew his efforts and hurried over to sit down with her.

He gave her a long searching look. 'You're not going to do anything silly, are you?' he asked. 'Only Aunt Agatha is afraid you might. She said that being jilted is a terrible thing for a woman to endure and you're very young and vulnerable.'

'No, I'm not planning to do anything drastic,' she said, wondering whether to laugh or cry. She had to face the fact that most of the English community would be discussing the fiasco of her abortive wedding and wondering about the aftermath.

'I said I'd keep an eye on you,' he told her shyly.

'Oh but Leo! That's not necessary!'

He waved a hand airily. 'It's the least I can do. Honestly, I've got nothing better to do.'

'Oh!' She struggled to keep her face straight. She tried to imagine him in his twenties and wondered how his unsophisticated manner would appeal to the women in his life.

He regarded her earnestly. 'Joanna says you're probably humiliated and will go back to England with your sister and it will be our loss.'

'Did she?' Lucy felt she should not be encouraging him to pass on these snippets but it was fascinating to hear what was being said.

'Are you dreadfully humiliated?'

She hesitated. No doubt anything she said would be part of his next conversation. 'I'm mortified, I suppose, but . . . but Mr Shreiker was in the wrong. Not me. I try to remember that.'

He considered her words carefully and then nodded. 'I said I thought you should stay and do something to take your mind off him. You could learn to ride a horse. Doctor Lourdes is a very good teacher. I'm going to learn to canter next week. He says I'm a natural horseman which is awfully gratifying because I'm not brilliant at school sports. He's got several horses and I'm sure he could find a very docile one for you.'

'Thank you, Leo. That's a very good idea. I'll think about it.'

'He says you're very bright and resilient and you'll survive. I think he rather likes you. He often talks about you.' He glanced up and saw his father walking in the direction of the Palacio. 'There's Papa! I need to ask him about my new school blazer. Aunt Agatha will have to order it for me. Excuse me.'

She watched him go and felt strangely comforted. It was good to know that people cared about her troubles and that Joanna thought her departure would be a loss. Good too to know that the doctor thought so well of her.

At last a faint smile lit up her weary face. 'I just might stay,' she murmured.

Twelve

It was November and the first rains had fallen. The parched plain had sprouted a fine sheen of new green growth which would strengthen as autumn gave way to the short Alentejo winter. As planned three months earlier, the library now boasted the two new mobile bookshelves Mr Garsey had made, and these had been wheeled to one side to make more room for the motley collection of chairs which had been begged and borrowed from members of the Ladies' Group. These were now being set out by Mrs Garsey and Joanna. The group had met once before to iron out their rules and procedures but this was to be the first evening with a speaker and everyone was in a state of high excitement.

A lady had been found among the English ladies who had admitted to having been a chorus girl in a music hall in Edmonton and she had agreed to give them a twenty-minute talk about it. Grace Frewin also had some photographs, which had been pinned to the library noticeboard, showing her posing in various costumes and also in a line-up of dancers. There were fifty-six members in the group and they all wanted to attend but there was room only for thirty so it had been decided on a first-come first-serve basis.

Sarah stood back and surveyed the room. Ten minutes to go before the door officially opened and she was becoming nervous. For the third time she inspected the card table at the back of the room on which thirty glasses waited to be filled with lemonade. This, with two biscuits, came with the ticket price of threepence and gave the group a profit of seven shillings and sixpence. The speaker would stand at the front behind a second card table on which Agatha was placing a small bowl of tastefully arranged bougainvillea.

Grace Frewin, a middle-aged lady, watched the preparations with growing apprehension for she had never spoken in public before and was beginning to regret her offer.

Sarah smiled reassuringly at her. 'Don't worry,' she told her. 'You will be a great success. All the members wanted to hear your story. We had to refuse twenty-six but we told them you might be willing to repeat the talk at a later date!'

'Oh! Do you think so?' The idea obviously flustered her.

'But only if you decide to do so. It will be entirely up to you.' Sarah glanced at the clock on the library wall. 'Two minutes to go!'

Lucy came in carrying a carafe of water and a glass and set them on the speaker's table. 'There's a small queue forming,' she told them. She smiled at Grace Frewin. 'This is so good of you. We're all looking forward to it immensely.'

The minute hand moved with a click and settled on twelve. Two o'clock exactly. Sarah opened the doors with a flourish and the members hurried in. Jane appeared and sat beside Lucy. The pregnancy was beginning to show and she sank thankfully on to the chair Lucy had kept for her.

She said, 'Hugh's quite disappointed that men aren't included!'

'So he should be.'

Ten minutes later the audience had settled expectantly on their chairs and a hush descended as Agatha rose to introduce the speaker.

Half an hour later the talk came to an end and Lucy, in the audience, was one of many who would have liked it to last a little longer. There was a hearty round of applause and Sarah rose to her feet again.

'Mrs Frewin has graciously agreed to answer a few questions. I'm sure we all have plenty to put to her.'

Grace helped herself to the water and sipped it with obvious relief. The worst was over and she must have known the talk had been well received. Stricken with shyness, however, nobody could think of an intelligent question. Nobody raised a hand and the embarrassing seconds ticked by. Lucy glanced hopefully along the row to Agatha but she was jotting down a few words for Mrs Garsey to say in her vote of thanks. Lucy thought desperately and then broke the awkward silence.

'What were your parents' reactions to your determination to go on the stage?'

Grace smiled. 'My father was rather shocked. He was a sidesman at our church and he worried about what people would think but my mother had been a dancer herself for a few short years so she understood.'

Agatha passed the paper to Mrs Garsey who seized it gratefully and read it through. Another hand was raised. Another question. Lucy watched the speaker with admiration. Grace Frewin had come out to Portugal with her husband, an assayer, seven years earlier but he had died from consumption within two years of their setting up home. Faced with the prospect of returning to England she had chosen instead to stay on. To earn a living she had developed a small catering business and served meals to some of the many English engineers who were single. Her cooking was excellent and she enjoyed it and treated them like the sons she had never had. In fact she had created a satisfying niche for herself.

Two months since the fiasco of her wedding, Lucy was still undecided about her own future. Marion had returned to England but Lucy had stayed on with her aunt while she came to terms with her situation. Now she was plagued with doubts about whether she could stay at San Domingos. She could not accept charity from her aunt now that her uncle was dead and their financial situation had changed but did she have Grace Frewin's talent for providing for herself? If only she could earn *something*. Enough to pay her aunt for her food and lodging.

Andrew's letter had eventually reached her and the wording left no doubt that he had finally fallen out of love with her – or that his former fiancée had fully reclaimed his affections. The letter rested in her pocket even now and whenever she felt particularly downhearted she would crumple it with her hand to remind herself how badly he had treated her and how fortunate she was to have found out the truth in time. She had no need to read it again because she knew it by heart.

> *'Dear Lucy,*
>
> *This has been a difficult letter to write as you can imagine. I couldn't face you when I made the decision to return to England so took the cowardly way out. I realized when I read Elenor's letter – Mother brought it with her – just how badly I had behaved towards her and felt obliged to put matters right between her and myself. I knew that whatever I did I would hurt someone badly and I'm deeply sorry it had to be you. I won't ask you to forgive me. I'm sure you never will.*
>
> *Elenor and I will be married in November and I shall stay in Redruth and continue teaching at the School of Mining. The adventure in Australia has been a victim of my changed circumstances as Elenor has never wanted to leave England. In spite of my caddish behaviour towards you, I still think well of you and wish you every happiness in the future, wherever it lies.*
>
> *Sincerely, Andrew.'*

With an effort she ended her daydreaming and tried to concentrate on what was happening around her. The questions had come to an end and Mrs Garsey rose to give the vote of thanks. She read nervously from the sheet Agatha had given her.

'I'm sure I speak for everyone when I say how much I have enjoyed the talk and how grateful we are to Mrs Frewin for breaking the ice, so to speak, and giving us our first talk. Everything she told us about life on the stage was a revelation and very humorous.' She folded the paper and looked round at the audience. To Lucy's surprise she added a few words of her own. 'I do think . . . we have had such a difficult summer . . .' her voice shook a little, '. . . and that tonight's laughter has come at just the right time. Thank you again.'

Loud applause came from the audience and then they all stood and stretched their legs and headed for the lemonade and biscuits. Agatha and Sarah congratulated each other and Mrs Garsey. It had gone well.

Lucy and Jane stood together, nibbling the ginger biscuits provided by Joanna, who joined them. She and Lucy had become closer over the past few months and Lucy knew that when the Staffords' baby was born, Jane's days would be very full and she, Lucy, would value Joanna's friendship more and more.

Jane told them that she had seen the new doctor whose name was Mendoza. 'Fransesco Mendoza. He's also Portuguese but nothing like your Eduardo except in . . .'

Lucy felt her face flush. 'He's not *my* Eduardo,' she said. 'Don't say such things. Someone might hear you.'

Joanna laughed. 'I'm hearing the same rumours.' She and Jane exchanged amused glances.

Jane, taking pity on Lucy, went on. 'Mendoza's very talkative but his English isn't quite so good so you do have to listen carefully – and yes, Lucy, since you were obviously going to ask, all's well with the baby!'

They all grinned.

Joanna asked, 'Have you thought of names for the child?'

Jane looked at Lucy with a straight face. 'You'll never guess what Hugh has chosen for a boy!'

Lucy hesitated. 'Not *Andrew*! Oh, he couldn't be so . . .'

'No! I was teasing you. It's to be Simon for a boy after Hugh's father and Amanda after my mother. Amanda Lucy, actually.' She looked at her friend and she was no longer being flippant. 'Lucy after a very good and understanding . . . and forgiving friend.'

For a moment Lucy's eyes misted over then the two women hugged each other. At that moment Mrs Garsey tapped Lucy on the shoulder. 'There's a handsome young man outside. He has two horses and seems to think . . .'

'Oh no!' Lucy pressed her fingers to her lips. 'My riding lesson! I forgot to say I'd be a bit late because of the talk. I'm not even changed yet.'

Mrs Garsey smiled. 'I wouldn't keep him waiting if it was me he wanted!'

Lucy made her apologies to Jane and Joanna, washed down the last of her biscuit and hurried outside.

Joanna looked at Jane. 'Are you thinking what I'm thinking about our charming Eduardo?'

Jane laughed. 'We all know it and Eduardo knows it. Lucy will probably be the last to know!'

CARIVAGIO